# The Book
# of
# Almost
# Anything

## K H Dawson

Grateful acknowledgement is made for
permission to reprint excerpts from the
following material:

I COULD WRITE A BOOK. By Lorenz Hart
and Richard Rodgers © 1940

INTO EACH LIFE SOME RAIN MUST
FALL by Allan Roberts and Doris Fisher ©
1944

ISBN: 9798557138734

# DEDICATION

To my wife, Kerry, and my daughter Ana.

# ~ CONTENTS ~

# ACKNOWLEDGMENTS

I would like to thank my mother and father because this book would have been impossible without them. Although they are no longer with me, I know that their spirits will live on through the stories I will continue to tell. Mum and Dad, I hope that I have made you both proud.

I am eternally grateful to my beautiful wife, Kerry. Thank you for your love, patience, support, and encouragement over the last six years. This novel has been a long journey, but you have been my light at the end of the tunnel.

A special thank you to Karen Stewart – a true angel. I am eternally grateful for all your help, love, kindness, and support.

And lastly, to my readers: I hope that you enjoy reading my story.

# Chapter 1
## ~ *THE OLD LEAN-TO* ~

Christopher wandered along the old white slabs of the
flagstone path. He wanted to escape to another place and
time, far away from the madness of the past few months.
He did not recognise his life anymore. Despite its size, his
grandmother's house had become like a prison to him,
where he was being punished by the memories of happier
times. Milaw House itself had not changed, but
Christopher felt the coldness now: an aching presence that
crept from room to room. It seemed to follow him
wherever he went. The only relief was being outside in the
fresh air, standing in the huge garden where he had spent
most of his early childhood.

The sun drooped lower in the sky and the first chill of
autumn danced its way through the air. Despite the
coldness, Christopher felt an unexpected warmth reach out
to him. It seemed to be emanating from the lavender
plants beside the garden wall. Their tiny lilac petals were
alive in the breeze, beckoning to him, begging him to
come closer. He had played at this part of the garden for
as far back as he could remember, but never before had
Christopher experienced this kind of sensation. He was
mesmerised. With his finger, he traced the outline of the
violet petals. For the first time, in a long time, he felt at
peace. He absorbed every detail of the garden, thinking
that it was unusual for the lilac buds to be still very much
in bloom at this late stage in the year. As he embraced the
soothing scent of lavender, he recalled the day he sat
outside in the bright April sunshine with his mother.
Christopher could still hear her voice clearly, telling him all
about the healing quality of the amethyst coloured plants.
It was as if his mother knew almost everything about
anything. That was just one of the things that he loved

about her, and it was certainly what made her everyone's favourite teacher at Ferncross Primary School.

Before he knew it, Christopher had hypnotically drifted towards the old white shed at the bottom of the garden. His grandmother – his Nana Kathy - had warned him so many times *don't go near that shabby lean-to*! But he could not help it. There was something drawing him in. As he ran his fingers across the worn slats of wood, specks of paint sailed slowly through the air, like white powder magically drifting through endless time, before settling into silence at the bottom of some wonderful old snow globe. Christopher thought that the lean-to must be as ancient as Milaw house itself; it was a miracle that both had survived two world wars. That was hard to believe looking at it now: one more gust of wind and surely it would be no more. He could vaguely recall his grandfather pottering about in the shed, mending old lawnmowers; sadly, it was now a mere husk and his Nana Kathy had locked the door many years ago.

Suddenly, something caught Christopher's attention. Although countless spiders had decorated the shed's ancient window with their silken labyrinths, he could just make out a ghostly white apparition. Through the panes of glass, two piercing azure coloured eyes stared at him. Goosebumps crawled over every inch of Christopher's skin. He knew that his Nana would be furious with him, but he just had to find out who - or *what* - was looking at him!

The light August breeze waltzed through air again, sending the heavenly scent of lavender in his direction, nudging him towards the lean-to door. Nervously, Christopher wrapped his hand around the rusting doorknob and turned it with all his might. Nothing. He tried it again, but this time he leaned against the door with his shoulder. Still nothing. The door just would not budge. It was going to be impossible to open it without the key.

Then something magical happened: the autumnal zephyr exhaled from above once more, through the garden, along the path and down to the old lean-to.

The door creaked slowly open.

# Chapter 2
## ~ *THE WHITE HORSE* ~

*What on earth?* Christopher thought, wiping disbelief from his eyes. It all seemed like some strange dream, but it looked like someone had deliberately pushed the door open as if to invite him inside. Suddenly, a shadow flickered from deep within the darkness. Christopher could just make out the silhouette of a small hand waving back and forth. Like a moth to a flame, he was helplessly pulled towards its haunting iridescence. A chill crawled up his spine. He could hear his heart pounding noisily in his ears. Christopher rubbed his eyes again in a hopeless attempt to clear the vision of this creepy apparition. But *it* was still there. Now the thin ghost like index finger moved repeatedly to and fro, like a little hook drawing him in. He tried to resist, but it was useless.

"H...h...h...hello?" Christopher stammered. He tried to say something else, but his mouth was mummified with fear. He could almost hear his Nana shouting at the top of her wee lungs - *it's dangerous son – keep oot*! But he just had to see what was inside. He swallowed down the lump of terror at the back of his throat, then ever so carefully he stepped inside the old lean-to.

Christopher's heart hammered painfully against his ribs. He felt like he was going to faint. He scrambled for the light switch, but there was no need. Sunlight shimmered through the misty panes of glass and thankfully its glow replaced the unwelcome darkness. Time stood still. Every ancient artefact seemed to hang suspended in the air, as if Christopher had interrupted some splendid celebration. The shelves were adorned with all manner of bric-a-brac: books, paintings, glass jars and board games of some decade past. In the corner lay an old gramophone with its records propped at the side. One object was still very much in motion: a white horse, rocking slowly back and forth, as if its jockey had leapt off merely seconds before. It actually appeared to be smiling at Christopher.

Another shaft of sunlight danced through the glass, catching the lustre of the horse's sapphire like eyes. Christopher was in awe. He smiled and whispered *"you are m…magnificent. Thanks for leading me h…here"*. He laid his hand upon the horse's saddle and felt an all-encompassing warmth wrap around him, causing his fear and anxiety to melt away. He forgot all about the impending horror of starting a new school; a miraculous thing given that only fifteen minutes ago he had burst out of Milaw house in search of some calming fresh air. These surges of panic had been sneaking up on him too much recently and he could not find the words to tell anyone about how he really felt. It all did not seem to matter so much now, standing inside this wonderful old relic. Christopher felt hypnotised being surrounded by such enchanting objects. He no longer felt alone. It was almost as if something, *or someone*, was trying to talk to him, to tell him their story.

The snowy steed continued to rock back and forth, but his momentum had slowed a little. Christopher was struck by how perfect the horse looked. It appeared to be made of solid oak and everything about it suggested that it had vaulted straight out of Victorian times. Temptation clutched at Christopher: it grasped his foot, placed it in one of the leather stirrups and helped him onto the trusted steed. Even though he knew he was too old to be sitting atop a timber horse, and the mere sight would cause him to be the laughingstock of his peers, Christopher could not help it. He felt like a king. As he grappled for the golden reigns, he noticed a line of jaunty words inscribed into the wood.

## Decemuir sacrorum libri.

There was something familiar about the strange inscription: Christopher was certain that he had seen it somewhere before. He placed his fingers over the deep lines of the letters. Suddenly, an overpowering current shot through his body, throwing him from the horse. A flash of white danced in front of his eyes.

When Christopher's vision returned, he discovered that he was lying crumpled on the floor. To his amazement though, there was no pain. He felt fine. In fact, he felt like cheering. And then he thought of his Nana. He was sure that his tumultuous clamour would have disturbed her, but the image of his Nana Kathy stomping down the path in her fluffy slippers made him laugh aloud.

*Dammit, what's wrong with me?* Christopher thought, trying hard to stifle his merriment. He lay on the floor, as still as his body would allow, hoping that his laughter would dissolve into nothing. But then he caught sight of the magic again and his belly summersaulted: the contents of the old lean-to appeared to float enchantingly in the air.

*Creak – creak – creak – creak.*

The silvery white horse gathered momentum again but there was no one sitting on his saddle. Christopher watched his pendulum like movement and followed the direction of his muzzle. It seemed to be pointing in the direction of a wooden box, on the shelf just below the window. He gingerly scrambled to his feet and crept towards the box.

The timeworn metal latch clicked open easily and Christopher pushed the lid up as far as it would go. A sprig of lavender rested on top of layers of yellowish, crumpled newspapers. The lilac scent drifted through air and warmed his very soul. Carefully, Christopher placed the lavender spray to the side and proceeded to pull out the scrunched-up balls of print. He noticed the date on one: *Tuesday 8th September 1959*. Not being one for history though, he put it aside and thought nothing more about it. Something far more interesting caught his attention. Underneath the layers of newspaper, Christopher found a wooden bound manuscript. On the front cover, the title *The Book of Almost Anything* was ornately engraved. He lifted the book from its wooden box and placed it on the shelf. At the bottom of the box lay a very decorative looking pen. Christopher had never seen anything like it in his life: it was encased in mother of pearl and its aurum nib looked like the beak of a majestic golden eagle. It had the initials *T. M.* engraved on the lid.

Christopher thought immediately of his grandfather, Thomas Muir. Although his Papa Tommy died when Christopher was only seven, he could still remember him vividly. He had played such an important part in his childhood. Memories resonated into life: he could recall sitting in the huge reception room in Milaw House, alongside his Papa, tinkering on the keys of the upright piano. His important job was to press the low C note when instructed, whilst his Papa graced the piano keys with his version of "Chopsticks".

The music faded along with the memory.

Christopher found himself holding the pen tightly between his thumb and index finger. He felt as though the pen had a story to tell, as if it was looking for something to bring its tale to life. Automatically, as if he had been commanded to, he opened the wooden bound book. The pages fell open at a page called *Sam*. Underneath the title, lay a magical story about a white Siberian husky. Christopher immediately became engrossed in the story: Sam was a wonderful dog with a loyal, loving heart, and deep blue eyes. The dog's story was spellbinding. As he read on, Christopher felt compelled to touch the words on the page, as though he was reading braille and it was the only way he would understand. Every expression about Sam and his young owner Tom appeared to leap out of the page and inject life into Christopher. He felt so alive and excited. Something magical was happening.

Then the story stopped.

Christopher yearned for another chapter, paragraph, sentence, word or even letter. The story could not stop there. Without thinking, he brought the nib of the pen to the paper and continued the *Story about Sam*. The words miraculously just appeared on the page, as if someone else was writing the tale. He could not believe it. Then the story changed: *Sam became Christopher's trusted dog and he followed him wherever he went.* Christopher had always wanted a dog, so the story naturally fell out onto the paper. From that moment on, *Sam slept at the bottom of Christopher's bed and chased away any of his nightmares or painful lingering memories. Sam and Christopher were inseparable.*

And then the story stopped. Again.

However, this time it was because Christopher had been interrupted by a scratching at the lean-to door. The hand of fear scuttled across the floor and scarpered up his spine. The scratching became more frantic. Christopher's heart leapt up from his chest and a mumbling whimper escaped from his mouth. He felt as if he was going to scream. But he thought of his father and how he would have been *incredibly ashamed of such feeble actions*! So, Christopher tried to *be a man,* in the emotionless way that his father would have commanded.

Christopher walked ever so slowly towards the rickety door. The clawing seemed louder and more aggressive. He gulped down what he thought would be the last breath of air he would ever experience. He opened the door.

Out of nowhere, a beautiful white dog darted forward, jumped up and knocked Christopher to his knees. As the dog greeted him with slobbering kisses, a glint of sunlight twinkled on its collar.

The dog was called Sam.

# CHAPTER 3
## ~ *SAM THE SIBERIAN* ~

Still on his knees, Christopher found himself staring into the beautiful blue eyes of the Siberian husky. He struggled to think logically, trying to dismiss the fantastical idea that he had somehow conjured up this wonderful snow-white dog called Sam. Was he just daydreaming? After all, his father was always criticising him for having *such an overactive imagination*! In the small village of Ferncross, everybody knew everything about anything, and so just about every pet was accounted for. It would also have been exceedingly difficult for anyone - or *anything* - to have crept by the eagle eyes of Nana Kathy. The more Christopher thought rationally about it, the more his original but outrageous idea seemed to make sense.

By this point, the striking Siberian had stopped adorning Christopher with slavering kisses; instead, he appeared to be listening to his new master's every thought. The dog's cerulean eyes were spellbinding. Christopher could *actually feel* the dog's paw firmly on his hand.

*"You are real"*, he whispered to the beautiful, white dog. Then, just like before, Christopher was embraced with a reassuring warmth. He felt as if this wonderful dog called Sam was sent from somewhere, as if he was meant to be Christopher's protector. Surely his Nana Kathy would understand. Surely, she would see that Sam was just the friend that Christopher had been yearning for ever since the loss of his mother. Surely, she would allow Sam to stay with them.

For as long as he could remember, his grandparents did not own any pets, but that did not stop them from being animal lovers. The garden of Milaw house was always bustling with life, from foxes to squirrels to hedgehogs even. Nana Kathy also loved taking care of her *wee feathered friends*, as she liked to call them; whatever the weather, she was always out filling up their little seed trays. This was just another one of the reasons why Christopher loved the garden so much. He looked at Sam and smiled, but at the same time he swallowed down his concern. He could almost hear his Nana's answer of *No son – and that's my final decision*.

If only looking after this huge bundle of white energy was as easy as tending to the little robins in the garden.

Christopher clambered to his feet and brushed the dust from his knees. He glanced around the interior of the old lean-to, checking that nothing had been broken or shunted out of its place. Thankfully, everything seemed fine, except for the old gramophone: its horn appeared to have swivelled round and it was now pointing towards Christopher. *It must have moved in all my calamity*, he thought. But when Christopher moved forward to push the cone back into its place, he noticed that there was an old shellac disc already in position in the turntable. *That's odd*, Christopher thought, as he stared at the strangely immaculate looking record. There did not appear to be a single scratch on the surface. Not even a speck of dust.

Sam nuzzled at his hand and awoke Christopher from his bemusement. He looked down and smiled again at his newly found friend. Then Sam nestled his nose again against Christopher's right hand. It was like Sam was encouraging his young master.

"A…a…and wh…why not?!" Christopher stammered aloud with excitement. Before he knew it, his hand found the arm of the old gramophone. He began winding it with all his might. The dynamic action caused a stir in the old lean-to, and every object in the room came alive again. Christopher stumbled backwards as the stylus slipped down onto the record's intricate spirals. A harmony of wonderful soft strings filled the air.

*If they ask me, I could write a book…*

The voice filled the air. The soothing sonorous words sounded so familiar to Christopher. Sinatra. Of course, it

10

was a Frank Sinatra; one of his Papa Tommy's favourite singers. The music and words swirled through the air, grasping a hold of Sam and Christopher.

*I could write a preface on how we met, so the world would never forget...*

Normally, this would have all seemed so ridiculous, and Christopher would certainly have been laughed at by any number of his so-called friends back in Leicester, but to be dancing foot to paw with a Siberian husky called Sam, in time to Frank Sinatra, seemed to be exactly the normality that Christopher had been looking for.

*And the simple secret of the plot, is just tell them that I love you a lot...*

Christopher stopped dancing. The words of the chorus resonated through to his very soul. Sam's prancing about also halted. They both stood motionless, listening to the soothing lyrics.

"A...a...am I losing m...my m...mind?" Christopher stuttered to Sam, as the stylus reached the end of the song. The silence brought back the reality of the afternoon's events, and it began to weigh down upon him. Exhausted, he slumped onto the dusty floor. Sam, sensing his dismay, curled up in front of his newly found master and began lapping his hand as an offer of comfort.

"I...if I am l...losing my m...mind, then why do you s...seem so real Sam?" The dog let out a little howl, as if he was trying to reassure Christopher that he was, in fact, sane.

"CHRISTOPHER!?"

Suddenly, Sam and Christopher were interrupted by the recognisable Scottish call of Nana Kathy from somewhere at the top of the garden. Christopher scrambled to his feet and stood at the door of the lean-to.

*Now I am really, really for it,* he thought. Sam was behind him, nudging him out of the lean-to and into the garden.

"I'll b...be there in a m...minute Nana. I h...have m...m...missed you.    J...just coming!" Christopher shouted, trying to cover up the strangled panic in his voice.

He thought that his forced but composed reply would buy him an extra five minutes. So, he quickly rootled back inside the old shed to cover up the unbelievable events of the afternoon.

*Of course, the book … how stupid am I?* Christopher thought. He carefully picked up *The Book of Almost Anything* and placed it back inside the old newspaper wrappings. He laid the lavender on top and shut the lid of the box. However, he kept his Papa's pen. He wanted to keep a hold of it for a while longer, just to prove to himself that the events of the afternoon had indeed taken place. He took one last look at contents of the shed and ran his hand over the wooden mane of the rocking horse.

"And you're coming with me. I don't care about the consequences!" Christopher said to Sam effortlessly, without any of his usual stuttering. Sam looked up at his young master adoringly. He was oh so grateful that he was not going to be left behind in the old shed.

As they stepped outside, and onto the old flagstone path, a heavenly force exhaled from above and sent its breath towards the lean-to, gracefully blowing the old door back into its place, causing the latch to shut.

Christopher and Sam began the dread filled journey towards the back door of Milaw house. With every step, he could feel his heart sink lower than the fading sunlight. Even though he knew his Nana Kathy's response would not be the one he wanted, he reached down and grabbed Sam's collar tightly.

"You're mine Sam. And I am keeping you. No matter what".

Sam's fluffy white tail thumped in agreement against the back of Christopher's legs. Yet again, his stutter had momentarily vanished, without him even realising it.

When they reached the back door, Nana Kathy appeared with a huge blue bowl in her hands. Her face lit up when she saw Christopher.

"There you are son! I was aboot to send a search party

oot for you." And then she placed a dish of meat down into the garden.

The name on the bowl was Sam.

# CHAPTER 4
## ~ *INCAENDIUM*~

Christopher played with the carrots on his plate. He did not feel hungry; he was too busy staring out into the back porch where Sam was sleeping. The fluffy Siberian was enjoying the last of the late afternoon sunshine. Christopher sat without eating a mouthful of food, trying to process the afternoon's events. He could not understand why Nana Kathy was behaving like everything was just "normal". What made things even more confusing was that everywhere Christopher looked, doggy paraphernalia lay, which suggested that Sam the Siberian was a long-established member of the Muir family.

Christopher almost laughed out loud at how ridiculous it all seemed. *This has got to be a dream*, he thought. However, he was too scared to say anything to his Nana Kathy about the appearance of his Siberian husky called Sam. He could almost hear his Nana say, *you've lost your marbles!*

"Whit's wrong son, are you not hungry?" Nana Kathy clucked over her grandson, placing her hand over his forehead to check his temperature. "You've no fever, but you look a wee bitty flushed. What's the matter?"

"I…I…eh, I'm …j…just thinking about s…starting school. I guess I am a little b…bit worried about it. Do you m…mind if I leave dinner until l…later. I think I n…need a walk."

Before his Nana could respond, the doorbell rang sharply. The harsh sound disturbed Sam from his sleep. He stretched out all four limbs and padded through to the kitchen to where Christopher was and flopped down at his feet. Nana Kathy had already vanished, presumably to answer the door. Even though she was in her winter years, she had an amazing talent for disappearing and then reappearing, as if she had magically teleported from one end

14

of the house to the other.

Christopher instantly recognised his father's rumbling voice resonating over the top of his Nana Kathy's hushed tones. Although he could not make out what she was saying, he knew that she was not happy to see him. His father, Aidan Brenton, was a powerful man and he knew it. Christopher always felt as if he did not really know his father at all. As a chief executive officer at Incaendium, a global computer and mobile communications company, Aidan Brenton had never been much of a father figure in Christopher's life. Before his parents' divorce and his mother's passing, he could only ever recall his father arriving home late at night, long after his mother had tucked him into bed. Latterly, he would pretend that he had fallen asleep; in truth, he was lying wide awake, listening for the click of his father's key in the front door. This was almost always followed by unpleasant exchanges between his parents, which usually ended with his poor mother in tears. The tension in the old Leicester town house seemed to swallow up every morsel of air; a choking, stifling presence that left Christopher bereft of any happy memories of his father. No matter how hard he tried, he could not think of his dad in a positive light. Sure, he was an extremely wealthy man, and he did financially provide for Christopher and his mother, but it all seemed to be in the name of something. If there were ever any problems, Aidan Brenton would merely throw money at it. But all Christopher ever wanted was his father to read him a bedtime story.

Perhaps though, most of all, Christopher wanted his father to take more care of his mother.

"What have I told you about slouching whilst eating your dinner!"

The suddenness of his father's voice startled Christopher and made him almost leap from his seat. Sam quickly stood up beside him and let out a disapproving growl.

"You will end up with a curved spine and a crooked

neck!"

"Enough Aidan! Christopher is no' bothering anyone. This is my hoose and I make the rules. So, Christopher can slouch when eating dinner, whether you like it or no'." Nana Kathy could cut quite a punch when she wanted to, and her words thankfully stopped Christopher's father from continuing his rant.

"Hi D…Dad", Christopher mumbled awkwardly as he hesitantly stepped forward to give his father a hug.

Instead, Mr Brenton pulled back from his son and offered his hand for what felt more like a formal business greeting. Christopher uncomfortably engaged in his father's handshake, but instantly regretted it.

"Your grip is weak Christopher; you need to man up! In the world of business, your handshake means everything. It tells people what kind of man you are."

"Aidan! Please leave my grandwean alone."

Christopher was ever so grateful for his Nana's input at this point in this awkward – and very unexpected – family reunion. Aiden Brenton shifted from one foot to another, as if he was trotting on the spot.

"Whit is it you are here for anyway? You've no seen your son for over three weeks, so you've got a bloomin' cheek to just appear and then try to behave like his faither!"

Mr Brenton ignored Nana Kathy's question. Instead, he placed his black leather suitcase on the table and clicked open the gold latches. Inside, there were several important looking documents all brandishing the Incaendium logo: the head of a black stag head with the letter "I" emblazoned at its centre. He put the papers aside, pulled out a little red box and then offered it to Christopher.

"There you go. You are now the proud owner of Incaendium's latest mobile phone. You will be the envy of everyone."

Christopher took the slim rectangular box from the hands of his father and stammered a very weak sounding "th…thanks". He was amazed how feeble his voice always appeared to sound in the presence of his father. It made his stutter even worse. Sam lifted his nose and sniffed the box, but quickly whipped his muzzle away. He snarled at Aiden Brenton, baring his teeth.

"Ahem. If I could continue?" Mr Brenton jibed. "When you set up the phone, you will notice that it has a first-class navigation and pairing device. This means that you can pair the phone to my phone, and we can literally see where we both are at any time. I will also see – and hear – *everything* that you do."

"Bloomin' cheek!" Nana Kathy interrupted. "You mean you can earwig in on Christopher's conversation and boss him around!" By this point, she appeared to be more than flustered, and the little lavender tints in her white hair almost appeared to turn a shade of crimson red.

"Th…thanks D…D…Da…" Christopher could not finish his sentence. He felt like he was suffocating. He needed to escape again. The heat was too much.

"Right Aidan, enough." Thankfully, Nana Kathy cut in again, just in time to save her grandson. "Christopher will do whatever later. But for the now, just leave the wee soul alone. He was just about to go for a wee walk." Nana Kathy hoped that Mr Brenton would take the hint and leave. It was all becoming too much, and she could feel the effect he was having on her blood pressure. Sam could sense her pain, so padded over to her side, nuzzling his cold nose into the heat of her palms.

"Ha ha ha!" Mr Brenton laughed slowly and malevolently. "I almost forgot, Kathy, how little – *or should I say wee* – everything seems to you." Mr Brenton's words were laced with scorn. "But this is no insignificant matter." He paused and then stared straight at Christopher. "Do not forget. Link your mobile to mine. Firstly, you must look straight into the camera so that it can scan your retinae. After that, the phone will tell you what to do…"

The technical jargon and harsh tones spewing from Aiden Brenton's mouth caused such an aching thump in

Christopher's brain. He felt a thousand voices scream out to him, telling him to leave, telling him to run far away from this man who was supposed to be his father. Time stopped ticking. Christopher found himself standing face to face with a man he no longer recognised. Fire and heat raged behind the eyes of this familiar stranger. It was a choking, agonizing heat; one that grasped tightly around Christopher's chest, squeezing all the oxygen from his lungs. The room was ablaze with crimson and amber. Angry flames lashed and whipped around him, like a lion stalking its prey, hemming him in on all sides. The flames whipped higher and higher, until their painful licks culminated into a high-pitched frequency shrieking in his ears. Christopher gasped for air. He held his hands over his ears and screamed "NOOOOOOOOOOO!"

The hands of time stirred, and the seconds moved forward.

"And for Dicken's sake, stop daydreaming!" Aiden Brenton shouted at his son.

Whether it was the strident force of his father's words, or the heat that still appeared to slap at his face, Christopher suddenly rushed out of the kitchen, with Sam following loyally behind him. He could not even find the words to say goodbye to his father. Tears prickled in eyes.

As he was pulling his jacket on in the hallway, his Nana appeared behind him. "Don't you take any notice of your so-called faither. He's just a very angry man. You're doing so well son, especially after everything that's happened to you. Your mother, my dear wee Peggy, would be so proud of you."

Nana Kathy then hugged her grandson lovingly and wiped away his tears. Her energy was so calming; it was just what Christopher needed in the aftermath of his father's presence. Sam was already at the front door, wagging his thick white tail, waiting patiently on his master to take him for a walk.

\*\*\*\*

Outside, the air felt unusually frosty, but it was a welcome relief to the inferno that had been building inside Milaw house. At that moment, Christopher felt that every fibre of his body was repelled by the presence of his father. At that moment, he hated him, loathed him even, as if he was everything that Christopher was not. At that very moment, he was not even sure if Aiden Brenton was actually his father. However, Sam's cooling nose suddenly brought Christopher to his senses, and the memory of his mother's words replaced his anger: *hate and anger are hot coals. Let go. The longer you hold onto them, the more they scald your hands.*

Christopher smiled. He inhaled the surprising soothing coolness of the air, allowing it to calm his racing heart. He looked upwards and smiled at the little swallows as they graced the sky with their late summer evening dance. Sam was fascinated by their high-flying antics and pulled Christopher forward. Laughter pushed the two chums even further, so much so that the two of them started running. Christopher sang loudly like the little feathered friends in the sky. They chirruped along Acacia Drive, until they reached the brook at the end of the road where the two of them stopped to catch their breath. Christopher was too busy ruffling the thick fur between Sam's ears to notice the beautiful vision walking towards him. It was only when Sam pulled forward again that Christopher noticed the exquisite emerald eyes of Kerry Robinson.

"Christopher Muir. How the heck are you?" Kerry flung her arms around her stunned friend.

Christopher stood in a state of disbelief, still holding Sam's leash, arms by his side. His face flushed beetroot.

"K…K…Kerry. Wow, you…you l…look amazing!" He smiled at Kerry, despite the awkwardness of his stutter. It appeared to attach every word he said.

Christopher had known Kerry for a long time, but he felt like a whole lifetime had passed since he last set eyes on her. Although she had not changed, and her long dark hair made her instantly recognisable, Kerry now looked even prettier that Christopher remembered. When they were younger, they would play for hours in the garden at Milaw house, pretending they were king and queen, ruling the village of Ferncross. It all seemed so silly now to Christopher.

"I'm so sorry to hear about your mum. We all were. I saw you the day of your mum's funeral, but I don't think you saw … me". Kerry held her hand out and delicately patted Christopher's shoulder. A hot flush swept up his neck and across his face. However, Sam's cool nose nuzzled his hand as it to give his master some comfort.

"I…I didn't s…see you K... Kerry," Christopher's heart slumped lower in his chest. Why did he not notice her on the day of his mum's funeral? Kerry had the most hypnotic green eyes that he had ever seen, so he usually fell into a trance whenever he looked at her. Perhaps if he had set sight on her that day, even for a split second, it would have momentarily appeased his feeling of loss and disbelief.

"Don't worry about it. It must have been so hard. It must still be. Margaret … I mean … Ms Muir was so caring. The school and village just aren't the same without her. How's your grandmother bearing up?"

"Sh…she h…has her days. I c…can tell that she really m…misses my m…mum, but she's s…so strong. I don't know wh…what I'd d…do without her."

Once again, Sam reassuringly prodded Christopher's hand and let out a little yowl. The adoring and encouraging look on Sam's face filled him with a short burst of confidence. Before he could think about what he was saying, the words popped out of his mouth "s…so you're a…at Oakwood Academy? I s…start there in a f…f…few days t…too. I'm going into Y…Year Eight."

Kerry hesitated for what felt like an eternity before she answered.

"Yeah, I'm at Oakwood. I'm just about to start Year

Nine. So, I guess that means we will be seeing a lot more of each other?"

Kerry's words danced in Christopher's head. His heart pounded in his chest again, but this time it was in a good way.

"I l...look f...forward to it. It's b...been n...nice c...catching up again".

"See you around then." Kerry smiled before popping her wireless Incaendium headphones back into her ears. She turned and then started her journey back along the tree lined Acacia Drive.

Christopher tried to remain calm, in case Kerry turned around to look at them; but excitement visited again, encouraging him to perform a little jig with Sam. For a split second, he was sure that he could hear the voice of Sinatra.

*The way you walk and whisper and look.*

# CHAPTER 5
## ~ *THE PEN IS MIGHTIER THAN THE SWORD* ~

On returning from his walk with Sam, Christopher came face to face with the ridiculous sight of his father's sports car, a black Belasco. Lurking to the right of the driveway, in his mother's old parking space, the car's stygian surface and private registration of **AB1** sneered menacingly at Christopher. The car was immaculate, almost too immaculate. Everything about it was preposterous. Aidan Brenton – and his car - had long outstayed their welcome. Christopher could feel his blood boil; he was certain that his father's actions were deliberate, just to add more fire to an already painful situation. However, Christopher's angst quickly faded when he heard the strained voice of his Nana Kathy.

"How dare you! You've no right to tell me how to raise him. That's my grandwean and my daughter's only bairn!"

"You are indulging in that boy's imagination too much Kathy. It is not normal." Aiden Brenton's sneering tone was instantly recognisable.

Christopher crept along towards the sill of the hall window and gestured to Sam to be as quiet as possible. The dog, as obedient as ever, followed. He even appeared to be listening to the voices coming from the gap in the window. The two chums then sat hunched below the ledge, trying to work out what was being discussed.

"Kathy, Kathy… calm down, I am just saying … the boy would be much better with me. He could come and work for me at my Leicester Office. It would be better for him *and* it might put a stop to his vivid imagination".

"I want you to leave. Now. I don't want you to be here when Christopher gets back. And I've already told you, stop calling me Kathy!"

"Well … *Mrs Muir*, you will be hearing from my lawyer".

An uncontrollable spasm suddenly pushed Christopher's foot forward, causing it to scuff along some loose gravel below the window. He tried to move and nudge Sam back along towards the side of the house, but it was too late.

"Christopher, it is very rude to listen in on conversations." Aiden Brenton's voice sounded so supercilious. "In any case," he continued before his son could reply, "there was nothing much to hear. I was just having a *nice wee* chat with your grandmother. I am sure you heard the gist of it."

"Eh … no … well, n…not all of it." Christopher screamed internally at how clumsy and weak he sounded. He wanted to be stronger. He wanted to shout at his father and tell him to leave. But he kept quiet.

"Your faither's just going Christopher. Goodbye. Mr Brenton."

Christopher could hear his Nana's voice waiver a little, so he walked over to the steps where she was standing at the doorway of Milaw house. Sam was already by Nana Kathy's side. In the fading light of the day, she suddenly looked so frail. The dwindling sunlight reflected on Sam's thick white coat, creating a halo around his prominent stature. For a split second, both Nana Kathy and Sam were surrounded by a white circle of light. Christopher felt like he was looking at an old photograph taken many, many years ago.

"Christopher!" Once again, the growling voice of Mr Brenton interrupted Christopher's thoughts. "The link up on your new phone. I will be waiting on your request later tonight. Do not forget!"

Before Christopher could say goodbye, Mr Brenton stormed off towards his monstrous motor car in the driveway. Christopher did not even wait on the sound of the outrageous rumble of the engine starting; instead, he ventured inside to check on his Nana. Sam led the way.

The hallway of Millaw House felt cold, aching, and

empty. An unwelcome darkness slithered out from the shadows. Christopher switched on the table lamp and instantly the hallway was adorned in longed-for light. He expected to see his Nana sitting on the chaise longue, but she was nowhere to be seen. Concern ushered Sam and Christopher into the sitting room. Nana Kathy was perched on her usual white chair facing the sliding patio doors. She was staring out at the violas in the garden, watching their little purple heads swaying in the evening breeze. Christopher did not say anything. He did not want to disturb her thoughts. Sam padded over to Nana Kathy and cuddled into the sides of her legs. The wagging of his thick tail seemed to awaken her from her trance like state.

"Oh son. I didnae hear you. I was lost in a wee world of my own there".

Christopher flopped down in the bean bag in front of his Nana. They gazed out at the fading light in the garden. The hypnotic tick of the grandfather clock echoed throughout the empty house, lulling Sam, Christopher and his Nana Kathy towards another place and time. Somewhere in the garden, a nightingale sang the first few notes of his sunset song. Nana Kathy stirred from her thoughts.

"You know, we used to think of your father as a *fairly* decent man. I don't know what happened to him. Sometimes I think it was all just an act."

Nana Kathy's eyes glistened with tears. In the setting sunlight, her eyes looked like precious amber gems. Christopher placed his hand over his Nana's and held it tightly.

"N…Nana, I'm n… not going anywhere. M…my home is here. With you. I d…don't care what he wants or says. It'll b…be all okay … you'll see".

The look on his Nana's face filled Christopher with such a painful sadness. It was like he was looking at his mother all over again. In the midst of trying to find the right words to say, his Nana thankfully piped up.

24

"What letter comes after S in the alphabet?"

"Eh… T?" Christopher chuckled. "Thanks N…Nana, I'd l…love a cup".

Fortunately, Nana Kathy's strength had made a welcome return, lifting her onto her feet and helping her through to the kitchen. Christopher stood up and stretched out any tiredness that had crept into his limbs before joining her. Sam, watching his every move, followed his master through to where Nana Kathy was standing. The kettle whistled softly, spouting steam up into air before settling and blanching the huge kitchen window facing the garden. Christopher wiped away some of the condensation from the glass and looked out at the changing light. Evening had finally arrived. The sky was awash with a whole palette of different blues and purples. Somewhere in the distance, the ominous bark of a solitary fox pierced the air. A cold breeze stirred, snaking its way through the gap in the hopper above, sending a shiver through Christopher's body. He shut the window and turned around to find his Nana with her arm outstretched, offering him a mug of hot tea.

"Mind the way you used to draw happy faces with your finger whenever the windows steamed up? But whenever I tried to give you into trouble, your cheeky wee chops would win me over and we'd both end up giggling." His Nana smiled at the memory before sipping her tea.

Christopher was glad to see that the rosiness had returned to her cheeks.

"It seems j … just like yesterday. D…don't worry though Nana, I have n…no urge to d…draw all over the windows t…tonight".

\*\*\*\*

As they drank the rest of their tea, Christopher and his Nana reminisced about the old times in Milaw house. Their laughter and merriment brought the memories of happier times alive, making Christopher feel at ease again. Sam lay by their feet, listening to their every word. Although his head was propped against his paws, the Siberian's bright blue eyes moved from Christopher to Nana Kathy and back again, as if he understood every word. There was no talk of Aiden Brenton and so it set the house at peace again. It was only when the grandfather clock chimed softly in the hall that Christopher and his Nana stopped talking.

"Well N…Nana, I th…think it's time for my bed. It's b…been quite a day…for all of us!" He wanted to say something about Sam, but he suddenly felt so stupid. Where would he even begin?

"It sure has son," his Nana replied, taking the mugs to the sink, and turning on the hot tap. "You go on up to bed, I'll take care of these."

Christopher bid his Nana goodnight and gave her a kiss on the cheek. He could almost hear the sneering jibes of *sissy* being shouted at him for doing so, but he did not care. Given everything that had happened, Christopher had no problem in showing how much he cared for, loved, and appreciated his Nana Kathy. He had learned one of life's hardest lessons: loved ones do not live forever. In the eyes of his so-called friends he might be *a sissy*, but at least his Nana knew how much he loved her.

Christopher climbed the stairs towards his bedroom, but he was so caught up in thoughts of his Nana and father's argument that he had not even fully considered the craziness of the day's events. The magnificent dog that he had somehow managed to conjure up through his writing was already sitting patiently at the end of his bed, keeping a patch of his bed warm. Christopher slumped down beside Sam and ruffled the hair on his fluffy head. His white coat made Christopher recall the wooden horse in the old lean-to and the strange engraving of *Decemuir sacrorum libri*. He had felt drawn towards every letter. He just had to find out what it all meant.

*"Perhaps tomorrow we will go back to the lean-to and explore a little further"*, Christopher whispered to Sam. The dog

26

wagged his bushy tail in agreement. His master's stutter had disappeared yet again.

**** 

Before climbing into bed, Christopher thought that he should tackle the new mobile phone. He knew that he should have been incredibly grateful for the gift, but it filled him with dread. He also knew that if he did not link the phone to his father's, then he would never hear the end of it. As he pressed the **on** button, the black screen flushed scarlet with the Incaendium logo: a black stag's head with the letter I emblazoned at its centre.

The phone felt alien to Christopher. He was not particularly good with technology and he always preferred to read paperbacks; staring at the harsh glare of an electronic book almost always gave him a headache.

**Request to read retina** flickered in red.

Christopher hesitated, and then pressed **OK.** He held the device in front of his eyes and gazed into its hollow darkness. Suddenly, a luminescent flare scored through his vision; Christopher felt like he had just looked directly at a solar eclipse. The pain forced him to drop the phone and hold his hands over his clenched-shut eyelids. White hot letters spelling out *IGNIS* cavorted in front of him. In the empty darkness, he felt another presence. Christopher quickly rubbed his eyes before opening them, but he still had trouble focusing.

Thankfully, there was no one else in his room. The mobile phone lay abandoned on the floor; its red glow eerily illuminated the corner of Christopher's bedroom. It was like a magnet. He was compelled to pick up the device and follow whatever instruction it decreed. Without even thinking, he obeyed a series of instructions before pairing his device to his father's. It ordered him to link up his email and old social media accounts. It had been years since Christopher had even logged into any of them. The next thing he knew, endless messages from his so-called friends back in Leicester appeared, asking **how's the stutter?** and **where've u bn?** Panic gargled at the back of Christopher's throat. It dragged him back into the land of living. He felt his heart beat out of time as he was bombarded with commands and orders. It was all too much. His head hurt and his eyes ached, so he switched the phone off and threw it in his wardrobe. Sam stared nervously at his master.

\*\*\*\*

Finally, in the comfort of his bed, Christopher pulled out his notebook and his Papa Tommy's pen. He had been looking forward to this part of the day, away from his father and the flashing lights of the horrible Incaendium device. Thankfully, his eyes no longer hurt. Sam shifted at the bottom of the bed, nuzzling himself into the feet of his master.

Christopher began writing.

Just like before in the old lean-to, the pen told the story. The nib effortlessly skipped across the paper. The words joined to make an adventure about a beautiful green-eyed girl called Kerry and how she would fall in love with a charming young man called Christopher. They would live a long happy life together with their dog Sam.

*"Well"*, Christopher whispered to Sam, his voice heavy with slumber as he put the pen and notepad on his bed side cabinet, *"if I can conjure you up from writing with this pen, then surely my story will make Kerry fall in love with me."*

Sam whimpered lightly in response.

And then the two friends fell sound asleep.

# CHAPTER 6
## ~ *THE GRANDFATHER CLOCK* ~

*BUZZZZZ ... BUZZZZZ ... BUZZZZZ!* A seething pulsation pulled Christopher from his slumber. He struggled to his feet. His eyes felt strained at the sunlight slicing through the window as he scrambled to where the sound was coming from. He flung his wardrobe door open in order to find the culprit: it was the Incaendium mobile phone. Its red obtrusive screen flashed impatiently with the message: **Dad calling.** Christopher quickly grabbed the device and pressed down hard on the power *off* button. The screen went blank. He could not face speaking to his father that early in the day.

Christopher slumped backwards onto the comfort of his bed. The silence calmed his galloping heart. He was worried that his Nana would have heard the racket, but there was not a sound to be heard in the house. Although the panic was beginning to leave, Christopher still felt uneasy: he was sure that he had turned the Incaendium phone off before he went to bed.

*"I knew it w…was a bad idea"*, he mumbled to Sam, turning around to see if his dog was awake yet. However, his heart leapt into his mouth. Sam was nowhere to be seen. Salty tears blurred Christopher's vision as he tried to make sense of what was happening. He swallowed down a huge lump of sadness. Was Sam just a figment of his imagination after all?

Before he knew it, Christopher was at the bottom of the staircase, frantically searching for his best friend. He was about to start shouting his dog's name at the top of his lungs, but he was stopped in his tracks by a wonderful white vision: Sam was sitting in front of the old grandfather clock in the hall, wagging his tail. Christopher fell to his knees and flung his arms around his dog.

"I…I thought I'd l…lost you", he whimpered into the Siberian's ears.

At first, Christopher was too caught up in his reunion with Sam to have noticed the folded piece of paper lying in front of the grandfather clock. It was only when the magnificent clock chimed once, declaring the time of quarter past seven, that Christopher spotted the wrinkled cartridge paper. This was the all-important wedge responsible for keeping the grandfather clock's door firmly shut – and it had been like that for years. It was only Nana Kathy that habitually removed the paper to wind up the gears. She took great pride in looking after the grandfather clock, so Christopher thought it was strange that she had not placed the paper back into the door to keep it shut. Standing majestically in the hall, the clock had witnessed many a happy occasion in Milaw house. Nana Kathy liked to call it *a Muir family heirloom*.

Before he jammed the paper back into the clock's door, curiosity nudged Christopher, begging him to open the worn cartridge paper. It was only at this point that he wondered why he had not looked at it before. As he unfolded it, tiny speckles of cartridge crumbled onto the floor, indicating its age. Inside, he found an elaborate handwritten note: *key ad alterum orbem terrarum in bibliotheca mendacium.*

Seconds turned into minutes. Christopher sat on the hall floor staring at the strange, but familiar writing. Although the words were written in ink, the handwriting appeared to be in the same style as the inscription carved into the hobby horse in the old leant-to. He had no idea what it all meant. Unfortunately, foreign languages had never been one of Christopher's strong points. At primary school, he struggled to pronounce any new French words his teacher threw at him. The mere thought of those uncomfortable lessons, along with the memory of his formidable French teacher, stirred a sickly feeling in his stomach.

*Clang – Clang.*

The grandfather clock struck half past seven. The floorboards creaked above. Nana Kathy was awake. Christopher did not want her to know that he had been prying, so he quickly refolded the thick paper and carefully placed it back into the door of the grandfather clock. He sat back and patted the fur of Sam's nape, content that his canine chum was by his side again. They sat staring at the clock's face, enthralled by its hypnotic rhythm. Although the strange words were now locked away from his view, Christopher could still envisage the writing when he shut his eyes. The ornate script danced in his memory like glitter falling through the air.

****

Upstairs in his bedroom, Christopher took out his notebook and scribbled down what he could remember of the strange words. Then he placed his Papa's pen back into the top drawer of his bedside cabinet and tucked his notepad into his jacket pocket. He crept back into bed and shut his eyes. He did not want his Nana to know about his early morning discovery; she would just think that he had been snooping around.

But all was to no avail.

"Christopher?" Nana Kathy's voice pierced the silence. Her footsteps followed her question, "whit were you doing up so early this morning?"

Before Christopher could answer, her dainty face appeared around his door. He nearly burst out laughing at the sight of her curlers and hair-net clad head.

"I ... eh ... I needed a glass of water Nana. Sorry if I woke you up".

Christopher expected his response to be met with a string of questions, but Nana Kathy just smiled and winked towards Sam and his master. Then she vanished from the doorway.

Christopher was curious. Did she know what he had

been up to? Perhaps, he even thought, Nana Kathy had left the paper there on purpose.

However, he was interrupted by the best question of all, radiating from the top of the hall staircase: "Do you want two bits of toast with your scrambled eggs son?"

Christopher popped his head around the door and shouted, "three bits please Nana."

\*\*\*\*

Outside Christopher's bedroom window, Ferncross Village was alive with the promise of a new day. He could just make out the faint whistle of the postman and the clinking of milk bottles. Everybody knew everything about anyone in the village and this filled Christopher with anxiety. Starting year eight at Oakwood Academy was hard enough but being the son of Aidan Brenton made it even worse. His father's success was plastered everywhere. There was no escape. This was the reason why Christopher insisted on using his mother's maiden name - *Muir* - for his surname; he did not want any of his prospective school mates knowing the truth. Besides, the folk of Ferncross thought fondly of his mother and many were still mourning her loss. He always felt more like a Muir than a Brenton.

Christopher tried to focus his thoughts on Kerry in order to stop the overwhelming lump of grief gathering at the back of his throat. He pulled out his notepad again to read the words of last night's story. The pages fell open at the words he had frantically penned earlier. Although it was his handwriting, the word *bibliotheca* leapt out of the page. Suddenly, white sparkles shimmered, blinding his vision. Christopher shut his eyes and sat on the floor beside Sam, waiting for his dizziness to disappear. He felt strangely calm though; in fact, he felt quite giddy, as if he was going to burst into hysterics at any moment. The excitement made him open his eyes again to find Sam sitting proudly beside the notepad. His paw seemed to be pointing to the words:

*library* and *book.*

*That's strange*, Christopher thought, *I don't recall writing that.*

It was only when he picked up his notepad to take a closer look, Christopher realised that another note had appeared underneath: *Siberian est protector.*

He recognised the style of handwriting instantly: it was written in the same script as the note in the grandfather clock.

# CHAPTER 7
## ~ *JUNIPER LUX* ~

The light pitter-patter of rain tapped on the windows of Milaw house, signalling the arrival of autumnal weather. Sam sat patiently in the hallway, waiting, watching Nana Kathy's every move. She did not appear to notice the beautiful dog; she was lost in the looking glass, fidgeting with her newly roller-curled hair. Christopher tried awfully hard to behave normally: he did not want to worry his Nana by letting on about all the peculiar events he had been experiencing. He still did not even know how to bring up the topic of Sam.

"Blast," Nana Kathy muttered whilst toing and froing with hairpins.

"Your h…hair looks f…fine. Just l…leave it," Christopher assured his Nana, as he pulled on his jacket. "It's r…raining anyway, so y…you'll need to cover your h…hair".

Strangely though, Christopher's words were not met with an immediate response; instead, Nana Kathy stood very still, staring intently at her refection. It was as if she was looking at something, or someone, far away in the distance.

*Tick – tock - - tick - - tock - - - tick*

The grandfather clock moved a slow hand. Time lingered, as if waiting on someone to arrive. Light twirled through the hall windows, illuminating tiny dust motes as they danced through the air. The rain had stopped. Milaw house itself seemed to relax, breathing deeply for the first time – in a long time - as if it was pleased to see the return of a dearly missed friend.

Christopher stepped towards his Nana Kathy and Sam. He put his hand on his grandmother's shoulder, but she stood motionless in front of the mirror. Then, just when he was about to break the silence, Christopher witnessed something magical. In the hallway mirror, Christopher saw his Papa Tommy. He was standing beside his Nana Kathy, smiling from ear to ear. He looked just like Christopher remembered: his dark rimmed glasses were perched on the bridge of his nose and his thick white hair looked like it had just been Brylcreemed perfectly into place. Christopher could not believe his eyes; he wanted to laugh, cry, hug his grandfather and not let go. But, before he could do or say anything, his Papa Tommy whispered something.

"Christopher, the key to our world lies in the book. You must learn the ancient language of Latin. *Decemuir sacrorum libri. Decemuir sacrorum libri. Decemuir sacrorum libri. Decemuir sacrorum libri.*"

With every word, the rhythmic chant became louder and louder, as if every plosive syllable pulsated deep down to the very core of Milaw House. It awakened something in the building, something that had been lying dormant for a long time.

*Decemuir sacrorum libri. Decemuir sacrorum libri.*

The floorboards began violently shaking; doors opened and closed in time to the enchanting mantra; books flew from their shelves and fell at Christopher's feet; the keys on the old piano even leapt into the air, performing a mesmerising Charleston dance of ebony and ivory.

*Decemuir sacrorum libri.*

Suddenly, the hallway fell into darkness and a piercing scream whipped at Christopher's face. The screech melted into a blaze of unwanted energy and he felt as if he was standing in front of an uncontrollable forest fire; the blaze leapt towards him with every hiss and crackle. The heat was unbearable. A ball of panic whirled in Christopher's stomach. He felt as if his heart was going to explode. To his horror, the darkness was swiftly replaced by a blinding light, flashing sporadically, painfully masquerading everything around him. Christopher looked to his left, but he could no longer see his Nana Kathy or his trusted dog Sam. He was petrified. He frantically gawped at the mirror, forcing his eyes as wide as they would go through the blinding sodium light, searching for a familiar face. But there was nothing. And then, without even thinking, he shut his eyes and screamed the words "DECEMUIR SACRORUM LIBRI!"

Silence settled around Christopher. When he opened his eyes, his vision was embraced by the sight of an amazing emerald green forest. He could not believe it. He was surrounded by a spray of beautiful lilac petals, as if Monet had just added his final touches to the serene ensemble of pine needles glistening in the sunlight. The trees reached out to Christopher, calming his hammering pulse. He shut his eyes and inhaled the recognisable scent of lavender.

*Tock - - - tick - - - tock - - tick –tock –tick -*

"Whit's wrong with you son?! You look like a fart in a trance!" Nana Kathy's Scottish slang cut through the silence and shook time from its slumber.

"I…I…eh, did you see…th…that?" Christopher mumbled, dumbfounded, thinking his eyes and ears were playing tricks on him.

"See whit? Christopher, whit have I told you about squeezing your spots? It's made a right bloomin' mess of that mirror!"

And then, before Christopher could say anything, Nana Kathy trotted off to the hall cupboard in search of her rain bonnet. Shock rendered him speechless. He stumbled over to the chaise longue by the hall window and sat down. His legs felt like they were made of jelly. His heart pounded in his ears, as if it was repeatedly chanting the strange but familiar words *Decemuir sacrorum libri*. Sam nudged his head into his master's hand, requesting some head patting. Thankfully, this comforted Christopher, making him feel almost normal again. He looked down at the dog's beautiful blue eyes and telepathically said, *I must be losing my mind!*

His thoughts were interrupted by Nana Kathy.

"You know son, there's times when I feel like your Papa Tommy is still here, in Milaw house with us. Does that sound daft?"

Nana Kathy's question warmed Christopher right to his very toes. Perhaps he was not losing his mind after all. Perhaps she did see his Papa only moments before. He tried to answer, but a lump formed at the back of his throat, clasping tightly around his words.

"He'd be so proud of you, so don't you ever forget that..." Nana's Kathy's voice followed her as she left the hallway and into the living room for her handbag.

Christopher stood up and moved towards the huge mirror in the hallway, still in awe with what had just happened. His eyes were drawn towards the carved initials of *AMM*. He reached out and let his fingertips trail over the elaborate carvings in the dark brown wood. Wooden flora and fauna found Christopher. He was pulled towards a magical time and place where visions of bramblings, wood warblers and robins bobbled beneath his fingers. Christopher let out a huge sigh, whispering his Papa Tommy's words *"Decemuir sacrorum libri."*

"What are you whittling on about son? You need to do a wee wee?! Well, that's what happens when you drink too much tea."

Christopher laughed as he was met with the reflection of his Nana Kathy's puzzled face, all wrapped up in her flower-patterned rain bonnet.

"Right, let's get a move on. Your uniform won't buy itself you know."

"I'm fine Nana, let's go." Christopher replied as flat as he could, trying to hide the crazy mix of emotions in his voice.

\*\*\*\*

Outside, the rain had returned, drenching everything in sight. Fernlock looked miserable, as though it was grieving over the memory of a long-lost friend. Great puddles had formed along the path into town and Christopher had a hard time guiding Sam away from them. He thought back to a time – in the not so distant past – when he would have galloped through the puddles in his bright blue wellies, accompanied by his mum's laughter at the sight of his splashing. Sensing the swelling at the back of his throat again, Christopher decided to redirect his thoughts.

"Nana, whose initials are AMM?"

Nana Kathy seemed to be somewhat taken aback by his question because she looked at him for a moment before answering.

"Well, that's a name I've no' heard for a long-time son," his Nana began. "Those initials belong to your great grandfather - Archibald Morton Muir. Everyone called him Archie though. He was a goldsmith by trade and was an excellent carpenter. Can you believe that he carved the mirror frame in the hallway all on his own? It's made of Juniperus Lux – an ancient family of tree that is now sadly extinct."

If it had not been for Sam mustering on ahead, Christopher would have stopped on the spot. He had no idea that the mirror had been carved by his great grandfather. But then he thought of the grandfather clock in the hall and the strange note.

"Nana, did he make anything else?"

"Yes son, he made the old grandfather clock in the hall. He finished it in 1914: the year that your Papa's father was born."

Christopher's thoughts started racing in his head. He suddenly had the idea that all the recent crazy events were in fact *real*; that they were not some silly figment of his imagination. He knew there and then that he just had to do as his Papa Tommy instructed. He must learn Latin. At least, that would be his starting point to unravelling the mystery behind the recent strange happenings. Surely such a thing as an "Idiot's Guide to Latin" existed. He wanted to jump up and down with excitement, but Christopher decided that such a reaction would make him look, what his Nana would call, *quackers*. Instead, he tried to hide his tumultuous thoughts by innocently asking, "what kind of wood is Juni…" but before he could finish his question, his eyes landed on the transfixing vision of Kerry Robinson. She was standing in front of the grand fountain on Main Street, looking even more beautiful than the last time he saw her. She was with a group of girls and they were all huddled underneath a frog shaped umbrella. An unfriendly looking girl held the green brolly and the other girls, including Kerry, appeared to hang on her every whim. Christopher found himself rooted to the spot. Even Sam stopped moving.

"Son? Is everything okay?" Nana Kathy's voice interrupted her grandson's thoughts.

Christopher had almost forgotten all about the story he had written about *Kerry and Christopher*. He suddenly felt so stupid. But the story was composed with his Papa's magical pen, so he clung desperately to that thought.

"Christopher, I am going into Taylor's to have a look for your new school blazer. When you have had a chance to catch up with Kerry, can you meet me in there?"

And there it was yet again: Nana Kathy's eagle eye and her amazing talent to see just how her grandson was feeling.

*Is it that obvious,* Christopher thought to himself as he mumbled something that resembled "okay" at his Nana. His legs had turned to jelly again, making it difficult to walk in a straight line towards Kerry.

\*\*\*\*

"Oh … eh … hi Christopher. What're you doing here?" Kerry's face turned what Christopher could only describe as pillar box red. A million thoughts raced through his head. Why was she so embarrassed? Was she ashamed to be anywhere near a boy in the year below her? Before he mustered up the strength to say something, anything even, his heart plummeted down into his stomach: he could see that Kerry's friends were giggling and rolling their eyes.

Sam nudged into the back of his master's legs as if to

encourage his master to say something. But Christopher pulled his raincoat hood down further to hide his awkwardness.

"I'm w…with my N…Nana. We're… I mean … I'm getting my new uniform."

His words were met with more sniggering and eye rolling. Sadly, he had no idea what to do, or say, next. Kerry just stood there. She did not utter a word. Christopher felt like he had blown everything because of his bumbling stutter. If Sam had not been by his side, then he would have run off in the opposite direction.

But then Kerry smiled. At Christopher.

"C'mon, we need to go now," sniggered the leviathan-like girl, standing beside Kerry. Her tall stature was crowned with a mass of fiery red curls and her long, pointed expression only added more insult to the condescending look she was quite clearly aiming at Christopher. She had what Nana Kathy would describe as *a face like a nippy sweetie!*

"I need to go Christopher. Sorry." And as quick as that, Kerry about turned to face her group of cackling friends.

The tall girl grabbed Kerry's hand and pulled her into a jog, as if to put as much distance as possible between Christopher and Kerry. The three other girls ran behind them, snickering and screaming like banshees.

\*\*\*\*

Christopher had no idea how long he had been standing at the fountain. It was probably only a matter of minutes, but it felt like hours. Water droplets trickled down his spine, making him feel cold and miserable.

*It's all nonsense. What was I thinking of?* He thought angrily to himself. *Kerry would never be interested in someone like me, and a stupid pen is never going to make it happen* he continued with his morose thoughts.

However, what Christopher failed to realise was that he had been talking to his loyal canine friend all along; Sam looked at his master with a reassuring azure gaze, as if he sympathised with his every word, every syllable, every letter. Thankfully, Sam's slobbery doggy kisses awoke Christopher from his miserable stupor.

*The pen and the story can't be nonsense because where did you –*

"Christopher?!" Nana Kathy's voice volleyed through the square. He almost laughed aloud when he heard her undeniable Scottish twang, still ever present and refusing to leave. "Just look at the state of you – you're like a droont rat! I've been calling you for ages son. Anyone would think that you've tumpshies stuffed in those lugs!"

Even though he still felt miserable, Christopher could only laugh out aloud in response to his Nana's words. She always had a way of making him smile and that was more important to him than anything at that moment. That and his trusted friend Sam.

\*\*\*\*

The afternoon melted into early evening. The autumnal rain had been hard at work, smothering the village of Fernlock, making everything look dark and forlorn, as if the buildings were dressed for a Victorian funeral. Christopher was more than glad to be back in Milaw House, perched by the log fire in the front sitting room. He thought of the not too distant past: a time when he would sit by the fire with his mum, both with a fork in their hands, toasting a thick slice of homemade bread. Christopher had such fond memories of those times. The images sparkled in his mind, like a piece of borrowed heaven that would always provide comfort during hard times.

He knew that his mum was not lost.

The zealous licks of brilliant white, orange, and red performed a fiery dance for Christopher and Sam. They sat in awe of the fire's dangerous yet alluring power to hypnotise and to chase away any unwelcoming chills. Christopher found it hard to believe that only yesterday he was out in the garden, enjoying the remnants of summer sunshine.

That, and of course, the magic of the old lean-to and his Papa Tommy's story.

Before he knew it, Christopher and Sam were bounding up the stairs towards his room. With shaking hands, Christopher hauled the top drawer of his bedside cabinet open to find his notepad and Papa's Tommy's pen. He fumbled with his notepad, trying to find the words of last night's story. By this point, Sam was almost howling loudly at Christopher.

"What's wrong boy?" he said, trying to reassure his doggy friend.

To his amazement, Sam then placed his paw on a page of the notebook. When Christopher looked down, he saw the all too familiar handwriting:

*The pen will only truly work on the Juniper Lux paper.*

The words jumped out of the page and paraded in front of his eyes. Christopher stumbled back in disbelief.

*Ring ---- ring.*

The sound of the front door disturbed the dancing words. The letters fell back onto the page and the notepad dropped to the floor. Christopher looked at Sam, his mouth still agape at what he had witnessed.

"Christopher!?" From below, Nana Kathy's voice commanded her grandson to *get your backside down here!*

For the moment, he decided the best option was to follow his Nana's order, so he left the mystery of the notepad for the time being and pounded back down the stairs, Sam following suit. To his delight, Christopher found Kerry and his Nana Kathy standing in the hallway.

"I'm so sorry about earlier Christopher. I was really rude," Kerry said pleadingly.

Nana Kathy winked at Christopher and began humming a familiar tune as she left them alone in the hallway.

Christopher could feel his cheeks burning.

"I blame Candice", Kerry went on. "The tall girl with the umbrella. She has to have all of the attention."

Christopher could still not believe what was happening. By this point, the flushing in his cheeks had crawled its way down his neck and arms. Sam howled softly again at his dumbfounded master, encouraging him to say something. Anything.

"No, no…you weren't r…rude. I j…just surprised you … no need to apologise," Christopher stammered, amazed that he had found his own voice again.

"Well, anyway, I just wanted to check that you were okay. Perhaps we can hang out tomorrow?

"Yes! That w…would b…be wonderful Kerry!" Christopher instantly regretted his over enthusiastic, geekish reply. But his worry quickly faded in the glow of Kerry's warm smile. Her eyes illuminated the dark shadows in the hallway.

"Great, I'll call by tomorrow, about midday."

And once again, Kerry had about turned and disappeared into the cool night air. However, this time it was different. Christopher felt like something had changed. He felt like he was walking on air.

****

Upstairs in his bedroom, everything was just as Christopher left it: his notepad was still sprawled on the floor with his Papa Tommy's pen to its side. Sam slouched down beside him and looked up with a wise expression. Christopher picked up the notepad, looking for the all-too familiar handwriting from earlier. He frantically searched through every page.

The writing had vanished.

# CHAPTER 8
## ~ PAPA TOMMY ~

From the minute his head hit the pillow, Christopher's mind was like a washing machine full of heavy sodden thoughts, all sloshing around in his brain, preventing him from sleeping. "*I can't work any of this out,*" he whispered to Sam, who was nestled at the bottom of his master's bed. Christopher thought about how easy it would be to just pull the covers back over his head and catch up on his lost sleep, but the mystery of the vanishing words hauled him out of bed.

Darkness prevailed outside his bedroom window, pressing its unwanted presence against the glass. Christopher had no idea what time it was; but then, as if right on cue, the grandfather clock chimed from below, declaring that it was two o'clock in the morning. The timing was perfect: Nana Kathy would still be in a deep sleep. Christopher crept out of bed and pulled on his sweatshirt and shoes. He did not care that he was still wearing his monkey patterned pyjama bottoms because he was not planning on going that far; he was only venturing out to the old lean-to at the bottom of the garden. Sam led the way. His thick white coat flashed like a torchlight in the darkness and his eyes appeared to sparkle. Christopher followed his protector.

In the upstairs hallway, the two friends tiptoed as quietly as possible as they approached the door to Nana Kathy's bedroom. Normally it would be quite difficult to awaken an elderly woman from the depths of her sleep – especially at two o'clock in the morning - but Nana Kathy was not your typical seventy-two-year old: she appeared to have an in-built radar that could detect any form of movement within a ten-metre radius. This was how she became affectionately known as *Radar* to some of the locals in Ferncross. There was no need for a burglar alarm if you lived next door to Kathryn Muir. So, this part of the operation was going to be like *mission impossible* for Christopher and Sam.

*Creak — crack*. The floorboards were not helping Christopher and Sam. In fact, they appeared to enjoy amplifying every step the two friends made. It made Christopher want to laugh out loud, which did not help matters at all. Sam looked at him as if to say *don't you dare*. Thankfully, his steely blue stare was enough to stifle Christopher's giggles, just enough to creep by the doorway of Nana Kathy's bedroom. However, they were still in precarious territory: his Nana's radar extended beyond the downstairs hallway.

Milaw house was fast asleep. The velvet, inky darkness cloaked everything in view, except for Sam and the snow-white glimmers of moonlight peering through the gaps in the curtains. Milaw house looked so majestic dressed in eventide. Even the furniture looked taller, like brave soldiers dressed in purple-black uniforms, standing on guard, ready and waiting on the enemy.

Christopher continued to follow Sam's silvery glow. The Siberian safely led his master out into the garden.

"*We're here Sam…without any stirring from Nana Kathy…or her radar*," Christopher whispered, again trying to curb his nervous laughter.

Sam quietly whimpered back, as if he was trying to tell his master something.

"What's wrong S - …" Christopher's question was abruptly interrupted by a bright light at the bottom of the garden. The door to the old lean-to lay open. A warm, welcoming glow called out to Christopher, inviting him in. At first, he rubbed his eyes, not quite believing what lay in front of him; but then the familiar and soothing sound of music pulled Christopher even closer. He could just make out the movement of the hobbyhorse at the window, rocking back and forth in time to the music.

*Then the word discovers, as my book ends…*

45

It was Sinatra's voice again, welcoming Christopher into the old lean-to.

*...how to make two lovers of friends.*

Once again, Christopher found himself inside the ailing lean-to. But this time he was not alone.

"Papa!" Christopher ran forward and wrapped his arms tightly around his grandfather. The scent of his Papa Tommy's woody aftershave transported Christopher back in time, to a happier place in his memory. His Papa hugged him lovingly and patted his back. It all seemed so real.

"There, there son. I am glad you finally found me. I knew that it would only be a matter of time," his Papa said, standing back so that he could have a proper look at his growing grandson. Christopher was speechless, partly because he could not believe what was happening, but mostly because he could feel the emotion swelling at the back of his throat.

"Ah, I can see the emulsion is getting to you son." His Papa Tommy's words made Christopher laugh. Emulsion was the word his Papa used to call emotion and it always brought a smile to even the saddest of faces.

"Look son, we don't have that much time. I have so much to tell you. You must listen carefully".

Even though Christopher had a million and one questions to ask his Papa, he heard the seriousness in his voice. So, he shook his head in agreement, eagerly awaiting his instruction. His Papa opened the wooden lid to a box Christopher immediately recognised. The smell of lavender leapt into the air, filling the old shed with its soothing aroma. Papa Tommy lifted out The Book of Almost Anything, placed it on the saddle of the hobby horse and turned to the back of the manuscript. To Christopher's surprise, there was a very rusty key taped to the last page of the book.

Then something really unbelievable happened.

When his Papa loosened the tape, and held the key in his hands, it gleamed brightly before transforming into shimmering gold. He placed the aurum artefact into Christopher's hands and whispered "*Sacrarium spiritus librorum.*"

Christopher had no idea about what his Papa meant, but before he could ask anything, the light in the lean-to started flickering. Without warning, the record stylus flopped onto its shellac disc, causing strange musical notes to screech out of the gramophone's cone. Undecipherable words were tangled around inharmonious notes. It was as if the record was playing backwards. Christopher reached out towards his Papa, hoping for some answers. But his Papa had vanished. Tears blinded Christopher's vision as he tried to make sense of what was happening. He called out for Sam, but instead of his canine chum's usual friendly howl, Christopher heard a static voice:

*Go to the library and seek out the silvery haired blind man who goes by the name Oliver Tiresias. He is one of us. He will show you the way.*

Although the voice was distant and sounded as though it had been recorded a long, long time ago, Christopher instantly recognised it. As strange as it was, his Papa Tommy's voice appeared to be speaking through the gramophone. His comforting tones reassured Christopher, calming his thumping heartbeat. Time moved a slow hand. The rocking horse stopped its galloping. The white light flickered once more.

And then the light vanished.

Blackness shrouded everything in the room. Christopher tried to step forward, but there was nothing solid beneath his feet. To his utter bewilderment he found that he was lying on his back. A scream grasped at the back of his throat; he could not remember falling backwards. However, the memory of his Papa's words quickly washed over him, cleansing away the fear. He rolled onto his belly and fumbled his way forward, in the hope that he could find the door to the lean-to and his trusted Siberian. But there was no door. Instead, his hands were met by something soft. He pushed further forward to find that he was cocooned in soft, familiar cosiness. A fluffy paw reached out to Christopher as if to tell him *it was all okay*.

And then reality hit him: Christopher was back in the safety of his bed, wrapped snugly in his duvet. Sam was sleeping at the foot of the bed.

Downstairs, the grandfather clock chimed twice.

\*\*\*\*

The first cheeps of a little robin chirruped just outside Christopher's window. It was morning already. The warm embrace of slumber had not graced Christopher with its presence. Yet again, he found himself lying flat on his bed, wrapped in a state of befuddlement. His head ached and his limbs felt heavy. He had heard almost every hourly chime of the grandfather clock downstairs. At one point, Christopher was certain that the clock chimed the words *get to sleep*. But sleep was the farthest thing from his mind. Although his body ached for some proper rest, his brain was working overtime, trying to make sense of what had happened in the old lean-to. What did his Papa mean by *go to the library*? And who the heck was Oliver Tiresias?

"*Perhaps*," Christopher whispered to Sam, "*I have totally lost my marbles. Gone gaga. Cuckoo. How do I even know if you …*" but just as he moved forward to pat Sam, a great clatter shattered the silence.

"WHIT WAS THAT?!" Nana Kathy's voice bellowed from the hallway below. So, she was awake after all.

Christopher's heart thumped uncontrollably in his chest. He had no idea what had caused such a cacophony. Even Sam's ears were even standing on end.

"It's…okay    N…Nana.    I    just    d…dropped my…eh…eh…phone."

"Phone?! Jeesy peeps! That sounded like a blasted anchor! I thought the roof was caving in!" Nana Kathy's voice sounded nearer now, as if she was on her way to her grandson's room to see what had really happened.

Christopher tried to say something else, but his eyes were suddenly blinded by a bright, brilliant light. His bedroom appeared to be decorated in ornate gold leaf: metallic orbs leapt through the air and parachuted downwards, landing just at the side of his bed. It was beautiful. Sam leapt off the bed, jumping into the air with his mouth open as if he was trying to catch the golden snowflakes on his tongue. Christopher gawped at the beautiful but unbelievable sight.

And then, as quickly as it had arrived, the gilded light vanished. The meek, early morning light returned to his bedroom once more.

Christopher's bedroom door creaked slowly open.

"Son, I'm away to put the kettle on. My heid's loupin' after that racket! Would you like a wee cuppa?" A vision of Nana Kathy appeared in the doorway, complete with roller-clad hair and a flowery-duvet-cover-inspired dressing gown. "Do you want a wee bit of cereal this morning?" Christopher could not speak; he could only nod his head up and down.

After his Nana had vanished, Christopher peered over the side of his bed. Sam was already there, sniffing the strange metal skeleton lying on the floor.

It was his Papa's key from the old lean-to.

# CHAPTER 9
## ~ ELLA AND THE KEEPER OF MILAW HOUSE ~

"*A B C D E F G, I never learned to spell, at least not that well...*"
Nana Kathy's singing voice lilted through the air, filling
Milaw house with warmth. The books, the paintings, and
the furniture all wore a look of contentment, listening to the
wee Scottish notes in her melody. Even Milaw House itself
appeared to hang on to her every word. It was early Sunday
afternoon: Nana Kathy's cleaning hour.

"1 2 3 4 5 6 7, I never learned to count, a great amount
..."

Sam was also listening to Nana Kathy. He was perched
outside the doorway of the front sitting room; his blue eyes
followed the movements of Nana Kathy back and forth.
The beautiful Siberian appeared to be smiling at her actions
– and her song. Nana Kathy's feather duster tickled the gold
ornaments in time to her singing, flicking away any soot
from last night's fire. It looked like they enjoyed the
attention as all her polishing brought the smiles back to their
tiny faces. This was Nana Kathy's favourite part of her
routine. She loved taking care of all the precious gold and
brass figurines – or wee treasures as she called them. Most
of them were heirlooms that had been passed down through
the Muir family tree.

As a young child, Christopher used to follow his Nana
around like a shadow, helping her to clean everything in
sight. She even taught him how to make the settee pillows
plumper, by smashing their heids the-gether. It was like a
sacred ritual to her: dusting everything, ensuring that every
part of the house looked spick and span. Nana Kathy always
said that she was the keeper of Milaw House.

Christopher tried to help his grandmother clean, but it
was useless. He could not even pretend. Tiredness gnawed

50

at his limbs. He felt the immensity of his Papa's key in his pocket; its cold, bumpy surface served as a reminder of the strange events that had taken place earlier. Just like Sam, the key was real, solid even; but both had appeared from the mists of make-believe. Papa Tommy's words swirled around Christopher's mind like a whirlpool. The eddy of emotions sloshed and splashed, creating a wavy rhythm just like the strange music from the old shellac disc. Christopher was daydreaming: he stood at the back of the sitting room, limply holding two cushions in his hands.

"I'll strike while the iron is hot…" Nana Kathy continued with her singing and cleaning.

Christopher recognised the tune but not the words of her song. He looked at Sam questioningly, in the vain hope that his canine chum would help him; but Sam offered no help. Instead, he responded by trying to yowl along with Nana Kathy's melody.

"CHRISTOPHER! Whit in the name of the Wee Man's wrong with you? You're right at the coo's tail this afternoon." Nana Kathy had stopped singing.

"S…s…sorry Nana," Christopher mumbled. He wanted to tell her about everything that had been happening; he wanted his Nana to explain everything that had been happening to him; but most importantly, he just wanted to hear that he was not losing his mind. However, all he could muster was, "have you ever had déjà vu?"

It seemed like an eternity passed before Nana Kathy answered. But then she smiled and said "Oh son, I get that all the time. Old age doesn't come alone you know." She laughed heartily and winked at her grandson before returning to her feather dusting - and her song "But my busy mind is burning to use what learning I've got…"

And there it was again, the all too familiar melody. The notes from her song pirouetted into the air and pranced around Christopher. He was captivated.

Suddenly, Christopher's mouth moved, and he began to speak; but he was not in control of what he was saying.

"Nana, wh…what are you singing? It sounds s…so familiar."

"Why that's just a wee ditty that both your Papa and I loved to sing." Before Christopher could ask anything else, his Nana continued "Your Papa was daft for the Frank Sinatra version, but I was more keen Ella's effort. Fitzgerald that is. Mind you, I've no played the record in a long time. In fact, I'm no' even sure where…"

Nana Kathy's words stopped abruptly. She stared out of the huge bay window in the sitting room. The soft afternoon light had surrendered over to an ominous rain cloud, casting shadows on the walls in Milaw House. An uninvited chill crept into the sitting room. The fading light made Nana Kathy look like a tiny silhouette, framed by the enormous edges of the bay window. She looked so small and vulnerable. Christopher tried to speak, but he was distracted by the low growl of Sam, who was standing beside Nana Kathy.

"Blast it! Your faither's here. Uninvited, may I also add."

Christopher felt the life drain from him. The image of his father's gift – an Incaendium mobile phone – still lay in its box up in Christopher's wardrobe. Switched firmly off. His father was the last person he wanted to see right now.

"Didnae worry son," Nana Kathy said reassuringly. "I'll get rid of him. Somehow," she declared, waving her feather duster in the air.

Christopher burst out laughing at his Nana's threatening promise, but his merriment was cut short by the overwhelming vision of his father standing outside the bay window. Anger was etched over his face. He aggressively pointed a black, leather, gloved finger at the front door. Sam pounded out of the sitting room and sat in the hallway, snarling at the door. Christopher had never seen Sam bare his teeth so aggressively before, but he understood his canine chum's reaction. He patted his trusted Siberian on the head before opening the door.

"At last Christopher, you appear to be the man of the

house. Well, a man, of sorts." Aiden Brenton stood menacingly tall in the doorway. Christopher thought his father's dark attire made him look like a gloomy raven, about to pounce and tear off its next piece of carrion.

"Congratulations for finally taking the initiative to open the door. Now, are you going to invite me in?"

"Aiden, you're a right bugger!" Nana Kathy shouted from the back of the hallway.

A finger of concern prodded at Christopher's chest; he could see that his Nana was visibly shaking. He was worried about her blood pressure.

"You should've called to let us know you were coming. Well - I suppose - now that you're here, you'd better come in and shut the door. But you can wait here. In the lobby." Nana Kathy continued to shake.

"Why thank you. Mrs Muir".

Christopher hated how every syllable of his father's words were laced with sarcasm. He stared at his estranged father as he sidled his way into hallway of Milaw House. Aiden Brenton sat, without asking, on the chaise longue.

"And, speaking of calling one, Christopher why haven't you set up your Incaendium phone and linked it to mine?"

Before Christopher could say anything, his Nana replied for him, "Aiden, enough. I warned you before. Christopher has a lot on his plate at the moment. He starts school on Tuesday and – I don't know if you remember – he's no long just lost his mum. So, a wee stupit phone is the last thing on his mind!"

Thankfully, Nana Kathy had stopped shaking. Perhaps, Christopher thought, it was because Sam was now by her side, with his thick white tail wagging comfortingly against her legs. Christopher wanted to say something to his father, but his stammer was still ever present at the back of his throat, grappling with his words.

Briiing. Briiing.

The doorbell of Milaw House rang brightly. Before Aiden Brenton could say anything else, Christopher sprang forward and opened the door. It was Kerry Robinson.

"Oh, hi everyone. I hope I haven't interrupted anything."

Christopher's heart thumped at the sight of her perfect white smile and the shimmering light in her green eyes.

"No, not at all Kerry. Come on in and come ben the living room," Nana Kathy said, before turning and smiling at her grandson. Christopher should have been mortified, but he was just ever so glad to see his Nana back to her usual self.

Aiden's face turned a more crimson shade of scarlet. "And what – why don't I get invited into the living room … Mrs Muir?"

"Christopher, you and Kerry go for that wee walk yous were both thinking of. Don't mind me. I'll just take your so-called faither into the kitchen for a wee chat." Thanks to Sam, Nana Kathy appeared stronger and back in control. It was as if she had something planned, or up her sleeve, as she would say. "And, by the way, we'll finish our wee chat about that record later on," she added, grinning at her grandson.

\*\*\*\*

"So, what was all that about? Talk about awkward! And your dad…whoa!" Kerry instantly regretted asking Christopher about his father because she could see the glow fade from his cheeks.

The silence was almost palpable, bouncing back and forth between the two friends. Kerry was not use to such tense situations: she was brought up in such a happy and warm family environment where she was lucky to have a father that behaved more like a human being. So, she could not help herself. Mr Brenton was quite different from Christopher; they appeared to have more of a headmaster-pupil relationship, rather than a father-son bond. It all seemed so wrong. Kerry instinctively thought of Ms Muir –

Christopher's mum – and how welcoming she had always been. Fond memories of Year Four at Ferncross Primary sprang into her mind, wrapping a glow of warmth around her. Ms Muir always went that extra mile to make her pupils feel special and welcome. Kerry almost laughed aloud at the memory of Christopher's mum turning the classroom into a haunted old house - all thanks to hundreds of shredded binbags and cotton wool.

"Your mum was amazing." Kerry thought that was the best way to break the silence. She moved towards Christopher, who was still standing at the patio window, gazing out towards the garden. He turned around to face Kerry and she could see why he had been so quiet. Tears glistened at the side of his eyes. Before he could say anything, Kerry wrapped her arms around her friend and patted him on the back. He stood still, again, with his arms by his side; but Kerry thought nothing of it because she had not given him much chance to move before hugging him. She then stepped back and asked, "are you okay?"

Christopher quickly rubbed his eyes with his sleeve and cleared his throat. "I…I…eh my dad…" Christopher's words were abruptly seized by a gurgle at the back of his throat. His face turned beetroot.

Kerry giggled uncontrollably because he snorted like a little piglet. She thought he looked so cute.

"S…sorry about that. Kerry, I…I have so much to tell you … I don't know where to start. I…I, eh … don't even know if you will believe me," Christopher stammered.

Kerry nodded to Christopher, encouraging her friend to continue.

"Well, the first thing is … is … the l…library. Can you go with me to F…Ferncross library? And then…th…there's this…" Christopher placed his hand into his pocket and produced the most prehistoric looking key Kerry had ever seen.

"Where on earth did you get that?" Kerry was in awe at how old it looked. She felt as if she was in the presence of something so old – and so important. Even though its thick coarse surface was encrusted in verdigris, it appeared to strangely sparkle in the soft autumnal sunlight.

"You...w... wouldn't believe me if I t...told you. But w...will you come with me to the library?"

Kerry nodded and smiled in agreement. She had a strange feeling about the key. She felt as if it was talking to her. And, thankfully, she had already forgotten about Aiden Brenton and all his fiery anger.

# CHAPTER 10
## ~ *OLD OLI AND AVIAS DERYN* ~

Christopher felt terrible about leaving his Nana alone with his father, but he had no choice. He had to. He felt his Papa's presence, urging him to go to Ferncross library. And besides, Sam was already thrusting on ahead, his muzzle pointed forwards, leading the way to Ferncross Library. But perhaps what filled Christopher with even more strength, was Kerry's genuine willingness to go along with him. She actually appeared to *want to* go with him. And that hug! Christopher's heart melted at the mere thought of it.

"*I'm such a wuss,*" he thought to himself. But his heart leapt once more when he looked at Kerry. She was smiling cheerfully at him.

For a Sunday afternoon, Ferncross village looked unusually alive. Thankfully, the dark clouds from earlier had vanished. The shops were bustling and outside Café Fern, people were supping their cappuccinos in the glow of the early September sunlight. In Balsamea square, local venders were packing up their stalls, content with their honest day's earnings. Christopher chuckled as he thought of his Nana Kathy and how she would have fluttered from stall to stall, buying little trinkets and early Christmas gifts.

"Thank goodness N…Nana isn't here, or w…we would be here all daaaaaaaawhooaaa!" Christopher found himself being hauled uncontrollably towards someone, or something! One stall had caught the eye – or rather, the scent – of Sam. The sun sat unusually low in the sky, binding Christopher's vision, so he shut his eyes and let Sam lead the way.

"Christopher! Wait for me!" Kerry's voice reverberated around the square, causing stall goers to stop and look.

"Well, at least I can still hear, Sa -"

"Good afternoon young man," Christopher's words

were suspended by a soothing voice. The lilt in the old man's expression sounded so familiar, so comforting.

"Oh, I'm, eh s…sorry. I can't see for the s…sun…"

"Don't worry my boy. You will find your way. Just follow your heart." The old man's words sounded so full of wisdom.

Christopher squinted and focussed on Sam's white fluffy mane. The ever-reliable canine chum led his young master to the back of the stall. When Christopher rubbed away the glare of the afternoon sunlight from his eyes, he could finally put a face to the welcoming voice. The man appeared to be in his winter years and, sadly, age had pecked away at his height. Nevertheless, Christopher was amazed at the youthful look in the old man's gaze: one eye appeared to be bright blue; the other looked almost silver. His congenial gaze was complimented by a huge white moustache and thatch of white bushy hair; both of which appeared to have a life of their own as the curly ends moved to and fro in the warm breeze. The familiar zephyr continually danced its way through Balsamea Square, twirling around the stalls, causing an explosion of crisp and fragrant notes.

"Lavender!" Kerry cried. Christopher was too busy staring at the old man to have noticed that the stall was full of lavender goods. "Ooh, I've never seen so many purple gifts before. Christopher, you should buy something for your Nana".

"Yes," replied the old man. "I think she would like this."

Before he could reply, the old man gently lifted Christopher's arm and placed a little purple parcel in his hands.

"Wow, it smells amazing. What is it?" Kerry inquired, just gasping to know what the little box contained.

"Now that would be telling," winked the old man. "But here is something for you Christopher – some lavender rock".

Christopher had no idea that there was such a thing. It

made him smile though as he thought of the many happy summers he spent at Millport with his mum, chomping on mint and fruit flavoured rock.

"And they are on the house. I don't want a penny," the old man said smiling. Perhaps it was the relaxing effect of the lavender, but up until that point, Christopher had not noticed the old man fumbling his way around the stall. It was only when he groped his way for a white stick that the penny dropped: the old man was blind! Christopher felt terrible for not noticing it before, but the old man appeared to see *everything*.

"I expect you're wondering what this is for," the old man chirruped, aware that his two young customers had fallen awkwardly silent. "I lost my sight, way before you were born, but thankfully my other senses sharpened up. It's a long story, but perhaps I will tell you all about that one day, my dear bot - Christopher. But, for now, I would be happy for you to take these." The old man handed Christopher a parcel for his Nana, along with the lavender rock, all wrapped in purple paper.

"Th…thank you, sir," Christopher replied, gratefully accepting his gifts.

"Sir?! Fiddlesticks! Pa ha!" The old man chuckled. "Why, that makes me sound like an old cob. Please call me Oli – that's what I'm known as round here."

"Thanks Oli" both Kerry and Christopher said in unison, laughing at the way that their voices merged like little schoolchildren saying good morning to their primary teacher.

"Now, you and Kerry run along, I need to pack up my goods. And don't worry, I have a little birdie to help me."

Christopher felt the need to stay and help the old man as he could not see anyone else at the stall. However, Sam had other ideas: he was already tugging at his lead, reminding his master of their planned visit to the library.

Just before Christopher could say goodbye, Oli nickered "and say hello to that wonderful Nana of yours. She's one in a million."

Christopher shouted, "I will do" as Sam pulled his master on ahead towards Ferncross library, with Kerry following suit.

The sun drooped even lower in the sky, indicating that time's hands were marching on. Sam pulled the two chums further and further away from the square, along the tree lined Balsamea Avenue, towards the library. It was nearing four o'clock, so Christopher only had an hour before the library closed. However, regardless of the tight time frame, he would not change the events of the afternoon. Meeting old Oli was a breath of welcoming fresh air.

"Wow, did you see his eyes? They were hypnotising!" Kerry exclaimed. "And I just can't believe he's blind! He appeared so confident as if ... as if he could *see everything*."

Christopher smiled at Kerry. He felt it and *saw it* too. Despite his ailing stature, old Oli somehow appeared to be tall and confident. He had made quite an impression on the two friends. But perhaps what was the most impressive aspect about Oli, was the way he actually *looked* at the person he was speaking to. It was as if he could really *see* them.

"Oooh, I wonder what's in the little purple box," Kerry exclaimed, as if her excitement was about to spill over.

However, Christopher's mind was too busy with the events of the last few days to think about the little purple box. Visions of the lean-to and the magnificent white horse pranced around in his head; his Papa Tommy's words, along with the strange Latin engravings eclipsed his vision; his mind was like a cornucopia of questions. Just how did old Oli know their names?

Suddenly, Christopher's thoughts were interrupted by a strange, sibilate voice:

*"Before you enter the library, can you please make sure you read the code of conduct in the hallway."*

There, just outside the doorway of Ferncross library, stood the most impressive figure of a woman: Avias Deryn, or *Ms Deryn* as she liked to be called. However, most of the locals referred to her as *the Deryn*. Regardless of her title, she had an important role in the community: she was the librarian at Ferncross library – the heart of the community.

In the low sunlight, her amber eyes appeared to be almost ablaze. For as far back as Christopher could remember, he was both terrified and in awe of the Deryn. She was well-known in the village because of her tall stature, her tendency to talk in whispers and - as she put it – her job to *fiercely protect the sanctity of books*. But she was beautiful. Her flaxen hair always looked immaculate, with a long plait swooping down from her prominent, ivory-like shoulders.

*Howoooooooooo.* Sam broke the library's silence. He let out an almost human howl. It was almost as if he was addressing this tall, blonde librarian.

*"Master Muir, come with me."* The Deryn quietly screamed.

Christopher shuffled forward, scared to say anything. He turned to look at Kerry, who was urging him, with a forced smile, to *follow the instructions of the almighty Deryn*. He inhaled deeply, filling his lungs with the late summer air before stepping forward. Just above him, along the keystone of the entrance, the words *Sacrarium Spiritus Librorum* were engraved into the stone. But Christopher was too wrapped up in the wings of Avias to have noticed the familiar words.

# CHAPTER 11
## ~ *FERNCROSS LIBRARY* ~

Ferncross library was quite a sight to see. Tourists flocked from everywhere just to see its spectacular form. The building itself was simply antediluvian. Having observed a myriad of past events, historical architects and researchers could not place the date of its origin. Even its blueprints had disappeared, lost in the labyrinth of time. As a result, a blue plaque adorned the wall beside the entrance, simply declaring "*Ferncross Library. Sanctuary of Books. Date of Origin Unknown.*" Its large, red clay like exterior stood like grand Chinese emperor at the bottom of Balsamea Avenue.

Inside, the silence was cathedral quiet. The grand atrium was the beating heart of the library, with countless artery like corridors leading from its core. Avias Deryn was already perched in the middle of the atrium, with her dark wooden desk wrapped around her like a protective nest. Kerry was already lost somewhere in corridor of fantasy classics, gazing on the row upon rows of tales, her eyes locked on stories from *Narnia* to *Neverland*. Christopher wanted to join her, but he could feel the eyes of Avias burning into the back of his head.

"Master Muir, I want you to have a look at this," the breathy voice of Avias summoned Christopher over to her bookish brood. She handed him an ancient looking clipboard with a piece of cartridge paper attached, as if it had just been freshly pressed from the finest of wood. The paper was full of names and addresses. At the top, Christopher read the title "Petition Against Installation of Incaendium Computer System in Ferncross." Further down, amongst a list of names he had heard of, but could not put faces to, he spotted a familiar name. "Kathryn Muir," he read aloud. "Milaw House, Acacia Dri…"

"*Shhhhhhhhh,*" squawked Avias. "*I don't want any unwanted ears to hear about this,"* she whispered. The tawny flecks in her eyes flashed like sirens.

"*S…s…sorry,*" Christopher whispered, terrified that Avias was about to swoop down from her chair and strike him over the head with a book. Although he recognised that this was a petition against his father's company, he wondered what he had to do with it. "Wh…what do you want me to do?" Christopher immediately wanted to withdraw his question because the Deryn's eyebrows formed an even higher arch above her amber eyes. She moved forward and began to whisper a series of questions into Christopher's left ear.

*"Do you believe in the sanctity of books?"*

Christopher nodded his head up and down. He was too scared to utter a word.

*"Do you believe that the cantankerous traffic and interfering noise of the world wide web has no place in the sanctity of the library?"*

Again, Christopher nodded in agreement. But he meant it. He thought of his father's so-called gift of Incaendium's latest mobile phone, his father's obtrusive manner, and the way he wanted to spy on Christopher's every move.

*"Well, I need your signature Master Muir. Your name will be the key in putting a stop to your father's combustive plans."*

For the last time, Christopher nodded his head. But this time, and because he meant it, he whispered "*yes*" and smiled at the almighty Avias. Without thinking, he reached into his pocket, pulled out his Papa's pen and placed the golden tip on the paper. Shards of sunlight trickled through the grand atrium window above, bathing everything in white and gold. The gilded nib of Papa Tommy's pen glinted in the watery sunlight. Christopher looked up from the paper to where his gaze was met by the formidable stare of Avias. In the light, her eyes glowed like two beautiful amber pendants.

Suddenly, a bolt of electricity shot up Christopher's arm, causing his hand to spasm. The tremors were so powerful that he lost control of what he was trying to write. Time slowed. Everything – and everyone – in the room floated aimlessly like lost objects in an empty vacuum. A blanket of nothingness shrouded every sound in the room. Sam was nowhere to be seen.

*Thump – thump. Thump – thump. Thump – thump.*

Christopher tried to focus on the beating of his heart, hoping that he would awake from this nightmare at any minute, but another jolt of electricity ricocheted through his body causing a deep-rooted paralysis. Dark shadows emerged from silent corners of the room, slowly snaking their way towards him. Before Christopher could shout for help, hot, sinewy fingers wrapped around his throat. He pulled and hauled and tugged with all his might, but the red-hot coils of necrosis twisted tighter around his neck.

A black veil slipped slowly over Christopher's eyes.

And then he was falling. His heart leapt up into his throat as his body plummeted down, deeper, and deeper into hostile blackness, down towards a never-ending abyss of loss. Christopher could not breath. He tried to scream again, but dark tendrils of silence strangled the last vestiges of life from his throat. Death was near. As he struggled for his last breath, he thought of his mum. Her memory illuminated the darkness, and all was not lost. Christopher was once again enveloped in the strange – but friendly and familiar – power, its magnetism lifted him from the dark void. He was no longer falling. Energetic waves vibrated up and down his arm, before finally culminating on his shoulder. The radiating current ceased and gave way to a warm, soothing sensation. It felt like a strong hand resting on his shoulder, both protecting and encouraging him at the same time. Christopher instantly recognised the feeling.

"*Well done Master Muir,*" Avias purled, her voice pulling Christopher back from time's dark chasm. "*Your signature really will make a difference.*" She smiled.

Christopher stood still, staring at the piece of paper in front of him. His mouth was agape. He had no recollection of writing, but there it was right under his nose: *Christopher*

*Muir.*

"I…I…eh…I don't remember wr…writing that," he stammered. His legs almost buckled with the force of Sam's tail, thumping against the back of his legs. His energy levels were still trying to return to normal, so he knelt, hugged his trusted Siberian and whispered, *"I don't know what I would do without you boy"*.

Sam let out a little howl of reassurance, instantly filling Christopher with some much-needed strength.

*"Well,"* Avias interrupted in a breathy whisper, *"I can assure you Master Muir; you did write your name on this here piece of paper. I saw the whole thing. And with your golden pen."* She smiled once more.

Christopher hauled himself back onto his feet. But the amber eyes of the Deryn were now locked firmly on Sam, instead of his master. Christopher was certain that the flaxen haired librarian was about to say something about his canine chum along a chain of library rules, so he quickly stammered "wh…what do you m…m…mean … you saw the whole thing?"

Avias Deryn's eyebrows arched, causing altogether the most disturbing effect: her amber eyes had turned into two smouldering flames, glaring at Christopher.

"Oh, I *see everything* that goes on around here Master Muir. And I mean *everything*."

Christopher wanted to know what she meant, and why she kept on repeating the word "everything", but before he could ask another question, Kerry appeared beside him.

"There you are. I was beginning to get worried about you."

Christopher smiled at Kerry's concern. Did this mean that she really did like him, and not just as a friend? Perhaps his story could come true after all. Despite the bleak events that had just occurred, Christopher could not stop smiling. He said nothing.

"Come on, I want to show you something," Kerry added, pulling her star-struck friend away from the Deryn's watchful eyes.

Thankfully, everything now appeared to be at peace in the library. Stillness replaced the dark shadows and the early evening light had turned the walls into a golden mosaic. The two friends, followed faithfully by Sam, stopped in the Classics Section.

Kerry stared at her friend. Her huge green eyes were mesmerising.

"K…Kerry, if you asked me, you wouldn't b…believe m…me," Christopher whispered questioningly, worried that the amber eyes of Avias Deryn might still have been watching and listening. "I…I will tell you l…later," he added, nervously. He suddenly thought that he was being very self-assured. Doubt visited, slapping him in the face. He hoped that Kerry would still want to still see him "later".

However, Kerry reached out and held his hand. Then, without warning, she pulled him along to one of the library's main arteries. Christopher loved the soft and delicate feeling of her hand in his as she led the way.

"Look, here it is!" Kerry silently exclaimed.

Christopher's eyes were drawn towards a shelf of the most ancient looking books he had ever seen. Their delicate spines were swaddled in a strange but sumptuous looking material.

"What's it bound in?" Kerry mouthed, carefully lifting one of the books from the shelf and handing it to Christopher.

"It f…feels like t…tree bark," Christopher whispered in return, but immediately he felt stupid for his suggestion because of the puzzled look on Kerry's face.

"Look again!" Kerry grabbed his hand tighter, her voice just one louder than a whisper. "Look at the name!"

Christopher was too taken aback by the feeling of Kerry's silky hands to notice anything. An elephant could have trumpeted into the library at that very moment, but he would not have noticed.

"Christopher!" Kerry shouted this time, trying to wake him from his trance. She hauled at him – this time, without any soft silkiness – towards the name on the shelf.

*"Tiresias. Oliver!"*

"OMG!" Christopher shouted. "It's Oliver!"

*"SHHHHHHHHHHHHHH!"* Avias Deryn commanded. She had appeared from nowhere. Christopher and Kerry were speechless. *"Will you please be quiet!"* Her voice was a soundless sharp scream, slicing through the air. Silence returned. Avias then looked at Christopher before declaring: *"I recommend that book."* One amber eye winked, and then she flapped away, back to her clutch of manuscripts.

"Wh…wh…?! - "

*"Shhh!"* Kerry interrupted Christopher. *"Do you want to suffer the wrath of the Deryn again?!"*

Christopher nodded his head up and down like a puppet. He swallowed. His mouth was desert dry. Despite his sweaty palms, he still had a firm hold of Oliver's book: *Unlocking the Impossible.* The title was ornately engraved on the front cover, as if it had been painstakingly hand carved into the strange wooden-like material. Christopher ran his hand over every nook and cranny of the letters, as if he was actually reading the title without even looking at the words. He felt as if the book was calling to him. Instinctively, he held it under his elbow and marched towards the checkout desk. With a shaking hand, he handed it over to the librarian, Avias Deryn.

*"Library shuts in seven minutes,"* Avias silently squawked as she climbed back atop her bureau. She stamped the book by Oliver Tiresias and then added *"Take this book also!"*

Christopher felt like he had no option. He smiled and politely accepted the book: *Cracking the Latin Code.*

# CHAPTER 12
## ~ *PICATSO* ~

Christopher walked a long way before he could think of what to say to Kerry. The ancient books felt heavy in his arm, along with the weight of his Papa's key in his pocket. Almost everything that had occurred appeared to be strangely linked. Christopher thought about what his next move should be, but his mind kept returning to Kerry - and the way she had held his hand in the library. His heart fluttered again. Sam looked at him and let out a little yowl.

The air still felt unusually warm for the late August evening. Notes of citrus and mint tickled the senses of the two friends as they had reached a standstill, just outside Kerry's house. Sam crouched down and rested across Christopher's toes, ready to move whenever his master declared. It was as if Sam knew. It was as if he knew that it was what Christopher had been waiting for – just like the happy ending in his story. Sam lifted his head and nudged Christopher's leg.

A comfortable silence floated in the air. The two friends gazed at each other. The crazy events of the afternoon melted in the balmy air. Christopher was so grateful for the line of high fern pine hedges: they were a welcome barricade shielding his embarrassed glow from all the properties on Fereneze Grove. And all the prying eyes. Christopher had so much that he wanted to say to Kerry, but all that he could manage was "Thank you for t...today. B...but I better be getting back. M....my Nana will have my tea on". Sam lowered his head back upon Christopher's shoes and let out a huge sigh.

"Christopher. Your stutter. It seems a bit better." Kerry thought that was the best thing to say in that moment, but she instantly regretted it. She could see that she had embarrassed him. She stepped closer to him. A warm breeze blew through the ferns. "Christopher, do y -"

"CAT! MY CAT!!!!!!" A ridiculous vision wrapped in a blue kaftan and pink fluffy slippers came flapping from the front gate of number 22 towards Christopher.

"Eh...erm...I...I...I haven't seen a c...c....c..." Christopher's sentence tailed off as he spied Sam sniffing around the wild bushes at the bottom of the grove. His nose seemed to be following a flash of blue, flickering amongst the greenery. Christopher instinctively clicked his fingers and slapped his knees, beckoning to his furry friend. Sam padded back over to Christopher with his tail wagging. The Siberian actually appeared to be laughing. Kerry placed her hand over her mouth to stop her giggles from escaping.

"PICATSO! CH...CH...CH...CH! Come to mummy, my darling!" The woman's stately figure floundered past Christopher and Kerry whilst shrieking "PICCY" at the top of her voice. Her short fiery hair looked ablaze in the autumnal light.

"Wh...who...who was that?" Christopher stammered, still in shock at what had just happened.

"*Meet Barbara Kenny – my nosey neighbour.*" Kerry whispered. "*She is a portrait photographer and artist, but if you ask me, she just likes to spy on...*" Kerry stopped mid-sentence. Barbara had reappeared. She was holding the most feminine looking feline Christopher had ever seen. The two of them looked ridiculous: Barbara looked like the more dominate yang to the tiny feline's ying.

"Kerry darling, how are you? And Christopher...I do believe that you have just met my Peterbald cat – Picatso. He's velour. Simply perfect." Barbara declared, thrusting the almost hairless cat into Christopher's hands. The tiny feline let out a squeaky little trill and bunted its head – quite forcefully - against his chin. "There, I can see that Piccy simply adores you already Christopher. Cats are very good judges of character - did you know?" One of Barbara's badly drawn eyebrows arched above her droopy eyelid. Christopher thought that she looked like a circus clown and it nearly made him laugh, but before he could say anything, the tiny feline had wriggled his way inside his jacket pocket. "I think Piccy has his eyes on whatever's in your pocket my dear. Have you been shopping at old Oli's stall this afternoon?" Barbara stared intently at Christopher's denim jacket pocket. Two large black pupils glared; their ominous fringes almost eclipsed the dark brown of their irises. It made Christopher feel uncomfortable, as if he was under surveillance. An awkward heat radiated from his cheeks.

"H...how...d...did you know?" Christopher asked, gently lifting the cat away from his pocket and handing it back to Barbara. He looked at Kerry in disbelief, but she appeared to be as puzzled as he was.

"Why, darling...the lavender scent was the big giveaway. I smelled it before I opened my garden gate." Barbara snorted then laughed, throwing her huge head back in such a melodramatic way that the sun reflected on the row of gold molars residing at the back of her enormous mouth. The glare momentarily blinded Christopher and Kerry, causing them both to shield their vision with their hands. "Well my dears, I must be off now. Piccy needs his dinner." Christopher felt relief wash over him. Just as he was about to reply, Barbara's penetrating voice cut in: "Oh, Christopher my dear, tell your *darling Nana* I was asking for her."

"I w...will," Christopher answered, but the wallowing stature of Barbara Kenny had already weltered her way back to her garden gate, along with her tiny feline Picatso, cradled like a baby.

"*Thank God!*" Kerry whispered. "*I thought that we would never escape the clutches of the Kenny!*"

"I can't b...b...believe that cat's name!" Christopher tried to stifle the laughter that was about to erupt from his mouth, but he could not help it. And it was contagious. Kerry put a hand over her mouth, but it was too late. Sam let out a low growl.

"WHAT? WHAT IS IT DEAR?!" Barbara Kenny's

piercing tones jolted the two friends out of their state of hysterics. A massive shadow skulked behind one of the tall pine fern bushes.

"*Quick Christopher! Run this way!*" Kerry tugged at Christopher's jacket sleeve and pulled him away from the prying eyes of number 22. Sam followed behind, looking back occasionally as if to make sure that the Kenny was not following. The three of them stopped at the bottom of Fereneze Grove, where the path met with the woods. "We'll be safe here. For now, "Kerry said, trying to catch her breath. Christopher hoped that their moment would magically return, here beside the protection of the trees. He put his hands in his pockets and crossed his fingers. He thought that he should just keep quiet this time and let the magic just happen. But it was not meant to be.

*BUZZ BUZZ.*

"I'm sorry Christopher. It's my mum. My dinner's ready". The moment had passed. Christopher pushed his hands further down into his pockets, like a pair of anchors trying to hold on the last vestiges of his dying moment with Kerry. He wanted this moment to last a little longer. But it melted away into the heat of time's cruel hands – and the annoyance of modern technology.

*BUZZ BUZZ.*

"Sorry Christopher. That's Candice. She's wondering what I am up to". Kerry sounded genuinely apologetic.

"It's okay Kerry. I n...n...need to be getting back to Nana anyway," Sam thumped the back of Christopher's legs, as if in approval for playing it cool. "Will I see you tomorrow perhaps?"

"Yeah! Defo! We have quite a bit to talk about. What a day!"

Christopher's confidence returned, along with his smile. Again, he forgot all about the madness of the day's events; he was more wrapped up in Kerry's serene green eyes. Perhaps that was why he did not see it coming – another hug. Kerry pulled Christopher towards her and whispered

*"I believe you"* into his ears.

BUZZ BUZZ.

The horrible interference of Kerry's phone cut in between the two friends. Again. What made it worse was that the phone was one of his dad's company's mobile phones. Incaendium. The intense image of Aiden Brenton burned at the forefront of his mind. Christopher suddenly remembered his Nana Kathy and the way that he had left her all alone with the imposing force of his father. Worry gnawed at his stomach, making it churn. He had a bad feeling. Christopher was too preoccupied with thoughts about his father and his Nana Kathy to notice Kerry's actions. All this time, she had been scribbling something down onto a diary she had taken from her pocket. She ripped the page out.

"Here, take this", Kerry handed Christopher her number. "Now, you can contact me, and we can arrange to meet sometime…tomorrow?" Kerry's question was followed by a cheeky wink. She smiled at Christopher and Sam before strolling back up along Ferneze Grove. Christopher forgot all about his dad – for the moment. He smiled like a young child trying to practice cheesy grins for the first time. He watched Kerry walk all the way back along to the safety of her house. He waited just a little longer, even after she disappeared behind the baroque wrought iron gate at the entrance of her house. Sam's thick tail thumped on the back of his legs and it stirred his master from his reverie. Sam let out a happy howl.

Christopher felt a skip in his step as he strolled back home. Despite the terrifyingly unbelievable events of the day, and the increasing worry over his Nana, all he could think about was Kerry. He felt guilty for being so self-obsessed, but there *was* a moment between the two friends. He felt it. He was sure that Kerry was going to ask him to kiss her! But the strident tones of Barbara Kenny shouting about her darn cat put an abrupt stop to that. Automatically, Christopher reached into his pocket and pulled out the little paper bag that Oli had given him. It had little chew marks at the corner where Picatso had chowed and chomped. Without thinking, he took the rock out of the bag and put his Nana's gift back into his pocket. At first, he did not pay much attention to the waxed brown paper wrapped around the lavender rock; he was too intent on scoffing the sweet before the eagle eyes of his Nana Kathy. *Sharing is caring* was her motto. Plus, it had been some time since he had eaten anything. He plunged the confectionary into his mouth and inhaled its soothing, sweet lavender scent. Christopher had never eaten anything that tasted like lavender before. He did not think that it was possible. His mouth was awash with mint, apple, and wood. He felt like he was walking on air. He almost floated all the way back along to Acacia Drive, with Sam trying to keep up with his master's drifting. Christopher had not felt this happy in a long time. He was not sure if it was the calming effects of the lavender rock, or the thought that Kerry might actually have wanted to kiss him.

But his happy thoughts were interrupted. Sam was howling at him and nuzzling into his hand. Christopher looked down at the waxen paper that he still clutched tightly between his fingers. He had not noticed it before, but right there, in front of his eyes were the words: "*Meet me outside the library tomorrow. I will be waiting at the tenth minute of the seventeenth hour. Bring the book and the key. Yours, Oli*".

# CHAPTER 13
## ~ *CHRISTOPHER'S NEW GLASSES* ~

Milaw house looked sad in the fading sunlight. The sun had slumped behind the proud structure of the old dwelling. A cold shadow crawled across the front lawn. Even the ranks of lollipop flowers had folded inward, as if to protect themselves from the creeping chill. Normally, Christopher would ring the doorbell three times: a little code that his Nana had invented, just to let her know that it was a friendly presence at the door. However, tonight was different. Christopher knew that something was wrong. He put his key in the lock and opened the door slowly. He was met with silence.

"N…Nana? Are y…you there?"

Sam brushed by his master and ran towards Nana Kathy, who was sitting on the old chaise longue in the hallway. He instantly nuzzled his head against her hands and howled.

"Oh son. I didnae hear you coming in." Nana Kathy sounded weak. The ticking of the grandfather clock echoed in the aching emptiness of the hallway. Christopher shut the door behind him and clicked the switch of the table lamp, illuminating the hallway in welcome light.

"Nana, h…how long have you been s…sitting here?" Christopher was concerned about how frail she looked. The last time he saw her look like this was on the morning of his mother's passing. "Here, h…have this." He took his jacket off and wrapped it around his Nana's shoulders.

"Are you trying to make me look like a punk?" She said, pulling the collars up and smiling. Christopher was glad to see that his Nana had not lost her sense of humour. A tiny bit of colour had returned to her cheeks. However, this brief happiness was quickly overshadowed by the elephant that still stood very prominent in the room. Nana Kathy was the first to break the silence. "It took me quite some time to get rid of your faither. What a bloomin' man!" Sadness tainted her usually lively and affectionate brown eyes.

"I…I should n…never have left you alone with h…him. I'm s…so sorry Nana." Despite the wonderful time that Christopher had experienced with Kerry earlier, he wished that he had stayed at home a little longer. He wished that he could have mustered up the strength to tell his father to leave. He dreaded the answer to his next question. "Wh…what did he want?" The grandfather clock chimed once before his Nana replied.

"Your faither has some halfwit idea about you going to live with him. I told him no. In fact, I told him he was a roaster."

Christopher could feel his heart thumping out of time again. A ball of panic gathered at the back of his throat. Sam, sensing Christopher's anxiety, nuzzled against his hand, and let out a small howl of reassurance.

"Look son, whatever happens, I don't want you worrying. I told your so-called faither that you were staying with me, and he couldnae dae anything aboot it." Thankfully, Nana was back on her feet again and the little lavender hints in her hair had fired up into a more vibrant violet hue.

It made Christopher think of the lavender rock and his visit to Oli's stall.

"Nana! I almost f…forgot. Check your…I…I… m…mean my j…jacket pocket".

They both laughed because Nana Kathy was still wearing Christopher's demin jacket. She took it off, but before handing it back to her grandson, she reached into the pocket and took out the parcel from Oli's stall. She instantly held it up to her nose and inhaled the parcel's fresh scent.

"I know what this is," Nana Kathy chuckled as she took herself out of the hallway and all the way through to the kitchen.

Christopher and Sam followed suit, inhaling the familiar scent as it drifted through the air. Nana Kathy placed the little parcel onto the kitchen worktop and then opened the third drawer down – the junk drawer. She rummaged around looking for something. Christopher was in awe. What was she going to do with it? All of a sudden, she turned around and looked at Christopher with beaming brown eyes.

"Ta-da! Takeaway! What do you fancy?" Nana Kathy thrust the paper menu into Christopher's hands. He could not stop himself from laughing, but he nodded firmly in agreement. "Well," his Nana said, "you know my usual. I'll let you choose, and then you can order for us".

Christopher took the menu through to the front sitting room and had a good look at the range on offer. He had forgotten all about Oli's parcel; his stomach had other ideas. Christopher's belly growled loudly. He already knew what he wanted to order – chicken chow Mein – but he wanted to have a look at the cornucopia of different dishes on offer. Just in case he changed in mind. However, Christopher's eyes were automatically drawn towards the corner of the menu. It was his mother's handwriting. She had scribbled down some numbers "*24. 27. 78. 88.*" – presumably order numbers from previous takeout meals. But underneath the numbers were the words "*Turn right twice…. turn left twice*" along with "*Stay away from him*". Christopher's blood ran cold. He immediately thought of his father. He felt an icy rage burn inside of him. This man, his own flesh and blood, had caused nothing but pain, harm, and sadness towards his poor mother. And now he was upsetting his Nana. Christopher wanted to tell his father what he really thought. "*One of these days,*" he whispered to Sam under his breath. His fist clenched.

"Aye, one of these days I might get my dinner Christopher!" Nana's voice cheeped from the kitchen. "Have you made your choice yet?" Christopher laughed at his Nana's radar ability to zone in on everything, despite her age.

"Yes, N…Nana. I'll order just now," Christopher

replied, returning to the kitchen where his Nana was standing over a steaming hot cup of tea. He was met by the vision of two foggy lenses nestled upon an unmistakable nose, inhaling the contents of whatever was in the huge teacup. It looked more like a soup bowl. "Wh...what's that you are d...drinking?" Christopher asked his Nana, but he intuitively knew as he inhaled the sweet woody scent.

"Thanks to Oli, I have my wee pick-me-up. Lavender tea. Here son, try it."  Christopher had a sip and was instantly warmed by a sweet, spicy kick coloured with fresh minty tinges. He felt invigorated. It had an instant effect: smooth jazz notes shimmied and sparkled all around him. Christopher shut his eyes and inhaled the sweet smell and the familiar music. He danced around in a circle, feeling Sam at his feet guiding his every move. After numerous pirouettes, Christopher opened his eyes to find his Nana dancing around a hot stove in time to Ella Fitzgerald's "'S Wonderful," coming from her record player. "Forget take-away Christopher! I'm making us a wee cheesy omelette and beans!".

The difference in Nana Kathy was night and day. Christopher rubbed his eyes, thinking that it was all just a delusion. But it was no dream. Oliver's tea really was a *pick me-up*, as Nana put it. As much as he was delighted with her turnaround, Christopher had no idea what to say. He was still worried about his grandmother.

"*My dear, its four-leaf clover time, from now on my heart's working overtime...*" Nana Kathy interrupted Christopher's thoughts with her singing. She had already started serving up their dinner – way quicker than Christopher could order take-out food for them.  She was glowing, a far cry from her earlier self. "Here you are son." She placed a hearty dish of food in front of Christopher. Sam padded through, salivating, towards his dish of food and water at the bottom of the breakfast bar in the kitchen.

Everything was at peace again in Milaw house. Notes of lavender danced in the air unnoticed, just like the sound of

Ella's soothing voice. Christopher and Sam sat happily, devouring the hearty home-made treat that his Nana had cooked up.

"You can keep that wee menu if you want." Nana Kathy piped up, as she took the plates over to the sink. Christopher wondered what she meant, but he quickly caught on when he realised that he had been holding the takeaway menu in his left hand, all the way through his dinner. He tried to speak, but his Nana beat him to it. "Sometimes it is nice to keep wee mementoes, it can help wi' the grieving process. When I saw your mum's writing on it, I couldnae bear to throw away that menu, even though the new edition came through weeks ago."

Christopher said nothing; a lump of sadness prevented him from saying anything. He was scared that he was going to start crying, so he ran his hands over his mum's handwriting instead, trying to draw strength from every letter. "Th…thanks Nana." Finally, the words came. "I…I would like that." He folded the menu carefully in half, but before he placed it in his back trouser pocket, he swallowed down the ball of grief and asked, "what did my mum mean by *stay away from him?*"

"Whit are you talking aboot?" Nana Kathy looked puzzled.

"Here," Christopher replied, unfolding the menu, and placing it in front of his Nana. "L…look."

But there was no warning. No numbers. Instead, the words *Saturday. 4pm.* were scribbled at the top. Even the directions had vanished. Christopher felt like he was losing his mind.

"B…b…but I s…s…saw s…something else.   I'm s…sure of it!" He felt almost hysterical.

"Awe son, didnae worry. These things happen to me all the time," Nana Kathy winked and ruffled her grandson's hair. "And besides, you were hungry. A wee empty belly can confuddle the mind!"

Despite his Nana's endearing words, Christopher still

felt overwhelmed. The crazy events of the past few days were really grating on him. He had so many things that he wanted to ask his Nana, but he was scared that it would make her tired again. Sam's tail thumped against his chair, as if to waken him from his state of confusion. It brought a strained smile to his face.

"Look son, why don't you treat yourself to a wee bath and an early night?" Nana Kathy's suggestion seemed so tempting, but all Christopher wanted to do was sit and talk to his grandmother about everything that had been happening to him. However, the look on Sam's face quickly changed his mind. His canine chum was already standing in the front room, wagging his tail ferociously as if to say "Upstairs. Bath!"

****

The sinister mantle of nightfall shrouded the happy village of Ferncross. One by one, the long summer nights were beginning to disappear, like grains of sand falling through life's hourglass. Christopher sat at his bedroom window, listening to the solitary hooting of owl, somewhere in the dark quietness. It soothed his busy mind, for just a moment. He felt somewhat relaxed after his bath, but confusion still lurked at the bottom of his stomach. He had so many questions but had no idea where to start. He could not make head nor tail of the past few days. His first task should have been easy and exciting: texting Kerry and arranging another *date*. He felt silly for even using the *d word*, but Christopher felt that Kerry liked him *more* than just a friend. He had already safely placed the paper with Kerry's number in the top drawer of his bedside table, beside his Papa's pen. All he had to do was start up his mobile phone and text Kerry.

"Easy peasy lemon squeezy," he whispered to Sam; but his canine chum thought differently. His sapphire eyes were clouded with concern.

"*Whyooooooooo!*" Sam howled as if to warn him about

something.

However, against Sam's warning, Christopher opened his wardrobe and scrambled through the pile of clothes that lay on top of his father's device. He just had to text Kerry, despite what happened the last time he tried to set up his Incaendium phone. He quickly pulled the mobile out of the box and switched it on. Automatically, Christopher became like a slave to its master, following the instructions that flashed on screen, entering the personal data requested. Automatically, he entered Kerry's number and then messaged "Hey, it's me Christopher. Text me back." And then, automatically, he allowed the device to scan his retinae. Christopher's phone linked to his father's.

*Sᵣᵣᵣᵣᵣᵣᵣᵣᵣᵣᵣᵣᵣᵣ!*

A scorching, scarlet laser beam of light ignited from the phone. Christopher dropped the device and covered his eyes, screaming in pain. The heat was unbearable. He shut his eyes and put his hands over his mouth to stifle his cries. "*Sam?!*" He half whimpered; half shrieked. Thankfully, his brave dog appeared at his side and nuzzled his cool, wet nose against his foot.

Christopher ever so slowly opened one of his eyes, just to see if Sam was okay, but he could not believe the horrifying vision that lay in front of him. Through one half open eye, his room looked like a blazing inferno of hell. His elephant wallpaper was on fire, peeling off the walls like melting wax from a furious flame.

Christopher then opened both eyes to see his trusted canine chum growling and snarling at something. In the corner of his bedroom, a dark, ominous presence prowled, leering over his bedside drawer. The unearthly figure had huge deciduous dark horns, like enormous antlers protruding from either side of its black snarling skull like face. Christopher rubbed his eyes in disbelief. His heart was in his throat. But his trusted dog gave him the strength he needed. Sam looked brilliant white amidst the hostile licks of crimson flames. However, the tall dark leviathan continued to grow; its long sinewy limbs stretched out towards every corner of the room. It wanted something. It needed something. Long nefarious fingers stretched out, towards Christopher's bedside cabinet, clutching at the handle. Scarlet fingernails tapped at the front of the top drawer. It then opened it. Sam growled and leapt at the feet of this malevolent force, but its limbs just dissolved into a pile of white-hot ashes. A flash of sickly fangs glared as it sneered at both Christopher and Sam. It was holding something golden in its hands. It was his Papa's pen. Sam clambered back onto all four paws and leapt at the evil creature again, but he was flung against the bedroom door.

Christopher felt an uncontrollable rage burn inside of him. He had never felt anything like it before. The anger charred his inner recesses. He looked into the lifeless eyes of the beast and shouted, "nolite nocere canem meum!" Christopher had no idea where the words came from, but the letters fell from his mouth automatically.

*PHEEEEEEEEEEEEEEEE!* A high-pitched frequency cut through the deafening silence.

*C-h-r-i-s-t-o-p-h-e-r. C-h-r-i-s-t-o-p-h-e-r.*

The leviathan intoned every letter, in a chilling chant, as if to say, "*you're next*". It looked at Christopher with such fury and hatred. Without thinking, he reached into his pyjama pocket and grabbed his Papa's key. With all his might, he threw it at the fiend. Suddenly, the room became pooled in soothing silver orbs; they absorbed the hostile heat permeating from the beast. It was so bright Christopher had to shut his eyes again. White covered red, soothing, and dousing the angry flames that had consumed Christopher's bedroom. Over in the corner stood a crooked dark figure, its stature somewhat smaller from before. Despite its shrinking size, malevolence still permeated from its dark black eyes. Christopher could not believe what he was seeing. He had seen that black stare before.

It reminded him of his father.

"Whit in the name of ever are you doing?!" Nana Kathy

peered around the door of Christopher's bedroom. Her voice quavered a little, despite its volume. She walked over to her grandson and cradled his chin in her soft, age worn hands. "Whit have I told you about those bloomin' phones son? They're no good for you. Just look at the state of you!" Tears trickled from Christopher's eyes as he opened them looking at the refreshing sight of his grandmother. He tried to speak, but his attempt was interrupted. "Follow me son." She guided her grandson through to the bathroom where she carefully wiped away his tears and put some drops in his eyes. "There, that'll help". And then she vanished, once again, her voice trailing up the corridor "and in the name of the wee man, tidy that room."

Christopher clambered towards the bathroom cabinet mirror and looked at his reflection. The whites of his eyes were covered in tiny, red thorny veins. He could just barely make out the blue light of his irises. He searched hard, but thankfully he could still see the light of his mother in his eyes. He stumbled back into the hallway and made his way back to his bedroom. He had to see if Sam was okay. But before he reached the doorway, his Nana reappeared with a pair of strange looking glasses.

"Here son, have these," she said, slipping a huge pair of spectacles over Christopher's nose, the type that only Buddy Holly would have been proud of. She spun her grandson around and looked at him lovingly, grabbing his chin between her thumb and index finger, "well, it'll no' go with your demin jacket, but at least it will stop you getting bloodshot eyes when you look at those electronic thingies."

Christopher's sight was saturated in soothing yellow tones. He looked at his Nana questioningly. "D...d...did you see any of that?"

"I saw enough son ... enough to know that you shouldnae use your faither's phone - and that it's bedtime," Nana Kathy declared, ruffling her grandson's head. But before she trotted back down the corridor and disappeared into her bedroom, she turned and said, "you know, those were your mum's specs. She wore them for the same thing." She winked and vanished behind the door of her bedroom.

Christopher raised his hands up to feel the square setting of the black frames, perched on the bridge of his nose. He almost laughed aloud at how ridiculous he must have looked, but his cheerfulness was curbed by the concern for his canine chum. He scurried towards his bedroom, flinging the door in a panic. However, Sam lay snuggled at the bottom of his bed, fast asleep. Christopher ran over and cuddled into the thick fur of Sam's nape, but his friendly pooch did not make a sound. He was too content with sleep.

Happy that his dog seemed unharmed, Christopher surveyed his room for damage. To his surprise, everything seemed untouched. No fire, no flames, no *father*. However, his gaze drifted to the corner where the *father-like* beast flamed. His stare was met by the sight of his Papa's huge, ailing lean-to door key. Despite its patina, it appeared to glimmer in the moonlight, shimmering through the gap in the curtains. Christopher carefully picked up the key and placed it back into his pocket. Along with the heaviness of the key, he felt like he had the weight of a huge responsibly placed upon him. This could not be make-believe.

The more Christopher thought about it, the more the crazy events of the past few days seemed to click into place. He lay back on his bed thinking of everything. Tomorrow would be more telling. Meeting old Oli would surely be another key in unlocking the many strange doors he had encountered so far. He just knew it. Thinking about this made his attention drift towards Sam. It brought a huge smile to Christopher's face, seeing his furry friend curled up in slumber. He tiptoed over to Sam and lay on his bed, listening to his rhythmic doggy breathing. Christopher shut his mind off from everything and anything, trying to focus only on his loyal chum's slow and regular heartbeat. And it worked. Sam must have been aware of his master's presence because he extended his paw over Christopher's hands. The two friends fell fast asleep.

\*\*\*\*

"*Christopher?*" Nana Kathy's voice whispered from behind his bedroom door. She was met by a chorus of snores. "Christopher?!" This time her voice was pitched more at her usual *Nana level*, just enough to wake her Grandson from his slumber.

"Wh…wh…what? N…Nana is that you?" Christopher mumbled, wiping the drool away from his mouth. Noticing that it was pitch-black outside, he looked at his Mickey Mouse watch. It was five minutes past twelve; he had been asleep for three hours.

"Your clothes son," Nana quipped, her voice trailing off as she moved down the upstairs hallway, "pick them up and hang them over the chair." Christopher laughed at her ability to see through doors.

"S…sorry N…Nana, j…just p…picking them up now," he mumbled, full of sleep, as he gathered his clothes up from the floor. Thankfully, his bedside light was still aglow: a little grey elephant lamp, still illuminating the darkness. It was ever present in his room from as far back as he could remember. His mum must have bought it when he was a baby. Sam lay snoring on his master's bed, his legs moving involuntarily. "*Probably chasing rabbits,*" Christopher thought, pushing away the darker thoughts of Sam fighting against the dark beast in his room earlier.

Christopher lifted his clothes over to his desk, but just as he was about to hang his jeans over the chair, a piece of paper fell out. It was the takeaway menu from earlier. Christopher folded his clothes over the chair and picked up the menu. After the frightening events of earlier, he had almost forgotten about his mother's writing.

*Sssnnnoortzzzzzzz.* Sam snored loudly, disturbing Christopher from his contemplation. Still holding the menu, Christopher returned to the cosiness of his bed. He lay back, looking at the all too familiar writing of his mother. He scanned the menu again, imaging what it would be like to have his mother here, just once more, to order a family take out dinner. This time though, it would be his treat.

*24. 27. 78. 88. Turn right twice …. turn left twice.*

And there they were. The numbers and inscription, written in his mother's unmistakable hand. Christopher robotically reached up to his eyes, but he was met by strange wooden frames. "What the?!" he whispered, as he pulled the old frames from his nose. He felt stupid as he fumbled around, pulling his Mother's glasses from his face. Sam had woken up and found the whole thing hilarious. Christopher rubbed his eyes and looked at the menu again. His mother's writing had completely vanished.

# CHAPTER 14
## ~ *THE RAVEN AND THE ROBIN* ~

Christopher could not finish his breakfast. The remnants of last night's terrifying ordeal still swilled around in his stomach. He felt very uneasy. Nana Kathy was nowhere to be seen; but for once, Christopher was glad of this. He wanted his restlessness to go under the radar. Her radar. He did not want to worry his Nana anymore, given the poor state he had found her in when he returned home yesterday.

A feverish chill clung onto Christopher, making him feel altogether miserable and anxious. He took another sip of his milky tea, but his mouth still felt as dry as dust. He could not shake off the chilling image of the beast that invaded his room. He had seen that dark, permeating look before and it filled him with dread. He thought of Sam and how the pervading evil creature had almost maimed him. Sam, detecting his concern, padded over from his empty breakfast bowl and licked his master's hand. It brought a smile to Christopher's face. He looked down towards his smiling canine chum and felt reassured. *"Perhaps we should both get some fresh air,"* he whispered.

Outside, the birds chirruped happily, welcoming the warmth of the morning. The sun stood prominently in the sky, full of promise for the new day. The sweet scent of freshly cut grass skipped through the air. Christopher inhaled deeply, allowing the verdant aroma to wash away his ails. The golden sunlight glistened upon the petals of Nana Kathy's yellow roses. Their blond hues contrasted with the rows of little pink and purple celosias. Christopher smiled as he looked at their tiny fluffy amethyst heads, gently swaying in the gentle breeze. He thought that they looked like the hair on little troll dolls, just like the ones that his mum used to have on her dressing table. *For good luck*, she used to say. Christopher missed his mum more than ever.

Since her passing, he would wake every morning with such an empty aching in his heart. And almost always, he would awaken to a damp pillow of tears. Christopher's mum had appeared in his dreams just about every night after she died. Sometimes she would occupy all his sleepy visions; other times she would just appear out of nowhere, with no warning. Christopher felt like she was trying to communicate with him. But that had all changed. Ever since Christopher's adventure into the old lean-to, his dreams had been filled with strange but familiar apparitions. His mother had left his dreams.

"CHRISTOPHER?!" Nana Kathy's declaration interrupted her grandson's thoughts. Yet again. "Can you carry this ootside for me?" She thumped down a huge basket of washing in front of him, full of duvets and clothing.

"S…sure Nana," Christopher replied, wondering how she had managed to fit everything in one load into the washing machine. He lifted the basket over to the whirligig in front of the patio stones. "Phew," he exhaled to Sam. "That w…was heavy!"

"No' as heavy as this!" Nana Kathy reappeared with another load of washing, this time it was all packed into a tiny little basin. She lifted it onto her head and carried it out to the washing line. Christopher was delighted to see that she had such a burst of new energy; such a contrast to the way she looked just less than twenty-four hours ago. It made him think of the pick-me-up lavender tea that Oli had given her. And then he remembered, he was supposed to meet Old Oli this very day. According to the note, Oli requested that they meet at ten minutes past five in the afternoon, outside Ferncross Library. Christopher could not believe that he had forgotten about this. It filled him with hope: perhaps the old man would be able to shed some long-awaited light upon the dark and confusing events of the past few days. Despite his ailing age and blindness, Christopher felt that Oli was going to answer a lot of burning questions.

He knew that there had to be some magic involved in this. After all, how did Oli actually write the note?

Christopher's thoughts were once again disturbed by his Nana, but this time it was because of her actions. A vision of Nana dancing around the whirligig, pegging up his new uniform made Christopher's mind immediately jump onto the horrible thought of school. Tomorrow marked his first day at Oakwood Academy. The few friends that he had in Leicester were moving onto Woodfarm High School in the town; but because Christopher had moved back to stay with his Nana, it meant that he had to attend Oakwood. Anxiety overwhelmed him. Normally Sam would be his comfort in these situations, but Christopher's misery increased because he could not take his dog to school with him. "*How w…will I c…cope?*" He whispered to Sam, who seemed to understand because he let out a little reassuring yowl and licked his master's hand.

*"Keehoooweee!"*

Sam's yowl made Christopher laugh. He could be mistaken, but it sounded like he howled *Kerry*. He hugged his dog tightly and then ruffled the thick white fur that covered the muscles on his strong back. Of course, he would not be alone: Kerry was already a pupil at Oakwood Academy, so he could hang out with her at lunchtimes. He patted Sam's head, grateful for the reassurance that his canine chum had instilled in him. Surely it did not matter that she was in the year above him.

Christopher pushed this nagging doubt to the back of his mind; instead, he focussed on the day ahead. Today he was going to meet Oli *and* Kerry. His heart fluttered again at the memory of yesterday and how keen she was to see him. There was only one problem: how could Christopher even contemplate using that mobile phone again after the terrifying events of last night. Perhaps he could just call round to Kerry's house? But then, she might be out. Or worse still, Candice could be there. Although Christopher had only encountered the fiery red head once, he had experienced enough of her to sense that she did not like him. She appeared to have a strange power over Kerry – and her other friends – as if they were scared to disagree with her in any shape or form. Like his mother, Christopher was a great judge of character, and there was something about Candice that felt wrong. Very wrong. In fact, Christopher could not shake off the feeling that she was actually jealous of him. There was only one solution to all of this: Christopher had to use the Incaendium mobile to contact Kerry.

"Right son, that's the last of the washin'. Whit a belter of a morning." Nana Kathy piped up. "I dunno what you've planned for the day, but I have a few wee things needin' done. Will you be okay?"

"Y… yes Nana," Christopher tried to act as if nothing was wrong.

"Jus' promise me one thing."

Christopher's head nodded in response to his Nana's request. He would do anything for her.

"Jus' promise me that you'll wear your mother's specs if you insist on using that blasted gadget of your faither's".

Christopher almost laughed aloud at how in tune his Nana's radar was. "Okay Nana, I p…promise".

****

Excitement pushed Christopher upstairs into the upper hallway. He was too busy dreaming about Kerry to have noticed a fluffy white vision scoot by his legs. Sam was already upstairs, waiting outside Christopher's bedroom door. Something was wrong. The two friends stood still looking at each other. Concern clouded Sam's usually bright blue eyes again, and it filled Christopher with fear. He placed a shaking hand on the doorknob to his bedroom, inhaled deeply and opened the door. Sam whined quietly.

Thankfully, everything looked normal. Well, as normal as normal could be for a young teenager's bedroom.

Christopher pulled his bedside cabinet open and took out his mother's spectacles. He placed them onto the bridge of his nose, hoping that their yellow lenses would miraculously work their magic. Once again, his vision was awash with soothing golden hues. Despite the cooling sensation, Christopher still felt nervous. He gingerly made his way over to his wardrobe, to where he had thrown the fiery mobile device the night before. "*Here goes. Wish me luck*" he whispered to Sam, as he picked up the phone. But his doggy chum sat staring at the Incaendium mobile in Christopher's hands. Sam was ready in case the nightmare returned.

Christopher tapped the crystallized glass. Nothing. The technological beast was still asleep. He swallowed hard, gulping down a mixture of fresh air and panic; he knew what he had to do. He held the device in front of his eyes and waited on it the eye recognition. One, two, three, four seconds passed. Nothing. Sam let out a yelp of despair.

*Beep ---- beep. Beep ---- beep.*

Suddenly, the phone flashed red. Christopher shut his eyes and dropped it, causing a huge clatter against his wooden floorboards.

"WHIT WAS THAT?!" Nana Kathy bellowed from below.

"N... NOTHING NANA!" Christopher shouted immediately, trying to hide the terror in his voice. He opened one eye, expecting to see flames leaping out from all corners from his room. Thankfully though, everything seemed fine – except that his room was bedecked in bright yellow. Christopher lifted his hands up to his mother's specs and let out a huge sigh of relief. He quickly picked the phone back up off the floor and looked at the screen.

A message from Kerry flashed: ***"Wat time do you want to meet?"***

Christopher jumped up in the air and then made a little fist pump.

"Whit are you up to now son?" Nana Kathy interrupted her grandson's celebrations. She was standing in the doorway. "I thought the pictures were aboot to fall off the walls…" she added, her voice trailing off into laughter.

Christopher stood still, with Sam by his side and the phone still in his hands. He was still wearing his mother's glasses.

"I'm fair chuffed that you are making good use of them specs. You look like your aff tae a Peter Sellers convention".

Christopher glanced over to the mirror on his wall, beside his bed, where he was met with the most ridiculous reflection he had ever seen. His face looked tiny compared to the huge black frames that almost dwarfed his face. He began to laugh along with his Nana.

"You know son…" Nana Kathy interrupted the laughter. "You look a lot like your Papa Tommy wi' those specs on. He had the same bump in the nose as you – it was great for haudin' his specs in place. Your mum had the same bump."

Christopher felt a huge swell in his heart. He felt so happy to hear those words: *a lot like your Papa*. He moved closer to the mirror and studied his reflection. He had never seen it before, but he could see a few similarities between himself and his Papa. He smiled broadly at the mirror.

"Is that Kerry your telexing?"

Christopher laughed again, unable to hide his amusement at his Nana's mistake. "Do you mean t…texting, N…Nana?"

"Aye, that's what I meant. Well if you are, telex her and ask if she wants to come for a wee bit o' lunch."

Christopher was about to reply, but his Nana vanished, just as quick as she had appeared five minutes before in his bedroom doorway. To avoid being rude, he shouted "I will d…do N…Nana", loud enough so that she could hear him from downstairs. There was no reply, but Christopher was certain that Nana Kathy's radar would have picked up his reply. He glanced back at his reflection in the mirror and realised that he still had the phone in his hands. Kerry! Of course, he was about to text her back and set a time for what he hoped would be a date. With trembling hands, he held the phone up in front of his eyes, allowing the Incaendium device to read the intricate detail of his retinae. It worked for a second time. Even with his mother's glasses, he could still operate the device. Without wasting anymore time, he tapped on Kerry's message, eager to respond. This was it. The moment he had been waiting for.

"Tell Kerry to come at the back of twelve." Nana Kathy magically reappeared in the doorway, smiling. She was carrying Christopher's freshly ironed gym kit. "Ah'll have a wee pot of soup on the stove ready."

"Th...thanks Nana," Christopher smiled at his Nana as she placed his clothes on his bed.

"Mind and roll them afore ye put them into your bag," she winked as she glided out of his room. "Ye didnae want crinkled sports clathes on your first day," she shouted, her voice trailing down the stairs.

Christopher was so grateful to have his Nana in his life. Even though the loss of his mother was too difficult to even think about, he felt more at peace knowing that his Nana was there to look after him. She loved making a fuss over him, even if it meant her interrupting him from time to time.

"*Khooooweee*," Sam howled at his master again, refocusing him on the task at hand. Christopher fumbled with the phone and was glad to see that it was still unlocked. No need for retinae recognition.

Christopher tapped on the keyboard and thought long and hard about what to reply with. *The back of twelve* was a great Nana-ism, and he still had no idea what it actually meant. He had always thought that it meant after half twelve, so he tapped on the luminous keyboard: **"What about 12.35? Do you want to come for lunch? My Nana is making soup."** He read the words of his message carefully and then clicked **send.** Christopher's heart leapt into his mouth. The message turned red, indicating that Kerry had read it.

A light breeze gathered outside Milaw house, blowing some of the premature yellowy leaves from their forlorn looking branches. Despite the cloudless sky, the cool zephyr reminded the locals in Fernlock that autumn was on its way. Christopher stood at his bedroom window gazing out at the fern trees. A nagging paranoia danced in the pit of his stomach. It felt like an eternity had passed since he sent his reply. He looked at the phone again. Nothing. Without thinking, he took off his mother's glasses and tried to focus on the flourishing green tips of the fir trees in front of his bedroom window. They appeared to be preparing for a long cold winter: little emerald seeds sprouted at the ends of each fern, like rows upon rows of tiny Brussels sprouts. It made Christopher think of Christmas and how this would be the first one without his mum. A huge well of sadness gathered at the back of his throat, almost choking him. Salty tears smarted his vision.

*Beep ---- beep. Beep ---- beep.*

Christopher hit his head off the glass pane of his bedroom window. He had no idea just how close he had been to the glass because his mind was running away with itself. He quickly wiped away the tears from his eyes and flung on his mother's glasses. He did not want to take any chances. He shut one eye and glanced down at the screen of the Incaendium device.

Kerry's reply was short and to the point: ☺

Christopher flung the phone on his bed and started dancing around in circles. Sam, who had been watching his master's movements all along, joined him in his celebratory dance. It was just like the first time they met, a couple of days before in the old magical lean-to. The two friends pranced foot to paw, back and forth, in time to imaginary music. And then Christopher stopped. He opened his bedroom door and listened to the music that was drifting up the staircase.

*If they asked me, I could write a book…*

Downstairs, Nana Kathy's old Dansette record player whirled happily, singing her favourite song. She was hovering over the cooker, or the stove as she liked to call it, cooking up a huge pot of her legendary vegetable broth. Christopher and Sam skipped downstairs, in time to the music. Ella Fitzgerald's smooth voice resonated around Milaw house. Her chanting cast a spell over the two friends, causing them to automatically saunter towards the source of the music; that, and the smell of Nana Kathy's home-made soup had lured them into the kitchen.

*Doo---roo---doo---root------do---do---do-----do---do---root.*
*Doo---roo---doo---root------do---do---do-----do---do---root.*

A punchier song exploded from the Dansette's speakers. Nana Kathy began waving the wooden spoon and soup ladle in the air. Christopher laughed hysterically at the sight of his wee lavender haired Nana, beating the cooking utensils in the air.

"A'm playin' the space drums son. C'mon – join in!"

Christopher chuckled even harder. He knew that his Nana meant to say *the air drums*, but this time he did not correct her. Instead, he grabbed two spoons from the top drawer and beat the imaginary drums along with his Nana. Sam gambolled around their feet, licking up the smattering of soup that had splashed down from Nana Kathy's flying soup spoon.

"A loved that," she chirruped, just as the record came to its end. "It's Ella's version of Sunshine of – Aiiiiieeeeeeeeeeeeeeee!" Nana Kathy dropped the utensils on to the floor, causing a huge clatter. She stood upright, holding her heart, gasping for a breath. Her face turned sickly white.

Christopher instantly knew what was wrong. Outside the kitchen window, a dark creature flapped wildly, its wingspan stretched almost the full horizontal length of the window. Two penetrating eyes stared ominously, clutching their black pupils like bottomless wells of scorn. Christopher had never seen a raven so huge, so terrifying.

"SHOOOO! Get oot o' here!" Nana Kathy shouted at the window, waving a tea towel. The sinister beast beat it wings ferociously, refusing to move. It stared at both

Christopher and his Nana, as if it was trying to intimidate them.

"*Grrooooooo!*" Sam growled, desperate to chase away the evil looking bird.

Christopher tried to say something to his Nana, but she was already opening the back-porch door, with Sam at her heels. She was shaking a wooden broom above her head. Christopher quickly ran to the door, but thanks to his Nana, her broom and Sam, the black feathered beast swooped above the rooftop of Milaw house and out of sight.

"Blast it!" Thankfully, some pinkness had returned to Nana Kathy's cheeks. "What a scoundrel – it gave me some fright."

She sat down on one of the patio chairs and patted her brow with her apron. Christopher pulled up another chair beside her. The two of them sat in the morning sun, allowing its delicate warmth to chase away the horrible vision of the black raven. No matter how he tried, Christopher could not help but think that the carrion creature was yet another disturbing event to add to all the others. He shut his eyes and put his hand in his pocket, searching for his Papa's pen and key. They were still there. They made him feel safer, as if his Papa's spirit was close by, ready to protect him. He opened his eyes to check on his Nana, but she had vanished.

Fine tendrils of clouds crept over the sun, dousing Milaw garden in shade. Christopher rubbed his eyes. Down at the bottom of the garden, he could see Sam sniffing at the base of the bird feeder. Nana Kathy was beside him, holding something in her hands. She looked so small and frail beside the powerful figure of Sam.

"Awe Christopher, I'm pure up to high doh." Nana Kathy's voice trembled as Christopher ran towards her. He could see tears forming in eyes. In her hands lay a little robin. It was dead.

"N…Nana, I d…d…don't know what to s…say." Christopher instantly thought that raven was responsible for the poor little bird's untimely death.

"That blasted raven." Nana Kathy's words agreed with her grandson's thoughts. "A wish I'd thumped it wi' ma brush before it killed this pure wee thing."

Christopher was worried about his Nana again. He could see how much she was visibly shaking. Sam, who was also aware of this, stood by her side, allowing his thick tail to thump against the back of her legs for reassurance.

"C...come on ins...s...side and I'll m...make some tea. You n...need a rest." Christopher took the robin from his Nana's hands and led her back towards the safety of Milaw house. He was unsure what distressed him the most: the sight of the lifeless robin or his Nana's weak condition.

****

The kettle whistled softly, as if it was aware of Nana Kathy's fragility. Christopher lifted it from the heat and poured the water into his Nana's mug. A plume of luscious, sweet, and fresh whispers tickled his nose. He was glad that his Nana had requested some of her lavender tea – he hoped that it would make her feel more like her usual self again. Christopher handed it to his Nana, and she sipped the hot lilac liquid slowly.

"I...I'll t...take care of the w...wee robin Nana," Christopher said as he rested against the sink in the kitchen. Without thinking, he had placed his back to the kitchen window, as if he wanted block out any reminder from earlier. Nana Kathy had still not said anything, which was not like her; instead, she merely nodded her head in between sipping her tea. Sam was still by her side. Christopher was worried about her sickly pallor.

*Ring --- ring.*

The doorbell cut through the silence. Christopher feared that it would be his father again. A mix of dread and anger broiled in the pit of his stomach. He could not face seeing him. Not today.

*Ring --- ring.*

Christopher looked at his Nana, but she appeared to be somewhere very far off.

"I'll g...get it N...Nana," he insisted, but she did not answer.

Sam walked his master to the front door, ready to defend him against any unwanted company. Christopher stood in the hallway for a moment, before gathering up the courage to open the door. A tall, dark, and strange looking shadow tainted the colours of the Charles Rennie Mackintosh stained glass window. Christopher shut his eyes, inhaled then pulled the front door open, as if he was ripping a plaster from a painful wound.

To Christopher's relief – and delight – Kerry was standing in the doorway. She was carrying a pair of rugged looking stepladders made of dark wood. She handed them to Christopher, who appeared to be as puzzled as she was.

"I found these in front of your garage - on the driveway. Oh, and I am sorry I am a bit early."

Christopher propped them against the wall in the hallway and automatically flung his arms around Kerry. He forgot all about the ladders for a second, choosing instead to inhale the sweet zingy allure of her perfume. However, he quickly realised what he was doing, and awkwardly stumbled back saying, "you a...are a s...sight for s...sore eyes."

Kerry nervously giggled and stepped into the hallway of Milaw House. She could not be sure, but she felt a different atmosphere, as if something had changed. Although the delicious aroma of Nana Kathy's soup floated in the air, welcoming Kerry, she also had the feeling that another presence lurked in the house; one that was entirely unwelcoming.

Christopher guided Kerry over to the chaise longue by the hall window. He felt like he had to warn her about his Nana – and everything else – before they ventured through to the kitchen. Christopher tried to speak, but it all became so overwhelming. There was so much more to tell Kerry; he had no idea where to start. However, Kerry's kind and caring look made him feel better. Sunlight glittered through the great hallway window, illuminating her beautiful green eyes. Christopher felt his heart melt.

"Right you two," Nana Kathy appeared in the hallway. "Your grub's up – it's soup-de-loop, wi' a coupla enders."

Kerry looked at Christopher with confusion. Aware that she was being impolite though, she smiled and said hello, but Nana Kathy had already fluttered out of the hallway.

But Christopher was the one that was more confused. He could not believe the quick transformation in his Nana. Thinking that it was best to leave it until later, he smiled at Kerry and said, "she m…means l…lunch....and it's…it's soup with bread."

****

In the kitchen, Nana Kathy was fussing over the cooker again, already preparing for dinnertime – or *teatime* as she called it. In between stirring the mince, she supped at her third cup of lavender tea. Her old wireless whistled away in the pantry. Christopher and Kerry sat in an awkward silence in the dining room. The reticence was almost deafening. Christopher was kicking himself from the inside. This was supposed to be a date, but so far, he had been as useless as what his Nana Kathy would call *a chocolate teapot*. He had to say something, anything, so he stuttered the first words that came into his head. "D…do you w…want to s…see the old l…lean-to?" He instantly regretted saying it and he worried that his Nana had heard him.

"Yes!" Kerry declared instantly, washing away any of Christopher's concern. "I'd love to," she whispered this time, in case Nana Kathy heard.

"Love to whit? Whit are you two love birds talkin' aboot?" Despite the afternoon jazz session crooning from her radio, Nana Kathy's radar still managed to zoom in on their chat. The rosiness had returned to her cheeks.

"N…nothing m…much Nana. J…just school s…stuff." Christopher's face burned bright red. He wanted to hold his hands over his cheeks. He could barely look Kerry in the eye, but when he did, she smiled at him and bit her lower lip. His belly flipped.

"Well," Nana Kathy piped up, taking off her apron. "I need to head into town for a few wee messages. If you are headin' oot, jus' remember to be back for the back of five - teatime. It's mince 'n' tatties."

"Th…thanks N…Nana," Christopher replied smiling, but his expression quickly turned into a look of pain. Kerry kicked him under the table. She only meant to tap his leg to catch his attention, but she hit his shin with quite some force.

"*Sorry,*" she mouthed slowly, before discreetly adding "*Oli?*"

Christopher instantly realised what Kerry meant – and why she had kicked him. "Eh…Nana…c…could we m…make it half p…past six instead?" Christopher hoped that would give him enough time to meet old Oli and then return home in time for dinner.

Nana Kathy was still trying to rearrange the Kirby grips in her thick purple-white hair; she had either witnessed the exchange between Kerry and Christopher, or she was pretending to ignore it. Christopher thought that it was the latter because her response was far too straightforward: "right son, that's fine." She winked at her grandson before adding, "I put the mince in the slow cooker, so another wee hour shouldnae make too much a difference. But mind – it's a school night the night. No too late to bed I should hope!"

"Thanks for lunch Mrs Muir," Kerry cut in, trying to smooth over any suspicion that lurked in the air.

"Awe, you're a bonnie wee lass. Your more than welcome. An' nae need tae call me that – call me Kathy." She turned to leave, but before she did, Nana Kathy ruffled the hair on her grandson's head - the very same hair that he had spent a whole ten minutes trying hard to look half decent after his morning shower. Christopher made a mental note to use some wax in his hair in future.

"My stepladders!" Nana Kathy's wee Scottish voice twittered from the hallway. "Whit in the name of the wee man are they doin' here?" She added, as she returned to the dining room.

"I found them Mrs Muir, I mean Kathy," Kerry was first to respond. Christopher was too busy rubbing his shin to respond. "I brought them to the door because they were just lying in front of the garage."

"That's queer. A couldnae find them anywhere." Nana Kathy looked puzzled. "They're a braw wee pair of stairs. Your Papa made them you know son."

Christopher looked up and smiled at his Nana. She was wearing her prescription sunglasses and they made her look a little like Dame Edna. He tried to hide his laughter.

"Whit are you rubbin' your leg for?" Despite the dark lenses in her elaborate frames, Nana Kathy could still see everything.

"I…I'm fine. I a…accidentally h…hit it off the t…table leg."

Kerry giggled at his unnatural sounding reply. His Nana just smiled, as if she knew more than she was letting on.

# CHAPTER 15
## ~ *THE THING IN THE CORNER* ~

When Christopher heard the front door click shut, the concern for his grandmother returned. Although she seemed more like her usual self, he could not stop worrying about the events of the morning. His Nana had been so distressed by the death of the robin and the sight of the raven. Thankfully, Kerry interrupted his thoughts.

"Well, are you going to tell me what the heck has been going on?"

Sam howled as if to say *finally*.

Christopher explained all the crazy events that had occurred over the last twenty-four hours. Kerry listened intently. There was something about his story that sounded so real. It was not just in the way he explained things, Kerry also could not shake off the unnerving feeling that something else was lurking in the shadows of Milaw house. When they had finished clearing up the dishes in the kitchen, Christopher took Kerry upstairs to show her his Papa's pen and where the *thing* had appeared in his bedroom. But he decided not to show her the yellow glasses. He was too embarrassed.

Sam was already upstairs on Christopher's bed, catching an early afternoon snooze. Christopher sat beside his canine chum and nuzzled his head into the thick fur of his nape. He wished that he had given Sam to his Nana for the afternoon: he would have been a great protector for her.

"Try not to worry about your Nana," Kerry read his mind. "She will be okay."

Christopher appreciated Kerry's words of comfort, but he could not help it: worrying was something that he was good at. He decided that now would be a good time to show her the pen: a perfect way to deflect his concern. For the time being anyway.

"Wow, it looks so old. So expensive." Kerry looked amazed.

Unexpectedly, something caught Christopher's gaze. Over in the corner, adjacent to his bedside cabinet, lay a sinister looking scorch mark. The wooden floorboards looked charred. Christopher knelt and touched the black charcoal with his hands. It still felt hot. He pulled his hand back in surprise and blew on his fingertips. He felt like he had touched a red-hot iron. Kerry was already by his side, staring at the stygian stain.

"*What the -?*" She breathed heavily, certain that she was in the presence of something evil.

Christopher grabbed a dirty tee-shirt from his laundry basket and scrubbed at the charcoal encrusted mark. When he pulled it away, the darkness still remained. However, his tee-shirt was filthy.

"Let's try washing it with some water," Kerry suggested, pulling out a bottle of water from her bag. She dropped a quarter of it over the mark then Christopher began rubbing his tee-shirt over it again.

And then something unbelievably horrifying happened.

The pool of charcoal water turned crimson red. Christopher's tee-shirt looked like it was drenched in blood. The two friends stared at each other in shock.

A low growl of concern came from behind them. Sam nudged in between Christopher and Kerry.

"I...I...I'm s...sure there's a v...very good explanation f...for this," Christopher suggested, but he was not convinced with his words.

"I'm going to get some kitchen roll," Kerry said, without even acknowledging what he had suggested. She almost sprinted downstairs.

Christopher stared at the place where the beast had invaded his bedroom. Goosebumps prickled over his skin. Even the walls in the corner of his bedroom were splashed in the murky red liquid. Although Sam was with him in his bedroom, Christopher could not bear to be near the blood bath that had consumed the corner of his room. He signalled to Sam to go with him through to the bathroom. He filled the sink and plunged his claret coloured top into the hot water. As he dried his hands on the towel, he noticed that tiny red blisters had appeared on his fingertips. The scarlet mark in the corner had burned him.

"Christopher, are you coming?" Kerry stood in the upper hallway landing, holding some kitchen roll and bin bags.

He decided not to show Kerry his burns, not until they had cleaned up the disturbing crimson tide in his room.

It took the two of them nearly ten minutes and almost two reels of kitchen roll to clear up the blood like liquid. Neither Christopher nor Kerry uttered a word whilst they scrubbed at the carmine coloured mess. Sam sat vigilantly behind them, keeping one eye on them and the other on the wardrobe, where the mobile phone lay.

Christopher could feel his heart pounding uncontrollably in his chest again. He had to get outside into the fresh air. He wondered what Kerry really thought of him. He wondered if she really believed him or if she thought that he just had an overactive imagination. Christopher was about to say sorry to Kerry, but she smiled and gave him a hug.

"Are you okay?" she said, as she pulled back to look at him.

"F...Fine. B...but can we get some f...fresh air?" Christopher lied. He was far from feeling fine. The tips of his fingers throbbed, and a ball of fear whirled in his stomach.

"What about you show me the lean-to?" Kerry thought that would make them both feel better. She did not wait for his answer; instead, she took Christopher's hand and led the way downstairs to the kitchen, where they washed the remnants of the sticky blood like substance from their hands. They decided to leave the bags until later.

Christopher forgot all about his tee-shirt soaking in the sink.

Out in the garden, Christopher looked nervously at his watch. He could not believe how quickly the day was disappearing. Dark clouds skulked on the horizon, indicating a change was on its way. A gust of wind whipped through Milaw garden, catching everything in its path and throwing it up into a dust devil. Sam chased after the dirty whirlwind, but it evaporated into the ether as quickly as it had appeared. Christopher looked at his watch again.

"Relax," Kerry said comfortingly. "You still have nearly three hours before you meet Oli."

Christopher took a deep breath and inhaled the fragrant aroma of lavender, allowing its fresh smell to calm his nerves. He smiled at Kerry, grateful for the heartening influence that she was also having on him. Despite how little time they had been in each other's company over the past few days, he felt like they had always been together. He smiled again at Kerry.

"Well, are you going to show me this lean-to?" She nudged him in a playful manner.

Christopher suddenly realised he had been staring at her with a big cheesy smile for the past few minutes, without saying anything. "Of c…course. Follow m…me," he finally replied. He wondered if other couples partook in such strange events on their first date. It almost made him laugh, but the sight of the lean-to stopped him. He could be mistaken, but it looked *even older* in the afternoon sunlight. As he stepped towards the door, he noticed that some of the wooden slats had decayed so much that they appeared to be crumbling into murky sawdust.

"Is it safe?" Kerry asked, as she too had noticed the poor state of the exterior.

"Y…yes," Christopher replied, trying to hide his concern. He was certain that once he opened the door, the interior would come alive and all would be revealed to Kerry. He could not wait to show her the old rocking horse and *The Book of Almost Anything*.

Slowly, Christopher pushed the door open.

"*Yeuch!*" Kerry held her hands over her nose.

The smell of dampness and rotten wood assaulted their nostrils upon entering the old lean-to. Christopher had not noticed when he was outside, but the window had been painted over with white paint, preventing any sunlight from entering. Kerry automatically pulled out her Incaendium mobile and activated the torch light function. Suddenly, the contents of the lean-to were illuminated by a powerful orange glow.

Christopher screamed in horror. He flung his hands up to cover his mouth as he surveyed the wreckage. Everything was covered in a thick coat of grimy dust, as if the lean-to's entire contents had been untouched in years. Decades even. Cobwebs covered every nook and cranny, as if the spiders had been trying to mend the broken slats with their strong silky stitching. The spinning top was on the floor. The board games on the shelf were covered in mildew. In the corner, lay the white rocking horse. It was broken. *The Book of Almost Anything* was nowhere to be seen.

"Nooooooo!" Christopher fell to his knees and covered his eyes. He tried so hard to stop the of tears exploding from his eyes. He felt Kerry's arms grip his shoulders. He could not hear what she was saying. And then everything turned black.

# CHAPTER 16
## ~ *CHRISTOPHER'S TIRAMAVEE* ~

"Oh jeez, oh jeez. Please let him be okay?!" Kerry patted the side of Christopher's cheek gently, trying to bring him round. Sam licked his master's hand, also trying to help. But Christopher was still out cold. Thankfully, he was still breathing, but Kerry was frantic with worry: he appeared to have fallen prey to a strange fit inside the old lean-to. She quickly pulled out her mobile and called for help.

"Emergency, which service do you require? Fir –"

"AHHHHHHH! CHRISTOPHER?!?!" Nana Kathy interrupted the emergency services. She had returned from her shopping trip. Her scream ricocheted from the patio to the back of the garden, and all the way up to Milaw House again, and then out towards Acacia Drive. She scarpered down to where her grandson lay unconscious.

"The ambulance … it's on its way Mrs Muir," Kerry said shakily, thinking that it was best to call Christopher's grandmother by her proper title given what was happening.

But Nana Kathy did not say anything. Instead, she took a little bottle out of her bag and held it under her grandson's nose. She waved it back and forth. Suddenly Christopher opened his eyes and turned on his side. And then he threw up. It was not one of his most glamorous moments.

"Smelling salts," Nana Kathy declared, passing the little purple bottle up to Kerry. "My wee pal Birdie - she's awfy prone to dizzy spells. She's been like that since the change. This wee concoction always brings her roond."

Kerry was about to sniff the bottle's contents, but Nana Kathy – who was still on her knees, holding her grandson's hand – suddenly stopped her.

"NOOOO hen! I wouldnae do that if I were you. It'll knock you clean oot!"

"Awk … aaugh!" Christopher rubbed his mouth and wiped away the last traces of vomit with his sleeve. Thankfully, his energy was returning minute by minute. Sam lapped at his master's face in joy. His bushy face tickled Christopher, making him smile. He tried to stand up, but he still felt a bit lightheaded.

"There, there son. You had another one of your tirramavees." For a change, Nana Kathy was the strong one. She had clambered back up from her knees – without the help of Kerry – and held her grandson's hands tightly in case he felt dizzy again. Kerry was speechless. She could not believe the forte that this little lavender haired woman possessed. She smiled at both Christopher and his Nana.

"What's a tirrama … eh, what's it again?" Kerry was intrigued.

"A tirramavee is a wee funny turn. Christopher's had them since … since his wee mam – my bonnie Peggie – passed away." Nana Kathy looked wistfully at the leant-to for a second before returning her gaze to her grandson. "I had the wee soul at the hospital and all that, but…" She paused and then smiled. "But they couldnae find his brain."

Christopher, who had been listening in, felt strong enough to speak up. "N…Nana thanks, b…but I'm n…not sure K…Kerry wants to hear a…all of this?" He did not want his Nana giving too much away. He thought that he had well and truly blown things with Kerry already, so this would probably be the final nail.

"Och, away and behave yoursel' son. I think Kerry should know about this, 'specially seeing as you two are a couple of wee lov- ".

"NANA!" Christopher almost shouted. His strength had returned, along with the embarrassment, which now burned brightly in his cheeks. "Th…thanks," he added, hugging his Nana, aware that he had raised his voice to her. "Thanks for s…s…saving m…me." Christopher was so busy expressing gratitude that he failed to notice the look of adoration on Kerry's face. All of this had been having the opposite effect of what Christopher thought. His anxiety was blinding him.

"So, this has happened before?" Kerry asked, more out of concern than anything else.

"Aye, many a time." Nana Kathy started again. Christopher could not even look Kerry in the eyes. "You just have to wait it out. Plenty of comfort's what's needed. No need to call the quack … CRIVVENS!" She was almost shouting. "The ambulance. You need tae call and cancel it".

Kerry fumbled with her phone, which she had in her hand all along, and dialled the number of the local police station. She explained what had happened and gave over all the details. When she ended the call, she looked worried. "I'm sorry about this Mrs Muir, but they are sending a few officers round here. They said it's procedure."

"Ach, no need to worry hen. I'll speak to the Bobbies. I'll set the record straight."

"I'm sorry Mrs Muir to have caused a fuss." Kerry felt genuinely terrible.

"Ach, wheest. And mind now – it's Kathy." She smiled and gave Kerry a hug before adding, "you just take care of my wee grandson. He's still a bit fragile." And then Nana Kathy shimmied back up towards the back door of Milaw house, humming one of her little tunes.

Christopher stood self-consciously, aware that he had hardly said anything to Kerry; aware also that his sleeve was encrusted in dried in sick. He tried to think of something to say - something that would redeem himself for his feeble efforts. But nothing came to mind.

"Perhaps, Kathy – eh, I mean your Nana – will offer the police some of her famous soup?" Kerry broke the awkward silence and Christopher was over the moon. She was smiling and that gave him a little boost of confidence.

"Do you wa…want to go f…for a w…walk?" Christopher needed some air in his lungs after his tirramavee. He put his hands in his pockets and crossed his fingers, hoping that Kerry would come along. He did not want to be alone. He had to salvage something of the time they had left. It seemed like a whole minute passed before Kerry replied. She was mulling over something. "This is probably the point I get the brush off," he thought to himself, feeling well and truly defeated.

"What about we head towards the old fountain, at Balsamea Square?" Kerry suggested cheerily. Her proposal sprinkled some fairy dust over Christopher's fading buoyancy. And then, without warning, she grabbed his sick encrusted sleeve and held it up to his eyes to show him the time. "Look, it's not long now until you meet Oli."

Christopher was mortified. He took Kerry's hands over to the spigot at the back of Milaw house and washed away any traces of his vomit. Her hands were so silky-smooth and soft compared to his. Just the feel of her hands in his stirred up a thousand butterflies, causing them to flitter and tickle the insides of his already sensitive belly. Aware that he had been very focussed on her hands, Christopher glanced up. Normally he would be too shy to look Kerry in the eyes, but this time he could not help it. The two of them stood gazing at each other for more than a minute. Sam chased the bees in the garden, giving them some time and space to be on their own.

"You need to change your shirt before we go anywhere." Kerry's voice interrupted the silence, but this time it was a comfortable one.

****

The police had already arrived at Milaw House when Christopher and Kerry entered the back door. Sam's claws scuttled on the kitchen floor tiles as he trailed in behind his master and Kerry. The beautiful Siberian headed straight for his water bowl. Playing tig with his little fuzzy airborne friends had puffed him out. Nana Kathy – being the perfect hostess – was in the middle of serving up two heaped bowls of her delicious soup. Christopher decided that introducing himself to the officers would be the right thing to do, given that he was the reason for the commotion in the first place. He mumbled a feeble "hello", but the two figures in blue were too caught up in their steaming plates of soup.

"Right boys, tuck in," Nany Kathy cheeped, as if she had just placed two bowls of food in front of two hungry pooches at the kennels. She wiped her hands on her apron and sat across from them. A cup of tea was already on the table in front of her. It was another fragrant cup of lavender. She smiled contently as they slurped at their soup. Christopher thought that the two policemen looked devoid of any authority, all thanks to the purple napkins that were tucked into their collars. He could almost picture his Nana tucking the serviettes in place for them and it made him laugh inwardly. He did wonder though, was it her intention to make them look so pathetic?

"Now then, let's see," the largest of the policemen began, wiping some soup away from his thick tawny beard with his purple napkin. His skin looked rough, pitted almost, underneath the thick mass of his facial hair. Christopher immediately felt sorry for him: he thought that the rather portly looking officer must have grown his beard to cover up his skin. "Ahem," the stocky policeman cleared his throat. "I think everything is in order then Mrs Muir." Nana Kathy looked at the officer as if she were chiding a little puppy. "Eh, I mean, Kathy." His voice was as gruff as his beard.

"And thanks for the soup … Kathy," the other officer declared. He was tiny and his voice almost screeched, like a cat mewling at its enemy. Every syllable sounded like it was laced with sarcasm.

Nana Kathy just smiled and lifted the plates away from her official guests. Sam scuttled through from the kitchen; he was certain that someone had just blown a dog whistle. The clever canine carefully studied the dainty appearance of the smaller officer. There was something about him that he recognised. It was his scent. It reminded him of something.

"Ssooo," the officer's voice almost hissed, "how are you

feeling, Christopher?" The slinky looking policeman appeared to enjoy his question, especially now that Nana was out of earshot. She was in the kitchen, clearing away the mess. But the little boy in blue had no idea about the power of Nana's radar.

There was something about the way this officer looked at Christopher that made him feel uncomfortable. He too had the same feeling as Sam.

"I…I…I…." Sam thumped the back of his master's legs as if to say hurry up. "I'm fine." And then Christopher remembered the blood-stained tee-shirt upstairs in the bathroom sink. His tee-shirt. Encased in a pool of blood. Paranoia seeped into his bones. He felt sick. "I…I…I" He struggled to speak.

"Christopher," Kerry cut in and saved the day. "Were you not about to go and change your top before we go?" She almost kicked him. "On our date?"

Christopher turned to look at Kerry and gave her the biggest, cheesiest grin. He caught his reflection in the dining room mirror and he almost threw up again. It was not an attractive look. He left without saying anything. He had to dispose of the evidence. But he had been too busy worrying about other things to have noticed Sam. In the mirror, the dog had no reflection.


Christopher made straight for the bathroom. He felt terrible for leaving Kerry downstairs with the two policemen, but he knew that his Nana would look after her. His heart was almost pounding out of the veins in his neck. A high-pitched whistling screamed loudly in his ears. He had to clear up the bloody mess before someone else found it. The sink would be full of crimson like soup by now, given how long his top had been soaking.

Christopher flung the bathroom door open, almost pulling it from its hinges. He inhaled deeply. But his jaw almost hit the lavender tiled floor with what he found; or, rather, what he did not find. The sink was empty. No blood.

No scarlet stained tee-shirt. The bathroom looked pristine, as if a little cleaning fairy had waved a magic wand and charmed away any of the disturbing mess. Christopher stumbled backwards into the hallway, where he met Kerry. She too looked like she had seen a ghost.

"Christopher … the bin bags! They've gone!"

# CHAPTER 17
## ~ *A PAIR OF DUMPLINGS* ~

In his bedroom, Christopher quickly changed his top. Kerry had her eyes shut, pretending not to look, but she had one eye half open, trying to sneak a cheeky peek at Christopher's torso. To her surprise, he looked so toned. Sam, who was well aware of this, padded over to Kerry and sat in front of her. It was as if he was trying to protect his master's self-esteem. After all, he knew how paranoid Christopher was about his appearance. Sadly, his confidence melted in the flames of his mother's accident.

"W…Well, what d…do you think?" Christopher immediately felt stupid for asking Kerry for her opinion on his top.

"I think you should wear this instead." Kerry smiled and threw a black and white checked shirt at him, from the ironing pile on his bed. "Your eyes will really suit this." She looked away from Christopher, towards Sam, trying to hide the red flush in her checks.

Christopher took this as a quick opportunity to change into his checked shirt – the one that Kerry liked. He was not quite sure what was happening, so he decided to change the subject whilst buttoning up his top. Sam looked at his master and rolled his cerulean eyes at him.

"Wh…what will w…we do about the m…missing bags a...and m…my bloody shirt?" His voice trembled. He was still shaken about the wreckage of his Papa's lean-to. Even though he wanted to, he could not bear to even mention it to Kerry. He worried about what she thought of him and why he had collapsed like that.

"Let's just get out of here." Kerry suggested. "And besides, you are meeting Oli soon!"

And that was enough to convince Christopher. He did not want to miss his meeting with old Oli.

\*\*\*\*

Christopher lingered in the hallway of Milaw house, waiting on Kerry – who was *powdering her nose* in the bathroom. He sat on the chaise longue, patting the thick white fur on Sam's back. Christopher's mind drifted over everything, trying to pick out the important parts. He thought about all the questions he was going to ask Oli, but his mind wandered. The sun glittered through the Mackintosh inspired cerise rose and verdant leaves on the front door glass. It produced a kaleidoscope of beautiful colours on the white walls in the hallway, as if the sun was an impressionist artist painting a beautiful mural for all to see.

"*Aye, he was there – skulking about ootside my garage! So, what are you gonna do?*" Nana Kathy's lilt interrupted Christopher's musing over the Milaw House fleeting art show. He shuffled to the edge of the chaise longue, so that he could hear better.

"*And I wouldn't be surprised if that bad bugger cut her brakes!*"

Christopher's heart leapt into his mouth. Sam lifted his paw onto his master's lap as if to warn him. But it was too late. The two officers – little and large – were at the doorway leading to the hallway of Milaw House. Nana Kathy's thick lavender locks twirled out from behind the odd figures of the policemen, indicating her presence.

"Young man Brenton," the thin one snivelled, "we meet again".

By now, the four of them – and Sam – were all standing in Milaw house's hallway. Christopher longed to ask what his Nana was talking about.

"My grandson's a Muir. Through and through. I thought I told you that." Nana Kathy's hair had turned a darker shade of indigo. She then muttered something under her breath. It sounded a lot like *ya eejit.*

Christopher felt extremely awkward at this exchange - and so did Kerry apparently. She was now standing at the bottom of the stairs in the hallway.

The heavier one called Inspector Gass tried to speak, but the thin one interjected.

"Right. *Thanks. Kathy*. And remember, my name's Ruiz. *Officer Ruiz*."

A threatening percussion of thunder crashed in the distance. The light faded, throwing the hallway into unwelcoming shade. It felt cold all of a sudden. Nana Kathy broke the icy silence.

"Aye, right," she replied to the scrawny officer called Ruiz. "Here son," she threw something at her grandson. "You'll need this." Christopher caught the kitchen roll wrapped package with both hands. He had no idea what it was.

"Can we just ask you a few more things, Mrs Muir," Inspector Gass requested. But despite his deep voice, he sounded much friendlier than Officer Ruiz.

"Dumplings!" Nana Kathy shouted. "A pair of dumplings!"

The two men in blue looked at each other in disbelief. Officer Ruiz took his radio out – the latest Incaendium model – as if he was about to call for back up.

"I made your pudding last night, but I thought I needed a wee pick me up after your tiramavee." Nana Kathy chuckled.

Christopher unwrapped the kitchen roll to find another layer of tinfoil. He carefully pulled back the edges of the crinkly, silvery wrapping to find the welcoming sight of his Nana's homemade dumpling. A thin layer of butter adorned the surface of the clootie delight. It smelled delicious.

"There's one there for Kerry too." Nana Kathy added.

Christopher felt another fit coming on. A fit of hysterics.

"Thanks Kathy," Kerry quickly replied for Christopher, putting her arm around his shoulders, trying to pretend that she was not pulling him out the front door.

"Mind now and tell Oli I was asking for him," Nana Kathy winked towards Christopher, Kerry, and Sam.

The three friends stood in the front garden of *Milaw* house, looking in on Nana Kathy and the two police officers. Christopher wanted to stay, at least until the officers had left, but both Sam and Kerry were almost hauling at his sleeves, telling him that it was time to go. He needed no more encouragement when Nana Kathy opened the front door and tossed his brown leather bag at him. She stuck her thumb up in mid-air and smiled, then she shut the door.

"I…I…I should g…go back," Christopher mumbled to Kerry, his voice full of concern. He had a bittersweet taste in his mouth: he wanted to be outside, spending his time with Kerry like normal teenagers would do; but he was worried about his Nana. He felt like two forces were pulling at him, equal and opposite in direction. Christopher was about to turn around and run back, but Kerry took both his hands. He was – again – taken aback at how smooth her hands were. She lifted his fingers up to her mouth and kissed them with her soft lips. Christopher shut his eyes. He was so embarrassed about the angry looking blisters on his fingertips, but Kerry's giggling prompted him to open his eyes. He was amazed to see that the tips of his fingers were smooth. No burns. No blisters. "I…I…" he stammered, but Kerry put her index finger over his lips and kissed him. Somewhere in the background, Christopher could hear fireworks, as if all his birthdays and Christmases had exploded into one.

*Hoooooowwwwaa,* Sam yowled, as if to say *at last!*

****

The three friends leaned against the ancient sandstone pillars of the Balsamea Square fountain. It looked almost brand new, despite its prehistoric place in history.

"Apparently, this is what inspired the Trevi fountain, in Italy. It says it here. Right on this plaque that was donated by the…" she paused for a moment before trying hard to read the Latin. "The Custodes Ober-something Liber people – I think. Whoever they are." Kerry's words merely floated around Christopher's head. He was more focussed on the sound of her voice rather than what she was saying.

Sam's thick white tail whacked him out of nowhere, as if to say *listen!* It worked, thankfully.

"*I believe you.*" Kerry whispered. This time, Christopher was fully aware of her words. She was now staring intently at him. "I feel it too. There's something…something different about your house. And the leant-to…" Her voice trailed off. Sam quietly whined.

"Wh…wh…what?" Christopher could not even articulate his question. It had been too painful up until now. He waited for Kerry's response.

"I … well I saw something, just as you opened the door, before I flicked my phone light on." Kerry's face drained a little of colour. Her eyes looked watery in the fading sunlight behind Balsamea Square's monuments.

"Wh…What is it Kerry?" Christopher felt stupid for asking again, but he had to know.

"I saw what looked like a beastly looking stag. It had huge horns. But…" she hesitated, "it had…it had a human face." The usual lustre of Kerry's golden skin vanished. She looked pale. "It looked a little bit like…" once again her voice trailed into nothing.

She did not need to say anymore. Christopher knew. He placed his arms around her shoulders and held her tight. Sam padded round and sat beside her, placing his huge head on her lap. All three of them shut their eyes for a moment, allowing the fading heat of the afternoon sun to ease their exhaustion. The dark storm clouds edged closer, like the calm before the storm.

*BUZZ --- BUZZ.*

Kerry's Incaendium phone disturbed the comfortable silence. She almost jumped out of her skin. She was still feeling on edge from the afternoon's events. Christopher could tell immediately that it was Candice. It was like Kerry became a hostage to the power of her phone the minute it summoned her attention: she robotically started typing a message without even looking or saying anything. Not being one for technology – mainly because of his mum's influence – Christopher could not understand why people behaved this way. It filled him with sadness that even Kerry could be manipulated by the powers of a mobile phone. An Incaendium phone at that.

Sam whined softly at Christopher and placed a paw on his hand.

"Candice is going to meet up with me," Kerry's voice sounded machinelike. She did not even lift her eyes from her phone. Christopher's heart sank further. "She's coming here in fifteen minutes," she uttered, her tone still mechanical. "Christopher!" Kerry suddenly came to life. "Look at the time! You only have ten minutes." She grabbed his hands and hauled him back onto his feet.

Christopher enjoyed the fleeting moment of her hands touching his. He would never tire of being close to her. Despite spending all afternoon with Kerry, he could not bear to say goodbye. The thought of school made it even harder: he worried that it would drive an uninvited wedge between the two friends. And then there was Candice. Christopher's shoulders sagged at the thought of the fiery red head: she even had the power to take Kerry away from him when she was not physically present, so what chance would Christopher stand if she was there. In the flesh.

"Hello?!" Kerry playfully tapped the side of Christopher's face.

Sam howled loudly; his cry echoed around the quadrangle of the almost empty Balsamea Square.

Christopher had no idea how long he had been lost in his worried thoughts, but he suddenly came to. He tried to speak, but the vision of Kerry's beautiful smile rendered him useless.

"Where do you go?" Kerry asked, giggling. Christopher's cheeks burned with awkwardness. "Well, wherever you disappear to, you need to wake up. You've so much to say – and ask – old Oli!

"Thanks Kerry." Christopher finally spoke up, amazed for once that he did not stutter. "I know, I have it all in h…here." He tapped the side of his head with his finger, trying to play it cool. Inside though, he was panicking. He was a mess. He did not know if he should make the first move. But Kerry put a stop to Christopher's worries. She pulled him closer and pecked him gently on the cheek.

"Now go!" Kerry almost shouted, "you don't want to be late for Oli!"

Christopher smiled and winked at Kerry – he thought that it was the coolest thing he could do in that moment. But then Christopher thought of his Nana's trademark wink. His face turned scarlet. Trying hard to hide his cringing, he turned away and shouted "s…s…see you t…tomorrow!" He did not have the guts to turn around and show Kerry what he was really feeling. He was embarrassed, sad, and scared all mixed into one. Sam could read his master like a book because he was already sitting ahead of him, cocking his head to the side, looking at him as if to say, "you're an idiot."

"Christopher!" This time Kerry shouted. He detected a note of concern in her voice, so he had to turn around. "Here, you forgot this!" Kerry threw his bag at him and then she winked. Sam yowled with laughter at the goofiness between the two friends. It made Christopher smile and helped his ailing confidence. "Remember to text me later," she added, before leaving Sam and Christopher.

# CHAPTER 18
## ~ *BREAH PARVA PARS* ~

Christopher ran all the way towards Ferncross library, with Sam leading the way. The dark clouds had almost obscured any remnants of blue sky, painting everything in unwanted murkiness. A chilly wind whisked through streets, stirring the sleepy village from its afternoon slumber. The bitter gust slapped against Christopher's face, as if it was trying to push him back, away from the direction of the library. He rubbed at his eyes, trying to wipe away the dust particles that had pervaded his vision.

*"Ooowwwliiii."* Sam's howl cut through the racket of the whipping wind.

Christopher rubbed his eyes again, but this time it was because he could not believe what he was seeing. Old Oli was standing outside the ancient gates of Ferncross Library – all by himself. No white stick, no dark glasses, no one was there to help him. Oli stood there like a man who could see *everything*.

"Christopher, my boy!" Oli was the first to speak. His voice sounded strong against the howling wind. "I believe you have something in your bag to show me?"

Christopher immediately handed his brown leather bag over to Oli. He forgot all about the dead robin in his bag. Christopher had placed the little feathered soul in his mum's old hair pin box. She used to keep all manner of good luck charms in there: buttons, old penny-farthings, dice, and some piercing blue eye shaped amulets. The box itself was yellowed and frayed with age but it had the most prominent looking white wolf on the top of the box. The striking she-wolf held a bright red rose in her mouth. She had the most exquisite looking indigo eyes.

To his horror, it was only when Christopher handed his bag over to Oli that he remembered the little dead robin. He was mortified.

"I…I…yes," Christopher stumbled. He felt like an idiot, lost for words despite the one thousand and one questions dancing in front of his eyes.

"Ahhh, now let me see," Oli whispered, delicately feeling inside the bag like a magician about to produce a rabbit from his hat. "Hmmmmm," he whirred, pulling out his mother's little lucky box from the brown bag. The she-wolf stared at Christopher.

*Dammit,* Christopher thought, cursing himself. *Oli thinks that's his book!* But his thoughts were interrupted almost instantly. Oli lifted the little box up to his mouth. Christopher had no idea what was happening.

Sam howled and thumped his master's legs as if to say, *this is the best bit!*

Oli blew softly over the top of the box and whispered "*breah parva pars.*"

Suddenly, a huge gust of wind whipped around Sam, Oli, and Christopher. It was like a white tornado, wrapping its powerful arms around the three figures. Every gust thumped quicker, louder, like the locomotive hum of a spinning top gathering momentum.

And then everything fell strangely noiseless.

But it was a comforting silence, similar to the sheer innocence resting under a windowsill on a snow-filled morning. Christopher could still somehow feel the strength of the wind around them, but he knew that it was a protective energy. And then it dawned upon him: they were in the eye of the storm.

"*Breah parva pars, breah parva pars.*" Oli's words beat like a pulse, reminding Christopher of something that he had heard before.

However, Christopher's thoughts were swiftly suspended by intermittent cheeping. It appeared to be coming from his mother's box. Without warning, the lid of the box flew open. A tiny brown beak pecked through blood stained kitchen roll. The little robin poked her head out of the scarlet stained paper, stretched upwards, spread outwards and emerged from the dust like a tiny phoenix from its flames. And then the little red breasted creature fluttered her wings and flew upwards. The white whirlwind suddenly scattered into the dust. Christopher rubbed his eyes. Again. This time, he really thought that he was daydreaming.

"Well, my boy," Oli broke the silence, "you must tell your lovely Nana that her little robin will return to Milaw garden once more. She is on her way there right now."

Christopher had no idea what to say. He was still in awe at what he had just witnessed.

Oli reached his crinkled right hand towards him and placed it on his shoulder. "You must listen very carefully to everything I have to tell you. We do not have much time. I hope that you have brought my book from the library?" Oli articulated every word, every letter, as if they were his last.

"Y…yes," was just about all Christopher could stammer. Sam whacked his tail against the back of his master's legs as if to say *listen carefully*.

Christopher reached into his bag and pulled out Oli's book. However, just as he was about to hand it to his blind friend, the old man smacked it out of the young boy's hands, almost knocking it onto the pavement.

"*Shhhhhh!*" Oli forcefully whispered. *"Put that back into your bag!"*

Christopher fumbled with Oli's book, following the old man's instructions.

"*Here*," Oli added in a hushed tone, as if someone - or something - was listening. *"You'd better put this away - out of harm's road."* He handed Christopher his mother's special little box. The she-wolf's eyes glowed like two sapphires in the growing darkness.

Christopher was about to ask why he should hide his mother's box, but the sight of Oli shuffling forward stopped him saying anything. He watched the old man carefully. Oli placed one careful foot in front of the other, cautiously climbing the steps to Ferncross library. The old man navigated his way towards the magnanimous entrance of the library.

Christopher half expected the doors to swoop open, only to find the overpowering stature of Avias brooding there. But she was nowhere in sight. Instead, Sam stood in the doorway, like a magnificent, bright beacon amidst the darkness. He stared at the ground, making strange clicking noises with his tongue and teeth. It was ever so subtle, but enough to be heard by the sharpest of ears. However, Christopher was too caught up in the sight of the threatening storm clouds above to notice that old Oli was making the same sound with his tongue and teeth.

*Brrrrrrrrrrrrooooooooom----boom----boom----boom!*

Somewhere, in the near distance, the low growl of thunder rumbled. It was followed by two blinding flashes of light. Sam howled loudly. Rain followed, pattering slowly against the old cobbles at first, coating everything in a dark, dank hue. The dampness crept from the darkness, like surly shadows slithering towards its prey. And then, the light tapping of rain transformed into a hammering of hail. Christopher felt like he was under attack, as if hot coals were firing at him from all angles. He held his hands up to his eyes, shielding them from the sizzling hail.

"Quick son!" This time Oli was shouting. "Follow me!" The old man placed his withered hands against the ancient wooden door of Ferncross library. His fingers disappeared into the dark wood as if it was made of melted toffee.

Christopher continued to wipe his eyes, thinking that the sting of the icy rain had blurred his vision. But he was wrong. The huge door creaked slowly open. A twinkling of warm light welcomed the three friends, illuminating the old terracotta-coloured slabs on the steps to the library. The light resembled the warm glow of the rising sun at dawn, announcing the hope of another new day.

Oli turned to face Christopher. He placed his wrinkly index finger vertically over his moustache coated lips.

"*Shhhhhh*," he whispered. "*We don't want to wake the sleeping Deryn. Do we?*"

Christopher swallowed his fear. Awakening the Avias was the last thing he wanted to do. Another crack of thunder reverberated, ricocheting around every object in sight. This time, the storm appeared to be directly above the three friends. Lightening sizzled, causing an almost palpable hum to pass through anything metallic. Christopher almost fell face first on the steps because of the searing pain that pulsated around the braces in his mouth. He held his hands over his mouth and lurched forward in agony towards the safety of Ferncross Library.

The library door screeched silently shut. Inside, everything was religiously still. No heavy rain. No rolls of thunder. No pain. Instead, the three friends were welcomed by the warm light of the library's interior. Christopher felt as if he had stepped into another realm, away from all the noisy interference of the outside world. He inhaled deeply, gulping down every molecule of oxygen. He could not be too sure, but he thought that he could smell freshly cut grass mixed in with another familiar woody scent.

"*Lavender. Do you smell it my boy?*" Christopher almost laughed aloud at Oli's surprise whisper. The old man took the words right out of his mouth. "*I don't have time to explain that just now, but you will find out all in good time. All in good time. We must find our way to ad ostium. It changes all the...*" Oli's whispery words trailed off into silence.

Christopher observed the old man's actions carefully. He appeared to be staring upwards – as if he could see something on the mezzanine level. Christopher squinted his eyes and looked up at the high balcony. It made him feel dizzy. The top floor seemed so high, so far away from where they were standing. Abruptly, a light flickered in one of the dimly lit rooms, as if someone had flapped their arms in front of the light source.

"*Wh...what th... -*" Christopher was cut off in mid-sentence by the whack of Sam's tail. He looked at his master and placed a paw over his foot. Christopher knew not to say anything else.

The light went out.

"*C'mon my boy, over here,*" Oli's command directed Christopher towards one of the many artery-like corridors that beat out from the library's atrium. Oli was already shuffling his way forward, clicking his tongue and teeth in the same manner as before. Christopher stared: he wondered about the old man's actions. However, he was so focussed on old Oli that he failed to see what was really happening: Sam was in front, leading the way again, making the same clicking noises with his tongue and teeth.

"It's called echolocation," Oli stopped and slowly turned around to face Christopher. He was no longer whispering. "It's a little technique I use to help me see where I am going. It's also a form of communication. An old friend taught me how to do it many, many years ago."

Christopher felt terrible for staring at Oli in such an ignorant way, but he was so much in awe at how this little white-haired man could skilfully navigate his way round this strange environment.

"Well, my boy, we are just about here." Oli interrupted Christopher's embarrassment. "I'm glad that we didn't wake Avias. I don't know if you noticed, but she was stirring in her quarters when we entered."

Both Christopher and Sam stood still, listening to their wise old acquaintance.

"She lives here now, high up in the mezzanine level. That floor shelters all the zoology books ever written. Her quarters are in the great golden room that houses the ornithology books. No one is allowed up there." Oli paused. "No one has been up there..." he paused again. "Since the fire." His words fell into the silence of Ferncross Library, as if the walls were trying to absorb the heartache of what he had just said.

A stifling shiver scurried up Christopher's spine. He immediately thought of his mother and the horrible way in which she died. Sam, sensing his master's grief, padded over and placed a friendly paw on his thigh. Thankfully, Sam's presence stopped the well of sadness from overflowing at the back of Christopher's throat.

It was the fading light that brought Christopher out of his daydream. The three friends now appeared to be standing in the dimmest part of Ferncross library. Thanks to Sam though, Christopher could just about see where he was going. His brilliant white coat beamed, lighting the way through the balmy darkness. From what Christopher could see, they appeared to be standing in the doorway to one of the library's old reference rooms. He could just make out the letters "ARCHI…" in gold leaf inscription. Christopher presumed that it said "Archives". He wondered why Oli would lead him to such an ancient part of the library.

*"I have so, so much to tell you my boy… but we don't…we don't have much time."* Old Oli was right on cue, as if he was listening to Christopher's thoughts – again – but this time the sound of his voice concerned Christopher. This time he was whispering in a forced manner, as if his words were causing him a great deal of pain. *"Give me my book,"* he commanded in a croaking tone to his young apprentice, *"and your Papa's key"* he added.

Instinctively, Christopher followed the old man's instructions. Thankfully, he still had his Papa's key in his pocket. He carried it with him everywhere, especially after the way it had protected him against the beast in his bedroom. In the crepuscular darkness, the key shimmered silvery white, causing Christopher to nearly drop it. It was positively glowing, completely different from its usual tarnished appearance.

"A…are you o…okay O…Oli?" Christopher's voice sounded feeble as he carefully placed the key into the old man's hands. Oli did not reply; instead, he delicately lifted the luminous artefact and placed it inside his book.

*"Et aperire librum et clavem ad ostium! ad ostium!"* Oli's voice

sounded unrecognisable, as it powerfully whinnied around the walls of Ferncross Library. He dropped his book onto the floor causing it to fall open at a chapter called *Reserans Ianuam*.

Suddenly, powerful bursts of white light exploded from the book. Gold and silver circles shot up into the air like fireworks gushing with excitement. Despite the magical light show, Christopher's eyes were fixed on his Papa's key. It sat neatly, nestled in amongst the pages of the book. It was like someone had cut out a special place for it to be - as if it had always belonged in Oli's book. It was a perfect fit.

"*Chriiiioooowwwwoooo!*" Sam's howl directed his master to the beautiful sight that lay in front of him.

Christopher averted his eyes away from Oli's book and looked ahead. A sea of lavender awaited, waving to and fro in front of him, like an old friend waiting for their chum to catch up on them. A familiar woody scent welcomed him.

Above the lavender, there rested an emerald green forest of trees, stretching out as far as the eye could see. Their pine needles glistened in the beautiful light shining above them. Unsure of what was happening, Christopher stumbled forwards, trying to find his bearings. Old terracotta-coloured flagstones lay directly under his feet. However, in front of him lay a smattering of sparse steppingstones: they disappeared in amongst the deep purple hues of lavender. At first, he was certain that there was a hole in the roof - and that the light above was merely the sun's rays. But, as he stumbled closer, Christopher realised that the sky – or whatever resided above - was lit by three silvery fragmented planets. They resembled three crescent moons, but they were all circled by rainbow coloured orbs. They were magnificent. He blinked again and again, taking in the beautiful sight that glistened in front of him. He felt like he was looking at a watery mirage on a hot summer's day, and he was certain that the vision would vanish as quickly as it appeared.

Christopher stumbled back. He had forgotten all about

Oli because he had been so caught up in the sight of this enigmatic, evergreen world. Guilt and terror seized a hold of him. He quickly spun around, his eyes searching the darkness. Behind him lay the remnants of Ferncross library. Oli had vanished. Christopher could feel horror almost digging its thumbs into his windpipe. In the darkness behind him, he could just make out the doorway that Oli had led him to.

Christopher wanted to run back, run as fast as he could to try and find the helpless old man that had brought him here. He knew he could do it. He knew he could find his way back. So, he slowly stepped backwards some more, in the direction of his Papa's key and Oli's book. The two artefacts were now lying side by side; they were no longer together as they were before. No light glistened from the key or the book. Christopher knelt onto the copper coloured slabs of Ferncross library floor, expecting to feel a damp coldness. Instead, he was met by a friendly warmth. Wanting to be sure though, he placed his palms onto the terracotta flagstones. Again, his hands were met by a pleasant heat. It felt wonderfully soothing.

Suddenly, two white paws appeared in front of Christopher's hands. He looked up to find Sam: his piercing azure eyes stared at him as if to ask, *what are you doing?* The Siberian even comically cocked his head to the side and looked at Christopher as if he had taken leave of his senses.

"*I don't know what's happening here my friend,*" Christopher whispered to his canine chum, "*but I am so glad you are here to see all of this too.*" Sam let out a small whimper and placed a paw over Oli's book.

Thankfully, Christopher realised what his dog was saying. So, he carefully placed his Papa's key in his pocket and Oli's book into his bag. Yet again, his stutter had vanished.

*Clip clop ---- clip clop. Clip clop ---- clip clop. Clip clop ---- clip clop.*

Suddenly, a beautiful – but small – white horse galloped

around Christopher and Sam. It sprouted from the remnants of Ferncross Library. Its high-pitched nickering sounded like gleeful laughter as it cantered out towards the blades of lavender-like-grass. Sam howled jovially and joined the little white cob. The horse looked almost dwarf-like against the tall stature of Sam's tall hound-like legs. Christopher stood up in disbelief: he felt like he was looking at two friends happily reunited. It made him smile. The cob and the Siberian danced in circles, through the swaying lavender, beneath the magical glow of the three crescent-stars. Christopher stepped forward, inhaling the sweet and comforting scent of lavender. He stepped forward again, allowing his hands to touch the tiny delicate lavender buds that sprouted out in front of him.

Christopher felt like he was standing in the back garden of *Milaw* garden. But he knew that was impossible.

In the clear, cerulean sky above, a myriad of islands floated like clouds, all bedecked with their very own luscious forests and waterfalls. Vast plumes of water trickled down from the lilac roots that gathered at the base of the hovering archipelagos. Christopher squinted his eyes and followed the direction of the water. In the distance, he could just make out what looked like a beautiful lake, or *loch*, as his Nana Kathy would have called it. Vitreous blue water shimmered like wonderful crystals. The indigo line of the watery horizon met with huge purple mountains and their snowy peaks reached up into the beautiful blue sky. Christopher sprawled forward and fell onto his knees, into the beautiful lavender like grass. He lay back, stretched his legs out and inhaled the calming scent of lavender. He should have been worried about the disappearance of Oli, but something told Christopher that his old acquaintance was okay. After all, he had led him here. To this beautiful place.

Christopher breathed deeply and slowly. Despite the strange setting, he felt unusually calm. He opened his eyes and looked at the azure sky. Just above him, he noticed the faint lines of what appeared to be another crescent moon, but it was so weak and pale. Studying its dying shape closely, he realised that it resembled the form of the other three crescent moons, but this one looked like its light had been extinguished a long time ago. No rainbow circled its semi-circular shape; instead, a dark shadowy ring circled the poorly looking planet. An overwhelming feeling of loss gathered in the pit of his stomach, as if he somehow knew that an inferno had caused the loss of so many lives. Tears formed at the corners of his eyes.

Christopher had been too busy staring at the lost crescent moon to have noticed that the little white horse was now cantering around him in a circle, with Sam following and frolicking closely behind. A soft breeze whispered through the blades of lavender grass. The friendly zephyr carried a strange high-pitched voice towards Christopher. It called to him. He sat upright. Laughter escaped his mouth as he watched the two white figures dance in front of him.

"*Follow the cob and the dog,*" a little voice squeaked, from behind the lavender reeds. Christopher looked to his right, but there was no one there.

"*Follow them, and they will show you the way,*" the little voice echoed once more. Christopher stumbled to his feet, in search of the speaker. But there was no one there. The two white figures of Sam and the little horse were now standing still in the lavender field in front of Christopher. They were listening and watching. Everything.

"*This way*" the same little voice piped up.

"*Over here,*" another dwarf like tone squeaked. Christopher looked to his right, to where the Lilliputian like words were coming from. There, in front of his eyes, were rows upon rows of purple and pink celosia flowers, dancing in the fragrant breeze like little lavender haired troll dolls. Christopher rubbed his eyes in disbelief. Yet again. He could not believe what he was seeing - or hearing. The lilac plumed plants appeared to be smiling at him. A sea of little happy faces beamed back at Christopher, awaiting his next move. He was rooted to the spot. He was awestruck with the sight of the smiling plants.

"*Listen carefully to what we have to say,*" a thousand little voices volleyed through the lavender. Christopher merely nodded his head up and down. Sam and the little white horse stepped closer.

"*Our message is short, just like us. Follow the path of the white haired animalium and they will lead you to the gateway. Follow their light. Follow them and they will ensure that no shadows follow.*" The sound of the thousand little lilac voices danced in unison through the air, echoing through the lavender like an endless chorus singing in harmony. Their tiny purple heads gambolled in time with the beat of the zephyr's rhythm.

Christopher fell to his knees again and reached out to one of the tiny lilac petals. "Where am I?" he asked, feeling suddenly very foolish for talking to a plant. But before he could berate himself any further for it, one little lilac flower reached out towards him. Its fluffy lavender fingers stretched forward and pointed towards Sam and the little horse.

"*Shhhhh. Don't ask where. Just follow the white haired animalium.*"

Another Lilliputian-like-plant pointed its pink feathery fingers towards Sam and the little white horse. The two fuzzy friends continued to trot around Christopher in a circle. Sam's tail thumped in time to the cadence of the little horse's hoofs.

"*Chriiiieeeeeweeee!*" The little white cob caught Christopher's attention. Its pony like hoofs cantered in time to the drops of water that fell from the floating archipelagos above.

Christopher glanced back over to the lilac plants, but their eyes were shut, lost in sleep. They could not help him now. So, he followed his gut instinct and clambered to his feet. However, just as he was about to reach out to the little horse's reigns, it galloped off in front of him. And then, before Christopher could do or say anything, Sam gambolled over to his master and pounced back and forth, in the same way that a clever sheep dog would try to direct his flock. Christopher, taking his dog's hint, stepped forward, following his faithful canine's lead. With this, Sam padded even further, in the direction of the little white horse, and again Christopher followed.

A few more steps later, and finally the fast dance ignited.

Christopher understood exactly what the tiny lilac plants meant.

Sam and the little white cob sprinted ahead into the wilderness, with Christopher following suit. The soft zephyr embraced the three friends as they skipped through the purple panorama of the strange but familiar place.

Christopher struggled to keep up with the speed set by *the white haired animalium*, but thankfully Sam faithfully turned around to ensure that his master was just one or two steps behind. The three white crescent moons glowed in the sky; their rainbow orbs splashed a whole palette of colours across the celestial sphere above. This was the longest and farthest Christopher had run in a long time without having to stop. In any other circumstances, his lungs would be flailing in time to his out-of-beat heart, causing his breathing to rasp like a locomotive out of control. This time though, he felt as though he was floating. He felt as light as a feather. There were no aching limbs, no pains in his chest, no gasping for air.

The three friends flitted freely through the strange but familiar vista. Christopher had such a strong feeling of déjà vu: it was as if he knew where he was going; yet, he had no idea where the little white cob and Sam were leading him to. Just ahead of his vision, he could see the white mane of the little horse fleeing in the wind. Christopher squinted his eyes and looked further ahead, but he could no longer see the purple peaks of the mountains on the horizon; instead, he was now in the thick of an emerald green forest. Lilac coloured grass still paved its way underfoot, but on either side of him lay rows of beautiful evergreens, glistening in the ever-changing light. Their tall statures stretched high up into the sky above. Christopher was in awe at how their pine needles caught the prism-like radiance from the planets above: their green points continually changed colours, like the tiny, oscillating lights on a fibre-optic Christmas tree. Below, their dark mahogany trunks dug deep underground, where their roots clung onto another life in the subterranean unknown. Christopher sensed that there was another world altogether underneath their wooden torsos. Somehow, he knew that he was only seeing a tiny part of what was really happening. He could almost sense another lifeforce, another planet even, stretching far out below his feet.

Christopher floated further forward, inhaling the fresh woody scent of lavender. He followed the white haired animalium without question. The gentle zephyr exhaled again and again, blowing life into the young teenager's fragile soul.

And then they stopped.

The little white horse and Sam stood motionless. Christopher almost crashed into the back of his faithful canine friend, but he managed to stop himself in the nick of time. He patted the thick fur of Sam's nape, but there was no response. Sam stood spellbound, staring at something in the not so far away distance. Christopher glanced ahead, expecting to see the little white cob. But the horse had vanished. Instead, a beautiful white she-wolf sat in front Sam and Christopher. Her cerulean stare was arresting. Her eyes settled upon Christopher with affection, just like a mother basking in the warm glow her child taking their first few steps. Tears smarted Christopher's eyes, blinding his vision. Sam padded away from his master, towards the beautiful white she-wolf. In the ever-changing light, the two canine figures looked like fading but familiar images from an old family album.

"*Hoooooooooowoooooooooo!*"

The she-wolf's cry silenced everything. Time moved a

slow hand as she stepped closer to Christopher. Even though she was larger than Sam – and that she was a wild animal – Christopher felt safe. Instinctively, he fell to his knees and reached out towards her beautiful face. She padded closer to him and offered her paw. Her pads felt wonderfully smooth and comforting, just like a mother's hands. She then lifted her paw towards his chest, trying to catch the tears falling from his eyes. Christopher suddenly felt embarrassed by what his Papa would have called *the emulsion*, so he let go of the she-wolf's paw and rubbed at his eyes.

When his vision returned, the she-wolf had vanished. He quickly looked down at his hands again, searching for her soft paws, but he was met with the sight of a single red rose. Despite its beauty, sadness welled at the pit of his stomach. The she-wolf had disappeared as quickly as she had appeared. To make matters worse, Sam was nowhere to be seen. Suddenly, Christopher felt alone. Extremely alone. More tears burned his vision, but he quickly rubbed them away.

And then Christopher no longer felt alone. To his astonishment, the old *lean-to* sat in front of him.

The white shed sat in the glade of lavender, surrounded by a thick protection of beautiful evergreen trees. It was the same lean-to from Milaw garden; only this was not Milaw garden. It had the same poorly structure and the same cobweb bedecked window, so Christopher was certain that it was his Papa Tommy's shed. He had never been so happy to see such an inanimate object in all his life. Without even questioning the strangeness of what was happening, Christopher stepped forward and pushed the ailing door open.

*Then the world discovers as my book ends, how to make two lovers of friends.*

Sinatra's voice welcomed Christopher. The old shellac disc clicked, and the needle returned to its resting place. Inside, everything looked exactly like Christopher remembered, unlike the last time he had entered with Kerry. The old white rocking horse was still volleying back and forth, as if it was still trying to go somewhere. It was wonderful. Everything sat its usual place as if order had been restored. However, nagging doubt still gnawed at the pit of Christopher's stomach: what if all of this was a figment of his imagination? What if it was just another *tiramavee*? He could almost feel the cool and soothing hands of his Nana, placing a cold flannel over his forehead and a *shakidoon* over his shivering body. But not even the memory of his Nana's magical *shakidoon* – pile after pile of cosy blankets – could stop Christopher from thinking that there was more to this. Something told him that this was no tiramavee.

"Christopher!" Out of nowhere, the Scottish command of wee Nana Kathy blared, sending Christopher into a tumult.

But surely *this* was impossible. Surely, this time, he was imagining things. Surely, he was hearing things. He quickly rubbed the misty pane inside the old lean-to, to see what was going on. But all was to no avail. Behind the thick opaque glass, he was met by a maze of cobwebs. So, he inhaled deeply and stepped slowly towards the old lean-to door. Gently, and very carefully, he opened the door.

"Whit in the name of the Wee Man have you been up to?" Nana Kathy's puzzled face met with Christopher's bewildered confusion. She was standing in the grounds of Milaw garden. Christopher was speechless. "And what's with the blush?"

Christopher quickly glanced down to see that he was holding a single red rose in his hands. It was the rose from before: the same rose that the she-wolf had placed in his hands. He had no recollection of holding it. But little did he realise, that it closely resembled the same ruby flower on the front of his mother's trinket box.

"I…I…eh…" Christopher stumbled with his words.

"Right, it's teatime son. In you get," Nana Kathy ordered

her grandson into the house.

Without thinking, he followed his Nana's command. But as he stepped into the grounds of *Milaw* garden, he was reunited with the sight of his faithful canine. Christopher was about to run over to Sam and adorn him with lots of hugs, but his loyal chum was too busy: he was running in circles, playing with a rather old and stooped old man. Christopher rubbed his eyes, doubting his vision.

"And oh," shouted Nana Kathy out of the kitchen window. "Oli's joining us for tea. So, you'd better set three places for us son."

# CHAPTER 19
## ~ *OLI'S SIGHT* ~

The kitchen of Milaw House was alive. Two huge pots broiled on the stove; their lids rattled like the percussion section of an orchestra warming up for their next performance. Christopher lifted the lid of the largest pot and inhaled the hearty smell of stew. His stomach growled violently, reminding him that he had not eaten in a while. Temptation grabbed him and forced the ladle into his hands. It scooped a huge spoonful of delicious meaty gravy onto the spoon and pushed it up towards his mouth.

"For heaven's sake, blow!" Nana Kathy entered the kitchen, realising that her grandson was about to swallow a spoonful of lava like stew. "A pair o' lobster lips isnae gonna make a good look for your first day at school son. And I'm sure Kerry wouldnae like her beau to have Botox chops!"

Christopher's face stewed warmer than the contents of his Nana Kathy's pots. He choked on his words before he could even say anything, but he was only glad that Kerry was not there to witness his embarrassment. He tiptoed with the stew-laden spoon over to the window of Milaw House kitchen and blew over its delicious, hearty contents. As he scooped up the contents into his mouth, he became aware of his Nana's presence beside him. Her mighty-but-little figure stood beside him; she rested her arm around his shoulder.

Outside in Milaw garden, Sam and Oli were still playing throw and catch. Christopher was too busy slobbering over his Nana's stew to realise that Oli was the one assuming the role of the catcher.

"Whit a right numpty!" Nana Kathy's words disturbed her grandson's slavering. "Oli looks like he sees everything. Just look at the way he's prancin' aboot that garden!"

Christopher felt her arm leaving his shoulder as she

stepped back towards her simmering stove. He thought that she looked tiny compared to the size of her cooker and oversized pots. But it was her spirit that made her seem larger than the tallest artefact in Milaw House.

"N…Nana, wh…what caused Oli to go b…blind?" Christopher's question was out before he even knew what he was asking. There was a moment's silence before his Nana said anything.

"It was a great fire. It happened a long time ago. He tried to…" Her voice trailed off into the distant past, back to a place where time had enclosed its careful hands around the pain.

Christopher could hear the sadness gargling at the back of her throat. He could not bear to see his Nana suffer, not again, so he stepped closer and rested his arm on her shoulders. They both stared out at the greenery in the garden. On the window ledge the red rose sat proudly, in one of Nana Kathy's ornate vases.

Dinner was served and an unusual silence prevailed. Even Sam sat in exhausted stillness after his afternoon's antics. Teatime in *Milaw* house was never this quiet; Nana Kathy always had something to say, at least something to bring to the conversation, no matter how trivial. It was like there was something lurking beneath the surface, something that not even any of them would dare to mention. Something unbelievable. Christopher was sure that he had suffered another one of his tiramavees, but he was too embarrassed to ask his Nana – or even Oli – how he had managed to travel from Ferncross Library to the old lean-to. It all seemed so ridiculous. Christopher could just hear his father's voice declaring *that that boy needs help!*

"Well Kathy," thankfully old Oli broke the silence, "your steak pie was delicious".

Christopher looked over at him, amazed at the way Oli could find the food on his plate. He studied the old man's smiling face. A brightness dampened any signs of weathering; instead, Oli's face looked altogether youthful. It was remarkable really, given his age. An inexplicable vitality radiated from the old man and it was somewhat infectious. His eyes glowed in the flickering candlelight. And then – ever so subtly, so much so that Christopher could not be sure – Oli winked at him. Christopher choked. Water sprouted out of his nostrils as he hacked and whooped, trying to clear the rogue liquid from his windpipe. The next thing he knew, Nana Kathy was patting his back, as if he was a baby being winded after feeding. He fell back into his chair in both laughter and embarrassment.

"Jeesy peeps son!" Nana Kathy declared as she sidled round to the front of her grandson so that she could look him in the eye. "Whit are you trying to do to yoursel'?!"

"S...s...sorry Nana" was all that Christopher could muster, but the sight of Oli winking and smiling - right in the direction of Christopher - caused him to explode into another fit of hysterical coughing. At that very moment, he was utterly convinced that Oli could see *everything*.

\*\*\*\*

Christopher offered to wash the dishes – *and* dry them – despite the plethora of pots and pans encrusted in stew and potatoes. To any other teenage boy, the thought of such a chore would turn their stomach, but Christopher Muir was no ordinary teenage boy. And besides, he quite liked it. It would give him time to think. The soaking, scrubbing, rinsing, drying, and stacking all felt quite therapeutic. Nana Kathy was not one for dishwashers or even microwaves; she thought they were just a *bunch of bloody new-fangled robots, waiting to take over my hoose!* Thankfully, Christopher liked it that way. It was such a far cry from all the gadgets that his father had installed at the townhouse in Leicester. Despite that being the house where he had lived with his parents, Christopher never felt at home there. It was too clinical. When he really thought about it, he never actually felt welcome.

"Ah son, you're just like your Papa standing there." Christopher turned around to see his Nana Kathy by the fridge. Her words caught him, along with the *emulsion*, so he just smiled back. Her amber eyes momentarily illuminated the fading light in Milaw House kitchen. Christopher wanted to fling his arms around his Nana and thank her for everything, but she had three bowls in her hand, already filled with dumplings and cream. She placed the dessert clad dishes on the sideboard and turned to face her grandson. She burst into laughter and turned to face her grandson. "A pair of dumplings." She chuckled. "Did you see the look on that wee, scrawny, good-for-nothing officer's face?!"

Christopher erupted into laughter along with Nana Kathy.

"Kathy?" Oli's poorly voice interrupted the merriment. "Can you help me?" He sounded weak.

Nana Kathy flew into the dining room before her grandson and Sam. She offered a shoulder to Oli, lifted him from his chair, and then walked him through to bathroom - next to hallway. She shut the door behind Oli but told him not to lock it in case he fainted. Christopher was flummoxed and worried. Oli had changed so quickly from being independent, as if he could see everything, to an ailing old man, in need of guidance for everything.

Sam sat in the entrance to the hallway. He was staring at where Oli had been sitting in the dining room. He let out a low growl. Christopher moved forward and sat down beside his Siberian, nuzzling his nose into the thick fur of his faithful chum's neck. He smelled of lavender.

"Kathy?!" Old Oli interjected; his voice muffled behind the door of the toilet. "So, when will you join me at the market? I could be doing with a beautiful smile like yours to sell my stuff".

"Och, away wi' yourself Oli," Nana Kathy protested, trying to keep an air of modesty, but her little crimson cheeks told a different story. "You've always been one for flattery," she added, as she fluttered towards the bathroom door where Oli now stood.

Thankfully, Oli looked altogether different, much stronger than just before. His usual pink glow sat rosily in his cheeks again. This time he did not need any guidance, and somehow Nana Kathy knew. Instead, he used the walls and felt his way over to the grandfather clock. Nana Kathy fell back into the chaise longue by the window and shut her eyes.

"Och son, I'm fair pecked oot. Whit a day." Sam padded over and lay by her feet. They both shut their eyes.

Christopher had so much that he wanted to say. He had so many things that he wanted to ask, to both his Nana and Oli. He thought that this might be the right time to say something, but the grandfather clock had other ideas.

*Clang----clang------clang--------claang.*

Something was different. The chimes sounded strange. With every tick of the clock, time appeared to slow down.

Oli was moving the hands of time. Backwards.

Out of nowhere, a snowy whirlwind whipped around Oli and the grandfather clock. Christopher could just make out the old man's ailing stature through the powerful gust encasing him. The clock no longer chimed; it had been replaced by a continuous thrum, like white noise echoing through an old wireless radio, radiating from some point in the distant past. Christopher glanced to his left, certain that his Nana Kathy and Sam would be awake. Both lay sound asleep. He tried to shout at them, to tell them to wake up, but no sound came from his throat. He tried to move towards them, but the magnetic force of the white whirlwind pulled Christopher into its vortex. He was back in the eye of the storm. He instantly recognised its protective force. He felt safe.

"*In tenebris est. In tenebris est.*" Old Oli's words beat out like a pounding drum. "*In tenebris est hic.* You must listen to me son." Oli dropped his hands from the face of the grandfather clock and turned towards Christopher. The white winded gyre still swirled around them. Despite its loud whistle, Christopher could still hear Oli's voice. "You did it my boy. You did it! You followed the light and found ad ostium. The gateway. You *passed through*." Christopher held Oli's gaze; the old man appeared to be looking straight at him. His eyes sparkled and his moustache twitched as he pulled Christopher closer. "A great many doors will now open in your life, but you must be careful. Beware of the tall dark one. *He* is here, in this house, in the garden. *He is everywhere*."

Christopher shivered. He knew exactly what Oli meant.

"*He* was just here, listening to our conversation. I felt his dark duress in the dining room. I don't know how, but *he* has found a way to listen to your thoughts. You must push him out."

"B…b…but how?" Fear swirled in the pit of Christopher's stomach. All the inexplicable events came together like a cryptic jigsaw puzzle: the lean-to, the dark vision in his room, the dark carrion bird that nearly scared his Nana Kathy to death, the dark pool of blood. The horned beast in his room. But there were many pieces still missing. Ever since the arrival of his father's gift – the Incaendium phone - things had not been right in Milaw House. Silence crackled through the white noise of the whirlwind. "Wh…wh…what…" Christopher opened his mouth, but he had no idea what to ask.

"You must smash it my boy." And just like that, Oli had read Christopher's mind. "It's his way of controlling you. You must never use it." Oli's grip tightened around Christopher's shoulder. "*Ever*."

And then, just as quickly as the whirlwind appeared, it faded into the hereafter.

"Whit in the name of the Wee Man are two playing at?" Nana Kathy was awake. "You two look like your about to do a wee jig."

Oli was still holding onto Christopher's shoulders.

"I was just giving your boy a few tips on how to impress

the ladies." Oli smiled and chuckled. "A little bit of the Tiresius charm never hurt anyone".

Astonishment had a firm grip over Christopher's mouth. How could his Nana not have seen anything of the last few minutes? But, as usual, he was too scared to say anything. Perhaps, if he even dared to mention the whirlwind, his Nana would put him to bed and call the doctor. The room around him appeared to swim and spin. He could just make out the voices of his Nana Kathy and Oli. Sam, who must have been aware of his master's troubled thoughts, padded over to him and nuzzled into his hands. His cool, wet nose was a welcome relief. His bushy white tail thumped rhythmically against his master's legs. Christopher knelt and nestled into the thick fur of Sam's nape.

"My grandson disnae need any of your advice Oli," Nana Kathy's chirruped loudly. She hauled herself up from her comfy spot, before adding, "he's already got himself a wee belter of an admirer."

"*Nana!*" Christopher found his voice, thanks to embarrassment. He clambered up from his knees, trying to hide the scarlet colour of his face. But it was no use, both Oli and Nana Kathy were laughing at his bashfulness.

"Och, away. You must know by now that Kerry's taken a wee shine to you."

Despite his reluctance, Nana Kathy grabbed her grandson's hands and twirled him around Milaw House hallway, in what she would call a *right good reel*. Oli was already at the piano, playing an upbeat but recognisable song, with Sam howling in tune.

143

# CHAPTER 20
## ~ *THE WILTING ROSE* ~

Evening alighted in the Village of Fernlock. The familiar fading blue of sundown was set ablaze with a strange crimson colour. The creeping carmine cast a horrible darkness over the sleepy suburb. Everything looked bloodshot. Despite the peculiar crepuscular activity, the people of Fernlock were oblivious; they were too busy preparing the younger generation for their first day back at school. A murder of crows cackled high in the branches of Fernlock forest, mocking and tormenting the creatures below. One solitary little robin perched itself on the roof of Milaw house.

Christopher lay on his bed. He was exhausted. He had ventured so far, but he felt like he had barely even figured out anything. His head was pounding. However, the cold flannel was helping to alleviate his angst. Nana Kathy had sent him to bed earlier, not long after their dance in the hallway. She was concerned about the *wabbit* look of her grandson, and so she declared that an early night was the *best treatment*. Despite his protest, Nana Kathy won. She almost always did.

Christopher was worried about Oli. How would his old acquaintance find his way home? He felt terrible: he should have been strong enough to walk the old man home, especially after everything that he had done for him. But the minute Nana Kathy ordered him to bed, Christopher fell into a fitful sleep. In between slumber and awakening, he heard murmured accents below his windowsill, but he could not make out who the voices belonged to. Sometimes they sounded like his Nana Kathy, other times it was Oli. Then he recalled another voice: the unwelcome mutterings of his father. Christopher sat up straight in his bed causing the flannel to fall into his lap. To his horror, when he opened his eyes, Sam was nowhere to be seen. He was sure that his faithful canine chum was nestled at the bottom of his bed. Sadness festered in the pit of his stomach. Perhaps he really had imagined everything. Even Sam. Perhaps it just his coping mechanism to deal with the loss of his mum.

"*Knock…knock…knock,*" Nana Kathy's distinctive triptych code signalled her presence. "How are you feeling son?" Her question was met with no reply, so she popped her head around the doorway to her grandson's bedroom.

Christopher's pale face caused his grandmother more concern. "I…I…I…" words failed Christopher. Tears smarted and singed the corners of his eyes.

*Whack!* Suddenly, the door flew open, smashing against the wall in Christopher's bedroom, knocking some of his books from the shelve and onto the floor. A fluffy white vision darted through the doorway and leapt onto the bed. It was Sam. He lunged forward, lapping at his master, wiping away his tears.

"Oh son, thank God." Nana Kathy peeped. "Your wee rosy cheeks have returned."

Christopher fell back onto his bed, allowing Sam to nuzzle in by his side. Despite the return of his faithful canine chum, Christopher could not find any words to say to his Nana. Had he been awake before though, he might have spotted Sam sneaking off, presumably to help old Oli on his way. But Christopher's thoughts were elsewhere.

"Tea and toast?" Nana Kathy interrupted her grandson's thoughts.

"Yes please. And some honey?" This time Christopher had no hesitation, and no stutter, in replying to his Nana's question.

"Okay, but then it's bed!" Nana Kathy's commands vanished behind the doorway as she left to prepare her grandson's supper.

Thoughts of delicious golden toast decorated with melted butter and honey warmed Christopher's belly. Even Sam sat salivating at his master's visualisations. Nana Kathy knew how to make the toast simply perfect. *Warm bread*, as she called it.

*BUZZ --- BUZZ!*

Christopher and Sam were pulled from their slobbering. The Incaendium phone burned fervently inside Christopher's beside drawer.

"*Hoooooooowwwwooooooo!*" Sam howled at his master as if to warn him about the dangers of his father's powerful device.

But something hauled at Christopher, something that he could not control. Without thinking, he pulled the drawer of his bedside cabinet open. The red glare exploded, splashing scarlet over everything in the room. Christopher instinctively slammed the door shut.

The cool moonlight from outside Milaw house pooled the room in calming silvery tones.

"Here you go son. Tea and toast." Nana Kathy entered her grandson's bedroom, this time unannounced. Concern was still stretched across her face. She placed the bedtime snack on his bedside table and turned to face him. "Are you okay? Do you feel okay about tomorrow?"

"Y…y…yes. A…and I w…will be fine," Christopher tried to lie, through mouthfuls of toast, but he did not sound so convincing. Sam yowled and thumped his tail against his master.

"Well son, you just go in there and smile. Anyone who is everyone in this blasted village will recognise that smile of yours. It's my Peggie's." Nana Kathy hesitated for what felt like an eternity. She sat down on the edge of his bed before adding, "and your mum's smile."

Christopher swallowed a whole piece of buttery toast to hide the gathering grief at the back of his throat. He washed it down with some of his milky tea. "Th…thanks Nana." He leaned forward from his bed and kissed her good night. "Th…thanks. F…for everything." He swallowed the last gulp of his tea, along with his sweet buttery toast.

Nana Kathy patted her grandson's head before she collected the empty cup and plate. She pulled herself up and headed towards the door of Christopher's bedroom. "Just remember to brush your teeth son. Nighty night. And don't let the beg bugs bite." She winked and shut her grandson's bedroom door over.

*BUZZ --- BUZZ!*

The Incaendium mobile sneered once more. However, this time, the bedroom cabinet drawer slithered slowly open, on its own, just enough so that Christopher could see the red frown bellowing from the angry device. Sam padded towards his master and howled softly. But from where Christopher was sitting, the temptation was too much. He could just make out Kerry's text message.

### R U ok? Plz text x

Christopher was drawn into the abbreviated words of Kerry's message. Despite him not being one for text talk, his eyes zoomed in on the **X** – that twenty-fourth letter of the alphabet that somehow denoted affection. A kiss. Christopher's stomach fluttered with butterflies. He furtively pulled the drawer open further and gazed at the phone in delight. He had forgotten to wear his mother's glasses. And he had forgotten all about Oli's warning.

Downstairs in the kitchen, a withered petal fell from the rose.

# CHAPTER 21
## ~ *CANDICE HAYDEN AND THE ROBIN* ~

Both Christopher and Sam were up early. It had been raining lightly during the night; now a damp morning mist was all that prevailed. A cool, early morning walk along to the brook at the bottom of the Drive seemed like a good idea at the time, but both Christopher and his canine chum traipsed sluggishly there and back. Their slow pace was not helped by the fact that every few seconds or so, Sam stopped to look up at his master with a strange sadness. It was a look that Christopher had not seen before, and it troubled him.

Nana Kathy, being her usual busy self, was already up when her grandson and his dutiful dog left for their walk. She swallowed down her worry with copious amounts of lavender tea, choosing to occupy herself instead with the preparation of her grandson's breakfast roll. She had made him another hearty breakfast of *tattie scones and scrambled eggs*, all wrapped up in a delicious morning roll. However, when Christopher arrived home, her heart sank.

"Th…thanks Nana. Really. Th…thanks. B…but I couldn't eat it. N…not just now." Christopher's stomach growled in unison with his words, but it was not from hunger. He felt sick.

"Well, I'll you what son. I'll put your roll in a wee bag for you to take to school. You can eat it on your way."

Christopher smiled, grimaced almost, trying to hide his nausea. Nevertheless, he did not want to appear ungrateful, not to his Nana, so he smiled and followed her through to the kitchen. He watched her fuss over his roll and her actions brought a smile to his face. He loved how she always had a plentiful supply of kitchen roll and silver paper to wrap food in. Sam sat at her feet, slavering, praying for leftovers. This time he was lucky: Nana Kathy had accidentally – or perhaps deliberately - dropped doggy sized dollops of scrambled eggs onto the floor. Sam tucked right in, wagging his thick white tail.

"Right son, there you are." Nana Kathy carefully placed the silvery bundled package of food into the top of his schoolbag and zipped it up. Christopher looked at the size of his rucksack and burst into laughter. It looked like he was ready to go on a yearlong trek around the world. And at that point, he felt like it.

****

It had been a quick goodbye. Christopher had been dreading the whole moment. The thought of leaving his Nana – and Sam – for a whole day filled him with dread. He kept reassuring himself that Sam would be okay with Nana Kathy. Or, maybe, it was the other way around. He could not forget the look in his dog's eyes: he looked so miserable. Christopher had whispered "*I love you mate*" into his ear before leaving, and Sam perfectly understood because he leapt forward and slobbered him with lots of huge doggy kisses. Although the two friends had only been together for a few days, Christopher felt like he had known Sam his entire life.

The rain had returned. It was a fine, misty webbing that clung and crawled over everything. Christopher felt wretched as he walked the seemingly short journey to his new school. He put one slow foot in front of the other, dragging himself along Gorse Drive towards Oakwood Academy. The school day started at ten to nine, so he had less that fifteen minutes to go. *A good brisk walk and you'll be there in jig time, ten minutes*, he remembered his Nana Kathy saying. So, Christopher tried to increase his pace, focussing on the positives; something that his mum had always encouraged him to do. He centred all his energy on the only beacon of light he had. *Kerry will be there,* he thought to

149

himself. *Waiting on me, smiling at me, blowing a kiss at me.*

"OI! WATCH WHERE YOU'RE GOING!"

Christopher could not see who he had bumped into, but his dreams of Kerry came tumbling down as he tripped face first into the ground. He quickly rolled around and tried to clamber onto his feet, but the pain radiating out from his nose was so painful. He could not hold in his suffering. "Ow...ow...ouch!!!!!" He held his hands over his nose to stop the stinging pain. Hot liquid seeped through the gaps between his fingers and dripped onto the collar of his crisp-white shirt. He pinched the bridge of his nose in a feeble attempt to stem the blood flow.

"What *are* you, some kind of idiot?" The red-haired figure spat out her question and it hit Christopher hard in the face. She stood still, looking down at him, arms crossed, offering no help whatsoever. Despite his injury, she showed no signs of sympathy towards him. Her brown eyes looked like two dark stones. It was Candice Hayden.

"I...I...I..." Christopher mumbled and stumbled over what he was trying to say. He felt sore, humiliated, and heartsick all in one go. He could not believe that he had tripped over Candice, Kerry's *so-called friend.*

"Ha, ha, ha, look at the *state* of you!" Candice cackled, as she whipped out her mobile phone and held it in front of her. "Everyone will get a laugh at *this*," she added, as she proceeded to record Christopher clambering about, trying to find his feet after his fall.

"Wh...wh...why would you d...d...do that?" Christopher could feel tears welling up at the corners of his eyes, but he quickly wiped them away, along with a handful of blood. Luckily, his school blazer was burgundy.

"*Wh...wh...why do you speak like that?!* Ha, what a big baby!" Candice snorted, mimicking poor Christopher. But then she stopped filming.

Christopher felt totally helpless. He naively wondered what her next move would be as she stared at her phone. It was the latest Incaendium model, just like the one his father had given to him.

**_Big baby crying at his first day at school!_** Candice fervently tapped her message into *Flare*, a social media app that would allow her post to be seen by an infinite number of viewers. Her profile was open to the public and she already had nearly 2000 followers, so she hoped that this upload would be enough to increase her fame tenfold. She was about to press **upload**, but out of nowhere a sharp, stinging sensation struck the bridge of nose. Her vision became intermittently blurred, so she instinctively waved her hands above her head to chase away the strange flapping above her.

It was the little red breasted robin from Milaw House.

The little bird continued her fluttering, pecking away at Candice's nose. Christopher could not help but giggle at the ridiculous sight of the tall, gangly red-haired girl flailing her arms around. He felt somewhat guilty, so he stepped forward to offer help. However, in all the commotion, Candice dropped her phone. It hit the concrete paving with such a force that it smashed into pieces. The little robin chirped happily and then she fluttered away. She perched on a horse-chestnut tree branch across the road.

"My phone!" Now Candice was the one on the ground, scrambling around, trying to pick up the pieces of her Incaendium mobile. "It's broken! And I didn't even get to upload your video!"

Christopher thought that she looked like she was about to start crying. He could not believe how attached she was to such a mechanical device. Why did it have such a hold over her? Despite her horrible actions, he felt sorry for her, so he tried to offer a helping hand again.

But he was only met by more anger, more rage. She slapped his hands away, declaring "you'll pay for this, this is all your —" but her heated words were cut short by the return of the little robin. She fluttered and chirruped loudly above her.

And then the little birdie pooped on Candice's head.

Christopher had to hold his hands over his mouth to stop his laughter. But it was all to no avail. Hilarity exploded from his mouth and it ignited red hot fury in Candice. Her freckles turned scarlet as she let out an ear-piercing scream. At the corner of his vision, Christopher was aware of a few onlookers gathering across the road, wondering what was happening, but the hatred radiating from Candice held his sight. The brown tint in her eyes turned crimson. She stared at Christopher, menacingly. She did not say anything, and it unnerved him more so than her thunderous screech. However, before he could break the painful silence, Candice sprinted off ahead of him.

"That girl was horrible to you. Are you okay?" It was one of the spectators from across the road. The tiny lady looked genuinely concerned. "She had it coming, if I may say so myself," she added, winking at Christopher.

"I...I...I'm fine...I th...think." Christopher was suddenly aware of his appearance: his nose and upper lip were smeared in his blood; his shirt was splattered with red spots.

"Here," the little woman held out a packet of wet wipes to Christopher. "Take the packet - you need them." She smiled and her face lit up with warmness. Two little dimples decorated her rosy cheeks.

"Th...thank you," Christopher replied, grateful for the help. He started cleaning his face with one of the wipes, but the spritely little lady plucked a few from the packet and began dabbing softly at his face. She sang a little song as she wiped away the blood. He stood like a naive child allowing a stranger to tend to his needs. But there was something familiar about this petite woman. Plus, her kind actions were more than welcome after his collision with Candice.

"The name's Primrose. Primrose Ruddock," the little lady smiled as she took a step back from Christopher. "I know your Nana. Me and Kathy go way, way back," she added, looking at Christopher's face closely. "There," she smiled. "you are all clean." She plucked a small mirror from her bag and help it up in front of him. To his amazement, he looked crystal clean. Not a spot of blood was evident anywhere. Not even on his collar.

"Th…thank you, ever so m…much," Christopher beamed. "How c…can I e…ever r…r…repay you?" This wonderful little woman had somehow managed to wipe away the damage unleashed by Candice and he was eternally grateful.

"Take this." Primrose handed Christopher a small card. A border of flora and fauna decorated her contact information: *P Ruddock. RSPB conservationist at Fernlock Bird Sanctuary*. "Tell your Nana I will pop by later on."

"I w….will do. Th…thanks Mrs R…Ruddock," Christopher replied, as he carefully placed her card in his pocket. The little woman was so helpful and so cheery; Christopher was almost sure that he had seen her before. But he could not recall his Nana mentioning the name Primrose. Suddenly, a light breeze waltzed its way up Gorse Drive, twisting around Christopher and the petite lady. It stopped his daydreaming. "Sch…sch…school. I…I am going to b…be late," but the time on his wristwatch told another story. It was only twenty minutes to nine. It was impossible. It was as if someone – or something – magically stopped the hands of time. Panic set in. He was certain that his watch must have stopped working when he fell over.

"Don't worry," Primrose piped up. "It's just after twenty to nine. You have plenty of time to get to school, but you'd better get going."

"Th…thanks Mrs Ruddock," was all that Christopher could manage. He was still in a daze over his apparent ability to time travel. But he listened to the little lady's advice and pulled his bag back up over his shoulder. Just as he was about to say goodbye, Primrose cheeped up.

"Right son, get going," she urged, pointing at her watch. "And it's Birdie. All my friends call me Birdie."

# Chapter 22
## ~ *DR VON BRANDT'S INSTITUTE* ~

Oakwood Academy looked thoroughly dismal in the morning drizzle. Christopher stood back from the huge gates and gasped. He stared solemnly at the concrete-and-glass fortress waiting in front of him. The entrance was like a huge mouth, sneering at him, waiting to swallow him up whole. It was a new build. No one really knew what happened to the old building, but it was clear that it had mutated into a new-fangled monster. At the top of the gates there lurked an overbearing sign: *Oakwood Institute, School of Supremacy*. It was yet another indication of change and Christopher did not like it.

A maze of burgundy blazers made the walk up to the school entrance seem impossible. Christopher zigzagged his way through pupil after pupil, some of which were twice the size of him. Perhaps though, the most unnerving thing was that no one was talking; instead, just about everyone appeared to be glued to their mobile phones. A spectral like silence weaved its way through the air. Christopher already felt like the odd one out and this made everything worse. *You stand oot like a sore thumb*, he could almost hear his Nana Kathy say.

Christopher had decided to leave his *Incaendium* device at home, in the bottom drawer of his bedside cabinet, beside his mother's spectacles. It seemed like the right idea at the time. He still had not decided what to do with it. Despite's old Oli's command of *smash it my boy*, it all seemed so confusing: Christopher wanted nothing more than to destroy his father's *gift*, but it was also a form of communication with the girl of his dreams. Kerry had texted him a couple of times before bed, but it took him some time to think of what to say - and his head ached. Badly. Eventually, he decided to keep his reply short: *I'm fine.*

***Can't wait to see you tomorrow. Xx*** But to his dismay, Kerry did not respond. He tried not to think anything of it. Common sense said that she had fallen asleep; anxiety had other ideas. It ate away at him, *all* night – that, and Sam's sad eyes – along with the thought of his first day at Oakwood Academy. And so here he was, standing outside the front entrance of his new school, like a complete outsider. Sadly, Kerry was nowhere to be seen, or Candice – thankfully!

Christopher stepped forward and placed his hands into his blazer pockets. With his right hand, he felt the rough exterior of his Papa's key, and it served as a reminder that he was not alone; with his left hand, his fingers tapped the smooth nib of his Papa's pen. He missed Sam and his Nana so much. *Everything will be okay*, he tried to convince himself as he looked up. Ahead of him, he saw one of the only pupils without a mobile phone. He was smiling at him. The happy boy was about Christopher's age and he was wearing a blue baseball cap.

"HURRY UP!" A sharp voice commanded the throng of Oakwood pupils to "Move forward! Get in line!"

Christopher stood on his tiptoes to see what lay ahead of him. Above the herd of burgundy, he could see a tall, gaunt, blonde woman shepherding mindless teenagers, one at a time, through some sort of electronic gate. With his toes tired, he plonked his heels back onto the ground. Once again, he felt so small, so insignificant; thankfully though the tiny figure beside him made him feel somewhat taller. It was the cheerful pupil with the blue baseball cap.

"*It's a security detector,*" he whispered. "*I was warned about this. I've heard it melts your brains.*"

Christopher giggled nervously, unsure if the baseball-capped-boy meant it.

"*I'm only kidding,*" he added lightly, nudging Christopher in the side playfully. The two of them were forced forward, following the flock. They were two steps away from the detector. "I'm Stevie. Stevie Malik," the boy in the baseball cap piped up, offering a handshake. Christopher was amazed at how small his hands were.

"I'm Chris…Chris…Christopher." Aware that this was the first time he had muttered any words to Stevie, Christopher felt so stupid. He felt so ashamed because he could not even say his own name without stuttering.

"Well, Chris, I'm pleased to meet you," Stevie smiled, playfully elbowing his new friend in the side again.

"ONE AT A TIME!" The transparent faced woman ordered, glaring at Christopher. Her long blonde hair contrasted with the dark cloak of her pin striped trouser suit. She held a long electronic device, presumably for scanning anyone that looked suspicious. Christopher thought that it looked like a cattle prod.

Stevie was next to step forward. Before entering, he turned around to his newly found friend. "I prefer Chris – the shorter version of your name suits you better. Well, see you on the other side buddy."

****

Christopher survived the metal detector. As he passed through, he heard what sounded like a thousand high-pitched voices screaming in his ears. It reminded him of Candice Hayden. He shuddered a little at the memory, but then giggled at the thought of the little red breasted bird's perfect timing. It also made him think about the village of Ferncross: it was renowned for its tranquillity, low crime rates and community spirit; so it seemed very strange to have such high security in the village's only high school.

Christopher looked down at the map, issued to him as he stepped out of the square confines of the detector. He was now in the central part of the school - *the Artery* – but to Christopher it looked more like a huge factory, devoid of any life and soul. It was so sterile. There were no wooden boards brandishing the names of previous captains or prefects in gold writing; instead, four huge screens shrouded the vast, white-washed walls, each displaying the message: *To ignite brainwaves and influence thoughts*. Christopher stared at one of the black mirrors above him, wondering how much money it would have cost just to install such a preposterous plasma screen. The words glowed in red, causing him to shield his eyes. He felt like he had looked at the sun too long; the word "*ignite*" scalded his vision, like a pyro of pain singeing his eyelids.

"Keep moving forward! Get to your house seats." Christopher opened his eyes. It was the tall, gaunt, blonde-haired woman again. She was now looking directly at him. "Are you lost?" she sneered.

"N…n…n…" Christopher's stutter was the worst it had ever been. He could not even reply to her simple question. She then smiled menacingly at him. Her row of strange angular teeth made her look like a shark, flaunting its grin at its next helpless victim. Christopher felt like he was about to dissolve into another one of his tiramavees. He longed for both his Nana and Sam. He missed them so much and almost cried aloud their names. He pulled out his water bottle and tried to sip the cool soothing liquid in a feeble attempt to calm his nerves.

"He's with me," a small and squeaky voice declared. It was Stevie.

"Th…th…thanks," Christopher stammered, grateful that Stevie had steered him away from the wrath of the tall, blonde, apex predator. He immediately realised how much he had underestimated the power of Stevie.

"*You were lucky there,*" Stevie whispered, pulling his newly found friend over to a row of orange seats. "*That's the Hak…Ms Hakan-Hughes,*" he added. "*She's second in command around here but she acts like she runs the whole school. Don't you think that she looks like a saw-fish?*"

Christopher nearly snorted his water everywhere with laughter.

Perhaps it was a turn of fate, or a clever card played by the friendly forces around them, but Stevie and Christopher just happened to be in the same schoolhouse: *Edan.* They were even in the same class set. They were directed to sit one of the seats marked *1E1*.

"Hey, do you think the *E* stands for Emo?" Stevie quipped, nudging Christopher in the side once again. The two newly found friends looked at each other, and then at the others around them, and then started laughing. Christopher and Stevie both stood out amongst the other Year 8 pupils in their *1E1* set; the others looked like immaculate imitations of what a Year 8 pupil should look like. Every pupil sat upright in their perfectly fitted burgundy blazers, complete with perfect Windsor knotted tie and crisp white shirt. They all wore the same supercilious expression. On closer inspection, Christopher noticed that they were all looking down their noses at something, but their heads were still strangely held upwards, alert, as if they were looking at what was going on around them. He then realised that they were all gazing at their mobiles; they were just pretending to listen and look in on what was happening around them.

"*Incaendium*" Stevie whispered. Christopher nearly fell off his seat. "*Do you see? I am convinced that the new device comes equipped with contact lenses, so that it looks like the user is actually looking at you…but they are really staring at the screen of their phone.*"

"Yes…I…I s…see." Christopher could not believe how perceptive Stevie was. He gulped down a ball of fear, aware that his father had just "gifted" him with the most up to date version of the device, more advanced than what his peers were currently holding. But Aidan Brenton not given his son any form of eye equipment along with the device.

"*My parents, they can't quite afford such a device, so I have to put up with this robotic Aster phone. It doesn't do half the things I want.*" The little baseball capped boy moaned quietly. "Hey, your stutter," Stevie voiced, this time with no whisper. "If you don't mind me asking, have you always had it?"

Christopher felt in no way offended at what his little

friend had asked. Strangely, he felt that this little awkward boy had more hang-ups than him. He could see it in the amber of his light brown eyes.

"I…I developed it a…after m…my mum died." And there it was. Christopher had never really said it aloud before. However, Stevie called him on it – and Christopher answered. Honestly.

"SILENCE!" The powerful tones of a soaring, sinewy looking creature bellowed from the stage. "LISTEN TO ME!" He commanded, in a fiery voice.

The artery of Oakwood Institute fell deathly silent.

"*That's the headmaster,*" Stevie silently nudged Christopher. "*Dr von Brandt, but nobody really knows wh –*"

"YOU BOY! STAND UP!" The ghostly dark-haired man shouted at poor Stevie. "REMOVE THAT HAT BOY!"

"Please sir," Stevie pleaded as he stumbled to his feet. Christopher thought that Stevie's reply sounded so feeble against the screaming noiselessness in Oakwood's artery. His voiced sounded so high-pitched, like a little squeak.

"*Well?*" The headmaster goaded, with a dangerously quieter voice, one that suggested something far worse was about to be declared. "Remove the hat!"

"But Sir." Stevie implored again. "I'm a… a… a… SHE! For just now." And with that announcement, the whole year group – Seraphimsan, Hugot and the rest of Edan – looked up from their mobile phones.

"WELL, WHATEVER THE HELL YOU ARE, TAKE OFF THAT HAT! And it is DR…DR von Brandt!"

All eyes fell on Stevie as she removed her hat, exposing a soft blanket of dark brown fuzz. She sat down and ran her right hand nervously over her short hair. Christopher took Stevie's hand. Now, he understood. He smiled broadly at his newly found friend, not caring what pronoun Stevie wanted to use. Christopher could almost hear is Nana Kathy say, "*you cannae just put people in boxes and label them. A person is a human being!*" So, Christopher smiled again at Stevie with one of the worst, cheesiest smiles ever. The most important thing was that Stevie was Christopher's friend.

Thankfully, the horrible headmaster appeared to have forgotten all about Stevie as he started on about Oakwood Institute's expectations and the demands of Year 8. He droned on for nearly half an hour, staring at every new pupil in the entire year group, as if he was recording every face and detail. From time to time, his attention would shift towards Christopher, holding his gaze before moving onto the next pupil. It made Christopher feel very uneasy.

"*I'm a she...for just now, but I want that to change when I'm ready.*" Stevie whispered to Christopher quietly so that Dr von Brandt could not hear.

"*You d... don't have to...to explain S...Stevie. You're m...my friend and that's wh...what matters.*" Christopher wanted to say more, but he could see the eyes of von Brant shifting back in his direction.

Despite this extremely formal and terrifying introduction, the first part of the morning passed by surprisingly quite smoothly. Christopher still had not seen any sign of Kerry yet, but he tried not to worry about it. The school was huge inside and everything looked the same. It reminded him of manufacturing company. The older pupils appeared to be like products of the Dr von Brandt business and the teachers were like the robots responsible for churning out the von Brandt-branded students. It made Christopher shudder. There was something very strange and unsettling about the headmaster's appearance. He had a sickly pallor, so much so that his skin appeared to be translucent. It made a stark contrast to his thick black hair, which started unnaturally low - just above his pointed eyebrows. Oil oozed from the edges of his slicked back hair and the overall effect was quite nauseating. Square framed glasses sat on the bump at the top of his hooked nose; two blue lenses obscured his eyes, making it impossible to work out what colour they were. Yes, Dr von Brandt was terrifying. Given his appearance, Christopher thought that the horrible headmaster should not be awake during daylight.

****

At morning break, the two friends sat outside, enjoying the fresh air. They had been herded out to the smallest of the three quadrangles in the school; a place designated to the Year 8 pupils only. Christopher's heart sank. There was no chance of seeing Kerry in such a place. He looked around him, in the vain hope that he might see the green flash of her eyes; instead, he was surrounded by the precipice of four grey rendered walls. There were no trees or greenery; only concrete. Prison like windows glared down at him. In the window directly above his head, he thought that he could see Dr von Brandt staring down at him. He was sure it was the horrible headmaster, there was no mistaking his apparition like appearance.

"Are you okay?" Stevie asked, aware that her friend had stopped talking and was staring into space instead. She patted him on the back, as if he needed to be stirred from his daydream.

"I'm f...fine," Christopher smiled, glancing back at Stevie. He was ever so grateful to have her by his side. He felt somehow safer with her. She had rescued him from the jaws of Ms Hakan-Hughes, so he felt eternally indebted to her. He looked back at the window above him, but the ghostly vision had gone.

"Hey," Stevie piped up, trying to distract Christopher away from his obvious uneasiness. "What did you make of our English teacher, Mrs Ash? To be perfectly honest, I thought that she was *sooooo* boring!"

Christopher laughed aloud at Stevie's honesty. She was particularly good at replying to her own questions, and it just so happened that her answers were identical to what he wanted to say.

"Y...yes." He agreed. "Sh...she was."

Again, there was something about Mrs Ash, just like the other teachers at Oakwood that made Christopher feel extremely uncomfortable. He thought that English teachers were meant to be renowned for their passion of poetry, novels, and drama, but Mrs Ash lacked any kind of literary spark. Her poker straight dark hair - a coiffure that Cleopatra would have killed for – along with her paper like white skin made her look like a fossil from Egyptian times. Her mouth looked like a letterbox slot. She lacked human expression of any sort.

"And what was with that eye patch?" Stevie declared, "that was enough to scare away Captain Hook! And all that about *Tiger, Tiger, burning bright*…what kind of poem was that? And who the heck is William Blake?"

Christopher collapsed into laughter because Stevie really had summed up Mrs Ash perfectly. "Y…yeah, I n…nearly fell asleep at th…that point!"

Without realising, Christopher had taken the breakfast roll his Nana had made for him out of his back and started chomping on it. It made him feel better. He was sure that his Nana Kathy and Sam would be simply fine back at Milaw House.

"Lucky you," said Stevie, as she pulled out a banana and apple. "My dad is trying to make me eat more fruit. Ha, what a cheek as well. I dunno if I said, but he is the manager at the "Shore Temple." He and his band of busy workers serve curries to the village of Fernlock, day in, day out. So, normally I'd be snacking on a little cheeky bit of Gulab jamun right now. But no sir, not today."

"Wh…what's gu…gu…," Christopher felt terrible for not being able to pronounce what Stevie said, but his stutter caught at the back of his throat.

"Gulab jamun is the most delicious thing you could ever taste. If you like anything sweet, then you will love it! Tell you what, I am going to take you to my dad's restaurant at the end of the day and let you try some. Deal?"

"D…deal!" Christopher replied eagerly. He could not

wait to tell his Nana. He thought Sam would love to come along too! "C…Can I bring m…my d…do… -"

*BEEP* ---- *BEEP* ---- *BEEP* ---- *BEEP*

A high-pitched buzzer blared, declaring the end of morning break. It rattled right through Christopher's braces and numbed his brain. He had grown accustomed to the sound a bell ringing, a familiar sound that set him off on his usual routine. However, this sound was entirely different, like an alarm that would always make you jump, no matter how many times you heard it. It made him realise how much he missed the stability of his old primary school in Leicester. It made him realise how much he missed his old life. And it made him realise how much he missed his mum.

"Hey, you?" Stevie pulled at his rucksack. "Where do you go in that head of yours? Well, no time to answer, we need to get going! You can tell me later what you were going to ask me. Deal?"

"D…deal." Christopher smiled at Stevie, again so glad to have such a small and mighty force to follow. She was already ahead of him, like a mite in amongst the towering giants of Oakwood. He focussed on her school bag, a little blue rucksack with the words *"BASS ROCKS"* scrawled over it in black ink. She continually turned around to make sure that her friend was following along. Christopher was glad that she knew where to go as he had no idea.

"Just follow the arrows," Stevie squeaked. "It's easy. We're off to art."

Christopher loved art. It was his mother's favourite subject. The image of her painting was like an old photograph etched on his memory. She loved nothing more than painting water colours in the back garden of Milaw House. She had always encouraged her son to join in, and very quickly he picked up his mother's skills. He had her talent. It seemed just like yesterday to Christopher.

He looked up, thinking that Stevie would still be there. But she was nowhere to be seen. Instead, he was faced with a wall of burgundy: a mass of Oakwood Institute pupils lay in front of him, scrabbling to find their next class. Somehow, Christopher managed to fumble his way to the wall on his left. His hands met the granular texture of sugar paper. It was a trick that his counsellor had taught him after his mum died: "find something real, something that you can touch, something that will bring you back to the here and now." He looked up to find a wall full of paintings. *At least I know I am in the art department,* he thought. With still no sign of Stevie, he stood on his tiptoes, straining to see ahead. To his horror though, just above the crimson sea of blazers, he saw what looked like his father. If it was him, Aiden Brenton was standing next to a fiery red head. She looked just like Candice Hayden.

"There you are," Stevie nudged Christopher in the side. "I thought I had lost you," she quipped, as she pulled him towards her. "I think I need to put reigns on you! You're like a little lost lamb."

Christopher laughed nervously but he was so relieved that Stevie had found him. By now, the corridor was nearly empty, and everyone had found their way to their class.

"Quick, we're in here," Stevie ordered, pulling Christopher into one of Oakwood's many art classes. How she had managed to find the room, he had no idea.

The two friends nervously stepped forward, aware that they were at least five minutes late. Dampness assaulted their nostrils along with a pungent and unwelcoming stench that smelled like paint that had well and truly passed its sell by date. In front of them sat two singular rows of robotic looking Year 8 students. Not one of them dared to look up at the two latecomers; the other pristine eighteen students were too busy looking at their tablets. Incaendium tablets. The walls were decorated in Picasso style painted cats: twenty-five different black and white images of the same cat, wearing a ridiculous black tee-shirt. The cat looked so smug in every painting.

"*There's no teacher,*" Stevie mouthed, looking at Christopher in wide eyed wonderment. "*What are we supposed to do?"*

Christopher could feel a bubble of giggles rising in his belly. He suddenly found it all hilarious and the sight of Stevie's face just made his merriment worse. She was pinching her nose, with cheeks puffed out, to stem her laughter. The silence in the room was piercing.

"Well, hello my *two-lovely late-comers*," a high-pitched voice screeched from within the art cupboard. Before Christopher or Stevie could say anything, the voice commanded, "Sit down…in front of my desk."

Like two little lambs they sat down and waited. Christopher recognised the shrill tone of the speaker and it sent a shiver up his spine. He tried to shake it off, discarding it as nerves. But he knew that voice.

"*What's happening?*" Stevie mouthed, whispering to Christopher in more of a concerned tone. The laughter had passed.

And then, quite without warning, a rather large, portly woman emerged from the art cupboard, wearing an oversized blue kaftan.

"Well, *heeellloooo* Christopher," she screeched.

It was Barbara Kenny. And she was carrying her blue Peterbald cat, Picatso.

# CHAPTER 23
## ~ *THE KENNY AND HER CRAZY CAT* ~

"Right class, today we are going to draw a *real-life portrait*," Barbara Kenny squealed. "I want you all to clap your hands and welcome our real-life model - my darling Piccy."

The formidable art teacher placed her scrawny little pet onto a red, velvet throne, and then she started clapping. The cat sat up straight, obviously enjoying the adulation. He looked so arrogant. Christopher and Stevie were the only ones not clapping; the other robotic children applauded along with Barbara Kenny, tapping their hands together in unison. It was all so bizarre.

Christopher wondered how this steamroller of a woman had managed to press her way into Oakwood Institute. He wondered if Kerry knew. But when he turned to face Stevie, he could see that her laughter was about to erupt again. Her hilarity was infectious: just one look at her cheeky grin was enough to set Christopher off into a gaggle of giggles.

"*What an ugly cat,*" Stevie mouthed to Christopher.

"CLAP! YOU DO AS I SAY!" Barbara Kenny growled at Christopher and Stevie. Her artificially sweet and high-pitched voice had vanished; it was replaced by a low growl that would have sent the hounds of hell running for cover. The other pupils continued clapping in unity, with blank expressions. Christopher and Stevie started clapping; they no longer felt like laughing.

"Yes, that's it *my dears,*" Barbara shrieked, her fake voice now back in full flow. "Clap, clap, clap!"

The cat, Picatso, sat staring at Christopher, with such a contemptible smile. *If only Sam was here*, he thought to himself. *He would wipe the smile from that hairless creature's face.*

"Right, right, that's enough now, my darlings." Barbara Kenny squealed. "Let's all start drawing little Piccy. I want you to open the art programme on your Incaendium tablets."

Christopher's heart shot upwards into his throat. He did not have an Incaendium tablet, so he could not take part in the lesson. And then his heart sank, right down into the pit of his stomach. He did not like the idea of "drawing" onto a screen; it seemed so mechanical and lacking in any talent or emotion. This was supposed to be art, his favourite subject; a place and time when he could really shine.

"And *what* seems to be the problem?" Barbara Kenny hissed at Christopher.

"I…I…I don't… -" Christopher struggled to say the words. He hated being put on the spot. He could feel the eyes of the other students burning into the back of his head.

"Eh, Mrs?" Stevie interrupted. Christopher was so glad. "I don't have one either. My mum and dad have ordered one, but it still hasn't arrived. So that makes the two of us, I'm the same as Chris." She smiled and winked at her newly found friend.

"Right oh, *darlings*," Barbara Kenny's so-called term of endearment was laced with acid. She vanished into the chasm of her art cupboard.

"Are you okay mate?" Stevie asked Christopher, worried that he looked like he was about to start crying. "*I lied, I do have one*," she whispered, leaning over, and nudging him in the side. "*But it's still in my bag, unopened and –*"

"Here we are," Barbara Kenny sang like a deranged opera singer as she reappeared from her art cupboard. "You can have this one, *Stevie*."

Strangely, Barbara Kenny looked straight at Christopher when she handed Stevie the Incaendium tablet. She sneered at him through a row of coffee stained crooked teeth.

"Eh, sorry Mrs, but what about Chris?" Stevie protested, aware of what was happening. "He can have this –"

"No, no, no!" Barbara Kenny shut Stevie down, thrusting the Incaendium tablet into her hands. "*Take this!*" She snarled. The veil of her synthetic voice had slipped again, allowing her Rottweiler like tone to appear. "My dear," she added in an artificial tone, realising that her mask had stumbled. The other students still sat in silence, sliding and tapping on their black screens.

Unfortunately, Stevie felt like she had no option. She felt so sorry for Christopher and she could see how upset he looked. With concern eating away at her, she stole her chance when Barbara Kenny swished away back to her desk. She watched the huge trail of her blue kaftan floating away, out of earshot, before she whispered "*I'm sorry, this is totally unfair on you. I think she is a big bully!*"

"I'm f…fine," Christopher replied, without whispering; he was trying to hide the embarrassment in his voice. "You've n…nothing to b…be sorry about. And thanks for t…trying," he smiled at Stevie, feeling once again ever so grateful for her help. "I will j…j –"

"Did *I* say that *you* could talk?" Barbara Kenny interjected, with a sour question that was not meant to be answered. "Christopher, did your *mum* not receive the memo? I mean, *every* soon-to-be Year 8 pupil at Oakwood *must* come equipped with *everything* stated in the *welcome* pack."

Christopher did not hear the rest of her squawking. At the mention of his mum, a whole hurricane of emotions hit him face on. Anger raged right at the centre of his storm. It was a feeling that he had not experienced before, and it scared him. This dreadful excuse for an art teacher knew *exactly* what she was doing and saying. Of course, she knew that Christopher's mum died before the summer holidays, so she was using this to pick on him. He felt his hands clutching his Papa's Key and pen in his pockets. The entire contents of the room swished around Christopher's vision. He felt sick again.

"Eh, Mrs … I think that you need to provide Chris with something to draw on if he hasn't got anything." Stevie brought Christopher back to his senses. He had no idea how long he had blacked out for. "You gave me something, so it's only fair you do the same for Chris."

Barbara Kenny's badly drawn on eyebrows arched up into two little blue hooks. Her face turned scarlet and her already puffy cheeks bloated even more, causing her scarlet lipstick bleeding lips to form a little spout. She stared hard at Stevie. She then stood up abruptly and marched off into the art cupboard. Stevie tapped Christopher on the elbow and then proceeded to give him the thumbs up. The sight of this made Christopher laugh; thankfully, his little friend had managed to melt his anger away.

Several minutes passed before Barbara Kenny reappeared. Christopher wondered what had taken her so long. The silence in the classroom was painful. Nobody said anything. The only sound came from the blue cat on the throne: he started purring like a little motor the minute Barbara Kenny re-emerged from the cupboard.

"Well, *Christopher*, I have emailed Dr von Brandt about this *unfortunate* incident. In the meantime, here is some scrap paper for you to draw on." She threw some cartridge paper at Christopher with such a force, that it skidded onto the floor. She then shuffled back to her seat. As she sat down, she added, "I presume you do have *something* to draw with?" Her question was barbed.

"Y…yes." Christopher had the perfect implement for drawing in his pocket. He picked up the yellowish paper from the floor, grateful that he had something to draw on. As he turned it over, he noticed the phrase *Oakwood Academy, Est 1451* stamped at the top. He wondered if this was perhaps the only relic left from the old school. It made him feel somewhat better, regardless of what state the paper was in.

"Right, good. Well *my dears*, you all have exactly thirty minutes to produce a drawing of my beautiful Piccy. When you have finished, please upload it to the *Oakwood Art, 1E1* folder in the *Incaendium Nebula*. Now - draw!" She clapped her hands and then clicked *play* on her sound system. Suddenly, the room reverberated with a strange frequency.

It sounded like a cross between a whooshing heartbeat and an old computer from the 1980s, struggling to load its programme.

"*What the?*" Stevie uttered to Christopher, but Barbara Kenny cleared her throat and raised one of her painted-on brows. That was enough to make Stevie return to her drawing, but she was not making much progress. Staring at the screen appeared to be causing her a headache.

"Oh, and Christopher, in *your case*, just leave your drawing on my table at the end," Barbara Kenny's row of condemned looking teeth reappeared. She smirked before picking up her dark tablet.

Christopher held his Papa's pen firmly in his hand and started sketching. He knew exactly what to do. He concentrated hard on the shape and definition of the scraggy looking cat. His Papa's pen made easy work of the drawing, and it was a delight to use. The nib coasted exquisitely across the paper. He took his time, paying attention to the subject Picatso. The supercilious cat stared at Christopher, but he shrugged it off and focussed on his work, adding in the shading of the funny looking feline. Even the colour of the ink was perfect in capturing the dark hues of silly cat called Picatso.

When he had finished, Christopher sat back and looked at the result. He was extremely chuffed. If anything, he had somehow managed to make the cat look better. He looked around, expecting the other students – and Stevie – to be finished, but they were all still busy working away. He looked at the red digits on the front wall: *11.20*. He still had twenty minutes left of the lesson. But how was that even possible? Christopher was certain that he had been drawing for at least twenty-five minutes but according to the time, his drawing had only taken five minutes. He glanced back down at the paper, just to check that he was not imagining it all. However, the blueish-black image of Picatso still sat smugly on the paper.

"Is there a problem, *Christopher*?" Another open question

from Barbara Kenny was not what he wanted to hear. She moved forward in her chair, causing the top of her belly to flop onto her desk.

"N...no, M...Mrs Kenny," Christopher answered as quickly as he could, deciding that attracting more attention at this point would be a bad idea.

"Well, get on with it … you little stuttering fool!"

The silence in the art room pulsated in response to Barbara Kenny's cutting outburst. Stevie stared at Christopher, widemouthed. She wished that she had recorded the whole thing, so that she could report the monstrous woman to the teaching council. However, her thoughts were cut abruptly short.

"And do *you* have something to say, *my dear?* I'm sure Dr von Brandt would *love* to hear about your input?" Barbara Kenny's venom silenced Stevie further.

"No Mrs." Stevie felt like all of this was so unfair. She wanted to do something to help Christopher, but for the moment she thought that keeping her mouth shut was the best plan.

However, Barbara Kenny's words planted an idea into Christopher's head. He could not help it. He put his Papa's pen to the paper and started writing underneath his drawing of Picatso. He started writing a story titled "*The Kenny and her Crazy Cat*". Underneath, the words just appeared on the paper...

\*\*\*\*

*"Meow-ow-ow -ow!" Picatso started mewling at the top of his voice. He looked very poorly. He was hunched over on his red throne. His eyes were almost popping out of his scrawny feline forehead.*

*"Oh, my dear, Piccy!" The Kenny screeched, turning her attention*

towards her beloved blue cat. "I'm – " but before she could reach her darling cat, she tripped over something.

A pot of white paint just happened to be lying open at her feet.

She plummeted down like a suitcase of heavy spanners. White paint splashed everywhere. The Kenny's kaftan no longer looked blue. And during all this calamity, Picatso proceeded to meow with such a sickly tone.

The whole class erupted into laughter, pointing, and jeering at The Kenny.

"Stop IT!" demanded The Kenny, who was now struggling to clamber back up onto solid ground. In her skirmish, she had lost her sandals, which made it even harder to find her feet.

Kahk - - - - kaahhkk - - - - kaaahhhkkk - - - - kaaaahhhhkkkk!

Picatso started coughing and heaving violently. It was a bit disturbing watching the little creature move back and forth in such a strange manner.

"NOOOOOOOOO!" Barbara Kenny growled like a Doberman.

And then, the once smug cat called Picatso gagged up a huge furball, complete with his breakfast, all over the red velvet throne.

Christopher sat back, reading the words he had written with his Papa's pen. He started chuckling quietly to himself, thinking how funny it would be to see such a sight. Stevie looked over at him, wondering what he was laughing at. And that was enough to set the two friends off again into hysterics. It had been bubbling up through the whole period. The nervous atmosphere between the two friends collapsed into a phrenzy of giggles.

And then the impossible happened.

Suddenly, the conceited cat started choking on a furball. Its eyes almost popped out of their sockets. The arrogant beast continued to wail loudly. Barbara Kenny waddled like a hysterical hippopotamus towards her raw-boned pet, howling at the top of her voice. She then tripped over a pot of paint, just like the one in Christopher's story. The whale like art teacher fell to the floor, face first into the white puddle. Her tent like kaftan turned a paler shade of blue. In the meantime, the ridiculous Peterbald cat started hacking and spluttering and convulsing.

Christopher rubbed his eyes. His story was happening - right in front of him.

"NOOOOOOOOO PICCY!" Barbara Kenny bellowed like howling hippo, swimming in a pool of white paint. "NOT ON THE BESPOKE VELVET THRONE!"

The cacophony came to its crescendo. Picatso expelled a mixture of fur and anchovies all over the red throne. The smell was disgusting.

Christopher put his hands to his mouth in disbelief. To his right, Stevie already had her mouth covered and she was holding her nose, in yet another attempt to stop her laughter. But it did not work.

Christopher felt bad for this horrid woman. He felt like he had – in some unbelievable way – caused this to happen. He wanted to help, but he did not know how to. But, at the same time, part of him just wanted to see how it would all play out. He looked at the other pupils, expecting their usual stony-faced silence; to his amazement though, they were all laughing - and *filming* their art teacher's misfortune.

# CHAPTER 24
## ~ *A BARBED REVENGE* ~

Barbara Kenny sat crying in the corner of the art classroom, clutching onto her little hairless cat. Picatso appeared to have forgotten all about his previous misfortune; instead, he was now bunting his tiny, bald head into Barbara Kenny. The whole classroom was covered in what Christopher's Papa would call *proper emulsion*. Eighteen burgundy blazered pupils danced around Barbara Kenny and her cat, whooping, and clapping like something straight out of a William Golding novel.

Christopher felt awful. As much as he wanted to seek revenge on Barbara Kenny for her horrible words, this was not what he imagined. Bile gathered at the back of his throat as he watched the throng of pupils; they were like a tsunami of lions snarling at their prey, thrashing about, brandishing their Incaendium devices. To Christopher's horror, they were still filming her. Despite her huge, overbearing size, she looked helpless.

Stevie too sat in silence. Her usual glow had faded. She knew that what was happening now was all wrong. She looked at Christopher and nodded. The two friends had to do something.

Christopher was the first one on his feet. He stepped forward, pushing through the mass of the other mindless pupils. It was like they were all brainwashed, as if they had no idea what they were doing. Right behind him, he could feel the tiny presence of Stevie, urging him on, pushing the other pupils away. Christopher held his hand out to his art teacher.

"Mrs Kenny, are y…you okay?" She pushed Christopher's hands away, but he tried again. "Mrs Kenny, take my hand."

Despite his smaller stature, Christopher managed to pull his hefty art teacher to her feet. He carefully placed her back onto her chair. Picatso hissed at the other pupils, and it was enough to stop the laughter. The blue feline's gaze then returned to Christopher, with an irritated look, as if to say, *that was my job!*

Barbara Kenny slumped back on her chair, glad that it was designed to take the weight of the heaviest of people. She fumbled around on her desk for something. Panic seized the dark pupils in her eyes. Christopher stumbled forward, trying to help her.

"What is it, what do you want?" Christopher articulated - perfectly. In return, Barbara Kenny pointed into her cavernous art cupboard. He was worried that she might be having a seizure, so, concerned that she was about to fall into a dark sleep, he lightly tapped her cheek and asked, "What can I get for you?"

"Chris, your stutter, it's gone." Stevie could not help herself. She knew it was the wrong time to bring up such a thing, but she was amazed. However, Christopher was too involved with what his art teacher wanted.

"Can you get my bag?" Barbara Kenny pointed again towards her cavernous cupboard. Thankfully, the baying pupils were all reformed, sitting like model Oakwood Institute students on their seats. It was like the little blue cat – Picatso – had somehow managed to order all eighteen pupils back to their art stools. Stevie stood, widemouthed, speechless for once at what she had witnessed.

"Stevie, can you get it? Mrs Kenny's bag?" Christopher's voice sounded calm and in control.

Stevie, who was still in awe at his pal's transformation, followed his instructions without question, and stepped forward towards the huge cupboard. She appeared to vanish the minute she stepped over the doorway.

Suddenly, two cold and clammy hands clamped around Christopher's neck, squeezing the life from his lungs. It was the vice grip of Barbara Kenny. She wanted to exact revenge. She stood up effortlessly and pushed her victim down. The back of Christopher's head battered against the ground, sending shockwaves through his skull and spine. He felt like she was holding a knife to his throat, but it was her whopping diamond set ring, grazing against his skin. He frantically looked all around him, in a weak attempt to look for help. To his right, eighteen model students sat, heads down, tapping away mindlessly on their Incaendium tablets. He mumbled a feeble "*help*". But Stevie was nowhere to be seen.

"You think you're so smart," Barbara Kenny snarled angrily, "but I know what game you're playing!"

The Kenny's grip tightened even more, causing Christopher's vision to blur. He felt like he was drowning. The tips of his fingers tingled. His body ached with pain. He looked for something, anything, that he could hit his assailant with. But there was nothing. Then, another figure appeared over him. Perhaps his eyes were deceiving him, but it looked like a police officer. A small, scrawny looking officer. Christopher squinted in attempt to focus, but it was no use. He eventually felt his body crumble into a limp state beneath the lumpy hands of Barbara Kenny.

A dark veil fell over his eyes.

# CHAPTER 25
## ~ *LITTLE STUVAN: CHRISTOPHER'S COMRADE* ~

Christopher felt like he was falling. He tried to open his eyes, but only darkness prevailed. A fiery but glacial like hardness surrounded him. Its aching coldness pulled him down, further into the dark abyss. Suddenly, a white light scolded his eyelids. He tried to move, but his body did not respond. *I must be dead*, Christopher thought.

Unearthly whispers danced around him, trying to confuse him, as if Christopher was the victim in some horrible game of blind-man's buff. The ghostly voices grew in volume. Then they quickly turned into sharp, punctuated inhumane tones, stabbing at his eardrums. He did not recognise any of them.

*But then if I can think, and I can feel, then surely, I am not dead.* Christopher's mind went into overdrive. He focussed on his mum, his Nana Kathy, Sam, and Stevie. Then he thought of Kerry. Slowly and gradually, a familiar force pulled him from the dark and fiery pit he had fallen into.

"Mate? Can you hear me?" Christopher recognised the voice this time.

"Wh…where am I?" Christopher could finally speak. He opened his eyes and gazed at his confined surroundings. Four white padded walls closed in on him. Above him, a huge white light glared in his direction. He felt like he was trapped somewhere between a dentist's surgery and a madhouse.

"Oh, thank Parvati you're okay!" Stevie screamed, as she took a hold of her friend's hand.

Christopher wondered who Parvati was, but the immediate warmth of his friend's hand chased away the coldness. It restored some energy back into his being. He tried to sit up, but a tightness in his chest prevented any movement. When he looked down at his hands, he realised what the problem was.

"I know, right?" Stevie said, realising that her friend could now see the leather shackles binding him down. "This is all wrong," she added, with tears welling up at the sides of her eyes. Without thinking about the consequences, she unfastened the straps that were holding Christopher to the stainless-steel bed.

"Wh…what's going on Stevie? Th…the l…last thing I…I remember…" and then Christopher's thoughts drifted off into another place and time, as if he had been deliberately injected with something to make him forget. "How l…long h…"

"Shhhh, don't worry mate. Just relax. Something really, really weird is going on here," Stevie tried to reassure Christopher, "but I intend on finding out. It's okay, we're alone. For now."

Christopher felt relief at his friend's words. Perhaps he was not going crazy after all.

"B…but what h…happened," he asked, desperate to know where it had all gone wrong. "And where a…am I?"

"Chris, I wish I had all of the answers but all I know is that something really weird happened when I stepped into that cupboard," Stevie's cheeks paled. "It was like time stopped. I don't how to explain it."

"G…go on," Christopher nodded to Stevie, urging her to continue.

"At first, all I could see were shelves upon shelves of art materials. And then, right in front of me lay a whole stack of Incaendium tablets – there must have been about twenty of them. I couldn't see the Kenny's bag anywhere."

"S…so, she was l…lying!" Christopher shot straight up with a newfound energy; his hands broke completely free from the loosened restraints. He grabbed Stevie's hand tightly, "g…go on. Wh…what next?"

"Chris, you won't believe it, but next thing was, I felt like I couldn't move. I felt suffocated, as if someone was choking me. I know it sounds silly, but believe me, I couldn't get any air into my lungs. And then, I heard you - I heard your voice. And then in front of me, a white light flashed. Four times. It was so blinding that I fell to my knees. So, I crawled … away from whatever it was. And then I got to my feet and stumbled forwards, out of the cupboard, and then…" Stevie fell silent. Her big brown eyes filled with tears again as she looked at Christopher. "And then I saw you, lying motionless on the floor. I was back in The Kenny's classroom."

Christopher pulled Stevie close in a friendly embrace, whispering, "*g…go on mate, I n…need to know.*"

Stevie sat back, wiping the tears from her eyes. She cleared her throat and then puffed out her chest to shake off her emotions. "I thought you were… gone. And all the while, the big, fat Kenny waved her hands screaming: *he's fainted, he's fainted.*"

A cold hand tickled the hairs on Christopher's neck. "B…but she was t…trying to s…strangle m…me".

"Mate, I know," Stevie responded. "The Kenny was standing over you, without even helping. I was the first to cradle your head in my hands." She stopped for a second, puffing her chest out again. The amber in her brown eyes glazed a little. "When I realised you were breathing, I turned you on your side into the recovery position. And then I turned to look up at the Kenny for help, but she was still standing there, staring at her fat, puffy hands. But the weirdest thing was, she held them out in front of her, fingers rigid as if she were clutching onto an imaginary ball. Her eyes were so dark. I've never seen anything like it. Then I looked at the red mark on your poor neck. And that was when it happened." Stevie's cheeks flushed. She pulled her hand away from Christopher. Her fists tightened with rage.

"Wh…what happened?" Christopher had to find the broken pieces of his blackout. The Kenny had caused this. This was no tiramavee.

"Chris, she lied. I saw it with my own eyes". Stevie's jaws

clenched.

Christopher was amazed at how masculine and feminine she looked at the same time: she was both beautiful and handsome. There was something so striking about her jawline: Stevie somehow resembled a pop icon or film star from the fifties; like James Dean and Madhubala intertwined.

"G...go on," Christopher urged, dying to know what really happened.

"Well, when Dr von Brandt stormed into the Kenny's room, she shouted something I will never forget." Stevie's face looked drained. "The Kenny said that *you* had *caused everything*. She said that *you* had *encouraged* the *other students* in the room to *shout and scream*. That was when I shouted, *noooo!*" Stevie sat back in her chair, covering her eyes with her fisted hands.

"It's o...o...okay Stevie. I c...cry too. D...don't hide your tears. My m...mum used to say that i...it was a sign of b...being human." Christopher held his hands up to Stevie and pulled her fists away from her eyes. She looked at him and smiled.

"What are we like? My father is always saying to me: *little Stuvan, if you want to be a boy, boys don't cry*. But Chris," Stevie clenched her jaws again, "these are tears of anger. I'm so angry at her. The Kenny lied. It's so unfair. They are interviewing a handful of the students right now, to hear *their* side of the story but they have not even considered mine. I was there."

"B...but Stevie. You w...weren't there, well a...at least, all of the t...time. You w...were in the c...cupboard. The K...Kenny will use that a...against your side of the s...story."

Silence skulked around them. Christopher was right and Stevie knew it. Whatever she could add to the events of what happened, it would not be enough. It would not be enough for Dr von Brandt. The two friends knew what lay ahead of them. Stevie did not see everything that happened between Barbara Kenny and Christopher, so her testimony would not stand.

Suddenly, the door of the tiny white room slammed open. A tall, sinewy figure stood at the entrance, staring menacingly at Christopher and Stevie. "WHAT IS GOING ON IN HERE?! You, *boy*! I thought I told you to wait outside my office!" It was Dr von Brandt.

"Sorry sir, but I wanted to see my friend, Chris," Stevie replied, aware that the horrible headteacher was talking – or rather shouting – directly at her. "I had to make sure he was okay. I hope you understand."

Christopher was taken by how polite Stevie sounded, despite the horrible way Dr von Brandt had spoken to her.

"Well, get out. Go to my office!" Dr von Brandt snarled, pushing his strange blue glasses further up onto the bridge of his nose. "I will deal with you shortly!"

Stevie made a fist and then mockingly punched her friend on the shoulder, totally ignoring the aggression unleashed by the horrible headmaster. She put a brave face on, trying to transform into the boy that she wanted to be, but at the same time, she had an aching sadness that still clung to her past. She was struggling with change – one of life's constant battles. Christopher was fighting the same war, so he was glad to have Stevie as his comrade.

"I'll see you on the other side Chris," Stevie winked, as she left the cold, cramped cell like room.

The door clicked shut.

Dr von Brandt stepped towards Christopher. He stood for what felt like an eternity, just staring at Christopher through the opaque blue of his glasses.

"So..." the horrible headmaster started, "what have you got to say for yourself?"

Christopher had so many things he wanted to say to this horrible man, but he did not know where to begin.

"*Shall I start for you?*" Dr von Brandt's rhetorical question was spiked with so much malice. It was a question that Christopher did not know how to answer. "Let's see," the horrible headmaster continued. "Hmmm, how about the point where you made a complete mockery of Mrs Kenny?"

Christopher's blood ran cold. He feared this would happen. He summoned all of his courage and spoke up, "I…I eh…, I didn't. I t…tried to help her. She had a s…sort of f…funny turn, so m…me and S…Stevie tried to help." Christopher hoped that his explanation was enough to appease the situation. Sadly, it did not help his case one bit. The horrible headmaster threw Christopher's handwritten tale onto his lap: *The Kenny and her Crazy Cat*. Christopher grimaced. The drawing of the scrawny cat – Picatso - added fuel to the already burning predicament he was in.

It really did look like Christopher had caused the calamity in Barbara Kenny's art class.

Time crawled forward awkwardly towards Christopher. He picked up the old Oakwood cartridge paper and mustered up a few words. "This …. this is n…not what it l…looks like, s…sir." Christopher tried to overcome his stutter. But it was useless. He felt like he was talking to his father.

"I think *this* says it *all*," smirked the horrible headmaster.

"B…but I w…wrote this story b…before it a…all happened." Christopher could see that his words were useless.

"I know exactly what you did, Master Muir. You wrote that story just to make a travesty of one of our finest art teachers. And what have you got to say for yourself?" Dr von Brandt gave Christopher no opportunity to respond, he just continued, like a snarling Doberman with a rag between its teeth. "And then you encouraged *every one* of those *impeccable* students to join in. I know. I interviewed them."

"That's a lie!" Christopher shouted at the top of his lungs. An unfamiliar feeling of rage broiled inside of him again, causing his stutter to disintegrate in his heat of anger. He was so outraged. He had been accused of a crime that he did not commit. "Y…you b…brainwashed those other pupils! A…ask Stevie for her side of the story."

*"You* are the *guilty party here Master Muir.* I *know,* and *this* is the proof. There is no need to ask Stevie."* Then the horrible headmaster snatched Christopher's story from his bed and placed it in his pocket. "I'll take this," he growled, "it's evidence. And I *know* all about *your wild imagination,* so *no one* will believe you!"

Christopher sat in silence. He felt broken. The horrible headmaster had cornered him, giving him no way out, no way to explain what truly happened.

"B...but why am I h...here? A...and wh...why am I enchained in these sh...shackles?"

Again, Christopher's words melted into the ether; Dr von Brandt had turned his attention towards his Incaendium tablet. It was flashing red, demanding his attention. He stared at the screen, lost in a blistering binary world. The lenses of Dr von Brandt's glasses turned red. Christopher was about to ask his question again, but the door of the tiny room creaked open slowly.

Christopher's father stood in the doorway.

# CHAPTER 26
## ~ *THE CELL OF THE THREE-HEADED SERPENT* ~

Christopher sat up, leaning forward in the direction of the ajar door. Strained voices slithered through the gap. It was just enough to hear what was being said.

"Titus, I think the restraints are a bit extreme, don't you?" It was the voice of Aiden Brenton. Christopher could recognise his father's voice anywhere.

"On the contrary, no Aid, *I disagree*. Your *son* was having a *strange turn*. The restraints were for *his protection*." Dr von Brandt sounded confident and calm. If anything, he sounded convincing.

"Yes, but all the same, you could have called me. *Right away*."

Mr Brenton's voice appeared to crack upon his final words. Christopher thought that his father sounded human for once. Perhaps he cared about his son after all.

"*Shhhhhh, you have to know ….*" whispered voices faded into the emptiness of the corridor behind the door. It was as if the two foreboding figures did not want prying ears to hear their words.

Christopher moved from his bed, towards the half-closed door. He stood as still freshly fallen snow on a winter's morning.

"*I warned you Aiden.*" Dr von Brandt's voice sounded strained, as if he was about to reveal a horrible truth. "Your son has a wild imagination. It is damaging him. But worst of all, it is damaging *to you – and your reputation!*"

Time recoiled. It waited on Aiden Brenton's reply.

"Are you aware – *Titus* – just *how much money me* and *my company* plough into your *so-called Institution?*" Mr Brenton sounded enraged.

"Yes, I do, but…"

Dr von Brandt's voice evaporated into the air.

Christopher could no longer hear his father's voice or the horrible headmaster's. Their tones were replaced with a high-pitched screaming.

Suddenly, it seemed like there was no air in the room. Christopher looked down at his arms to find that they were doused in pearly beads of perspiration. He felt feverish. His vision blurred. Weakness attacked his body. He fell back, thumping against the hard-metallic bed, causing the wheels to screech away from him. He landed with a thump on the floor.

Darkness obscured Christopher's vision. Again.

\*\*\*\*

"Wake up! You're an embarrassment!" Aiden Brenton slapped Christopher's face with the full force of his right hand. He had never been one for compassion, not towards anyone. The release of aggression towards his son caused his face to crack into what looked like an evil Jack-o'-lantern smile.

"Wh...what the?" Christopher rubbed his cheek. His face ached, as if he had been stung by a scorpion. "D...d...dad?"

"*Do not* call me *that*. You know that I do not go for terms of endearment!" Aiden Brenton's words snapped at his son's face; they were more painful than his physical strike.

"Do you have *any idea* the lengths I went to just to get you enrolled into this school?"

Christopher sat in silence, holding his cheek like a little lost puppy. His face felt like it was on fire. He looked at his father with sadness, trying to search for any morsel of empathy. But there was only anger.

"I take it from your stupid silence that you have no idea. None?"

Christopher had nothing to say. At least not to his father. He wanted to be back home, with his Nana Kathy and Sam.

"*You're just like your mother,*" Mr Brenton spat out his

words with venom. "She was always giving me the silent treatment. I don't know how - *or why* - I put up with it for so long!"

"Shut up!" Christopher's sudden command put a stop to his father's insult. His mother was such a good soul – in everyone's eyes – so there was no way that Christopher would allow his father to speak ill of his mother. "How DARE you!" Anger broiled inside Christopher.

"Well, well, well. Look at *my son*. This is what I have been looking for: a man in the making. No stutter. No weakness. Your anger impresses me."

Christopher flinched. He felt cold. He felt horrible. He longed for his mother's soothing voice, just to say: *it will all be okay.*

But it was not going to be okay. Not this time.

"Y…you have n…no right to speak about mum like that." Christopher shivered; his unwelcome stutter returned. He wanted to say more, but he could not find the energy. The power of his father's force was unbearable.

"Sooo, the cat's got your tongue again." Mr Brenton laughed maliciously.

A shudder skipped across Christopher's heart. His father had used one of his Nana Kathy's sayings. He was clearly trying to incite yet another fiery reaction from his son.

"Since your stutter has returned, I will finish off our little discussion. I am going to leave here in a minute, and when I do, I want you to go and apologise to Dr von Brandt. I also want you to type up a letter of apology to Mrs Kenny."

"N…n…no I – " Christopher's jaws clenched tightly with anger. He was about to shout and scream at his father, but Mr Benton did not let him finish his sentence.

"And then I'm going to see your Nana, to tell her all about your embarrassing behaviour this morning. But, most importantly, I'm going to tell her that *you are coming to live with me!*"

Christopher started shaking uncontrollably. His father's words evoked a strange energy, something that he had never felt before. Something propelled him forward. He landed on his feet, one step away from his father. Automatically, he raised his index finger and pointed it into his father's face.

"I will never, *ever*, come to stay with you. Never!"

But Christopher's outburst of confidence was not enough to smite the powers of Aiden Brenton. The tall, dark figure cackled malevolently.

At that very point, Christopher felt a divide rupture between him and his father. Aiden Brenton seemed so far away from his son, even though they were standing less than a metre apart. Both father and son had never been close, but something had occurred, something had shifted, something more powerful than life itself. Christopher stared at the dark, almost black, inkiness of his father's eyes. They appeared to swirl like two magnetic whirlpools, pulling him down into a shadowy place of torment. The fluorescent lights above them flickered. Once, twice, three times.

The room plunged into darkness.

Christopher's heart pounded uncontrollably. He held his hands out in front of him, trying to fumble his way towards the corner of the small room. Somehow, having two walls to hold onto would be better than clutching at nothing in the dark. He tried to keep his composure; he did not want his father to sense his fear. But something was not right. This was no power cut. Despite the tiny space of the room he had been occupying, Christopher could not find any walls.

"*Mwah ha ha ha!*" Time and space blended with Mr Brenton's cackling. It recoiled around the room like a snake about to pounce on its prey.

"*Christ-opher?*" a horrible, devilish voice intoned, almost as if to say: *I'm coming for you.*

Suddenly, something scorching fell upon Christopher's shoulders, clamping around them, pushing him downwards. Strangely, his knees did not clash with the ground; instead, he plummeted uncontrollably into an even murkier darkness. It was like the end of some horrible nightmare.

But this time, he could not come around from his bad dream; this time, he felt awake.

Splash!

Christopher collided with something, but it was not solid matter. An icy cold entity slithered around his body. He tried to shout for help, but a wall of water caused him to gargle and splutter. Somehow, someway, he had plummeted into the depths of darkest waters. He felt like he had been thrown overboard, with no warning, into the clutches of some unforgiving sea. Panicking, he kicked, flapped, and flailed through the dark water. His lungs felt like they were on fire. Then, from the abyss below, an unearthly scream shuddered, sending watery shockwaves towards Christopher. Something was coming for him. Its shrill squall swirled in circles, tormenting him, confusing him, as if it was trying to pull him down towards the nothingness below. Numbness gnawed at his fingertips as he thrashed in the water. But then he thought of his mum and remembered how she had taught him to swim. He focussed on that one time where she had lifted him above water – on holiday, many years ago - when he thought he was drowning. It was a fading memory and it all seemed so far away, but it was the beacon of light that Christopher needed now. So, he beat on, further, harder, determined to reach the light above the water. Every part of his body ached.

Finally, it was all worth it. He was above the surface of the water. He inhaled the welcome air around him, allowing his heart to relax and his breathing to return to normal. Despite his leaden limbs, Christopher hauled himself out of the water and onto dry land. He clambered to his feet and shivered uncontrollably as he surveyed his surroundings. He could smell the fresh scent of lavender.

He was in the garden of Milaw House.

Darkness cloaked everything, except for the white light of the full moon accentuating the natural beauty of the garden. Silvery droplets of dew coated the lavender buds beside the old lean-to. In the moonlight, they looked like jewel encrusted treasures. Christopher stumbled forwards. The door of the lean-to was open. Warm, welcoming light glowed from within, beckoning to him. Familiar music danced towards him. Christopher knew that it was his Papa, leading him to safety, away from whatever was preying on him.

"*EEEEEEEEEEEEEEEEEEE!*" Without warning, two nefarious talons flew towards Christopher, pinning him to the ground. In the darkness above, a disgusting creature snapped at him, stinging his face and neck. It was so strong, so powerful, it pushed him down into the murky wetness of the grass. In the fading moonlight it looked like a huge scorpion. Suddenly, water emanated from everywhere, plunging Christopher back into a pool of darkness.

Nothingness gnawed at Christopher. He felt tired, empty, numb. But just before he shut his eyes, he saw what looked like a three-headed serpent.

Aidan Brenton was one of the three heads, snarling and snapping at Christopher.

# CHAPTER 27
## ~ *THE PAINTED INTERLOPER* ~

When Christopher opened his eyes, he found himself in the office of Dr von Brandt. He knew instantly where he was because of the ridiculous oil painting hanging in front of him. It was obscene. But Christopher was so strangely taken by the detail of the artwork. He stood up and moved towards it, leaving behind a murky puddle of water on the plastic chair.

The stature of Dr von Brandt stood smugly, drenched in a dark red cloak, complete with an evil looking raven perched on his outstretched arm. The carrion bird's eyes were obscured by a black mask; only the prominence of its knife-like beak burst through its tiny hood. The brush strokes were so intricate. Depending on how you squinted at it, the portrait looked like a relic from the past; in other ways, it looked like the artist had just painted it. The overall dark hue of the paint was overwhelming. It was so sombre. It reminded Christopher of a Rembrandt painting, like an image he had seen in one of his mother's art books. He remembered it so vividly because it terrified him as a young boy. This painting had the same effect: it was draped in obsidian shades, all except for the contrasting light shining upon the subject's face. The expression on Dr von Brandt's face was so indignant, so arrogant, but so strangely familiar. He looked unearthly pale along with his hollow cheeks and blue glasses. Christopher stared at the darkness of the painting. He reached out his hand and touched the oil on canvas.

The paint was still wet.

"Chiaroscuro!" Dr von Brandt shouted as he entered his office.

"Ciao!" Christopher replied, grateful that his Nana Kathy had taught him how to say hello in so many different

191

languages.

"You silly boy! SIT DOWN!"

Christopher fell back into the seat behind him. He was suddenly aware how wet he was. His uniform was soaked right through to his vest. Horripilation prowled all over his skin. He then remembered the three headed serpent and the dark, endless pool of nothingness. His teeth began to chatter. It was like his mind had momentarily blackened out, as if he had been drugged.

"I was not saying hello in Italian." Dr von Brandt halted Christopher's malaise. "Chiaroscuro is Italian for light and shadow. It's a classic technique that creates the illusion of illumination from a specific source shining on the figures and objects in the painting. I have my contacts - my artist is a secret," he declared, tapping his beaked nose.

Christopher stopped shivering. Instead, he actually felt bored, as if he was being lectured at. Without his control, his mouth fell agape with yawning tiredness. Out of politeness, he held his hand over his mouth.

"Am I boring you, Master Muir?" The sudden nastiness in Dr von Brandt's voice stopped Christopher's feeling of tedium. "*Or, should I say, Master Brenton?*"

Christopher's fingers dug deep into the arms of the hard-plastic chair he was sitting in. He wanted to stand up and scream in his horrible headmaster's face, but he could hear his mother's voice of reason: *hold onto your integrity, not the hot coals.*

"My...my second name is Muir. Not Brenton." Christopher forced every letter, every word out with all his might.

"Well, whatever you are, whoever you are, we are going to have to make this work. Because your father says so."

And there it was. It was the admission that Christopher was waiting on. He had heard it when he had been eavesdropping earlier, but he could not believe how forthright his horrible headteacher had just been with him. Perhaps, though, it explained the way he had been looking at him so intently during assembly.

"So, shall, I continue? Again?" Dr von Brandt's face pursed into a tight spout of superiority, as if he was a person that was always in the right.

Christopher had no choice. He sat in a shambled mess. His uniform was drenched in water and his damp hair was still plastered to his head. He still had no idea where his bag or belongings were.

"Can you like to tell me what this is for?" Dr von Brandt held up Papa Tommy's key. In the artificial light of the horrible headmaster's office, it looked like something from Egyptian times. "This looks incredibly old. And awfully expensive. So, do explain."

Christopher gulped down a wave panic. He inhaled a deep breath and tried to speak, without his stutter.

"Th…th…that's" Christopher swallowed down another lungful of air. "It's my Papa's key. I carry it for g…good luck. I want that back. Or…or… I…" Christopher could not think of a consequence.

"Or what?" Dr von Brandt smirked, pushing his glasses further up onto the bridge of his hooked beak.

Christopher thought quickly. He recalled the discussion between his father and his horrible headmaster. It gave him the strength that he needed.

"Or … I will tell my father!"

Thankfully, this was exactly the exclamation that Christopher needed. Without hesitation, Dr von Brandt handed over the key. He looked like a browbeaten bird of prey. So that was his weakness: Aiden Brenton had control over the horrible headmaster. Christopher was relieved. He placed his Papa's key back into his blazer pocket. He was even more relieved to find his Papa's pen, still snuggly nestled in his pocket.

"Master," there was a pause, "*Muir.*" Another pause followed. Despite the threat of Aiden Brenton, Dr von Brandt looked like he had climbed back atop his perch of confidence.

Christopher knew that an unspeakable instruction followed. He sat back, further in the hard-plastic chair, feeling the water ooze out of every entity of his being. He was expecting the next few words to be all about the strange dark waters in the small cell. Surely there was an explanation for what had happened. He felt like he had been drugged. But the horrible headmaster did not even utter a word about it.

"When you leave my office," Dr von Brandt declared, "you will go directly to the gymnasium locker room and sort out your appearance. I don't care how you do it but tidy yourself up and make yourself look like you are more worthy of attending Oakwood Institute. Then, from there, you will go to the Incaendium library of computers. In there, you will type up a letter of apology to Mrs Kenny."

Christopher's thoughts travelled to his Nana Kathy. He sat back, once again in the wetness of his horrible blazer and shirt. He felt so sad at how he would have let his Nana down. But he felt deep down in his stomach *a gut feeling* – as his Nana would say - that something was very, very wrong. He knew, that despite the horrible nature of everything, his Nana would see the truth. Surely, she would believe her grandson.

Unfortunately, Dr von Brandt started again, "And then, from there, you will type up an absolute declaration of how privileged it is to be –"

*RING--RING—RING--RING*

Dr von Brandt almost dropped the vibrating Incaendium device out of his hands. The lens of his glasses flashed red as he tapped the glass of the device. And then, at that very moment, he turned into a more robotic form of the usual von Brandt. At least two minutes passed before he said anything.

"Yes. I hear you. So, what do you want me to do?"

Christopher sat wondering who the mysterious caller was. He moved further forward, trying to listen in to his horrible headmaster's conversation.

"Yes, yes, yes," Dr von Brandt dismissively added, "I have all the information." He paused and then looked up at Christopher.

*Tap - tap – rap - rap.* Dr von Brandt's long fingernails drummed on his desk. It was such an unnerving sound, like an unwanted visitor tapping on a window. Christopher had never noticed it before, but the horrible headmaster's nails looked like they had been painted with dark grey nail polish.

*Tap - tap – rap - rap.* Dr von Brandt grinned at Christopher. It was so ghastly and grim that it turned the air denser.

"I will tell him now." Without as much as a goodbye, the horrible headmaster hung up on his caller.

Dead air dangled heavily above the horrible headmaster and his student. Christopher shivered uncontrollably in his damp uniform. He knew something terrible was about to happen. He crossed his fingers.

"Well, I shan't ramble on with this." Dr von Brandt started. "There's no point in sugar coating what's happened. That was Aid, I mean – your father. Your grandmother has had some kind of accident. Fell off stepladders, or something to that sort."

Dr von Brandt continued, but Christopher could not hear any other words. His mind shut off after *grandmother* and *accident*. His head swirled with negative energy. It reverberated around and around like an off cycle washing machine, declaring that *Christopher was the culprit, it was all his fault, Nana Kathy fell off the ladders the minute she heard what had happened.* Sadly, Christopher went to his go-to mode of panic and guilt. He was certain that he had caused Nana Kathy's accident.

"CHRISTOPHER!" Dr von Brandt squawked in Christopher's face. It was enough to bring a poor soul out from its shadow.

Christopher opened his eyes. He felt like he was floating on the floor in front of the horrible headmaster. He dug his short fingernails into the artificial arms of the plastic chair again. Just touching the synthetic surface brought him back to his senses. It was another one of the calming techniques he had been encouraged to perform in counselling after his mum died: *find something mundane. Count the number of brown shoes in the room. That will bring you round.*

"Right, so you are awake." Dr von Brandt continued, with no concern for Christopher's blackout. "I will repeat this again, seeing as you did not hear the first time. Your father will be outside in approximately ten minutes. He will wait for you in the main car park. He will take to the hospital. To see your grandmother."

Although the horrible headmaster almost cackled out his last sentence, Christopher felt better just to hear the words *hospital* and *see your grandmother*. He hoped that meant that she would be okay, that she would survive whatever had happened to her.

Such words were never uttered when his mother died.

Christopher stumbled to his feet. He felt dizzy and sick all at the same time. He held his hands to his temples and shut his eyes. He focussed on the vision of his poorly Nana and summoned up all his strength. He inhaled deeply and exhaled slowly. He was ready. When he opened his eyes, Dr von Brandt was already in front of him at the door.

"How on earth did Aiden ever manage to have a son like you?" He declared, thrusting Christopher's school bag into his hands.

****

Christopher removed his blazer as he stepped into the corridor outside Dr von Brandt's room. Despite the dampness of his clothes, he felt hot, almost feverish. Automatically, he rolled up his sleeves. Thankfully, his collar had already been loosened. His tie was nowhere to be seen but presumably it had been removed after the incident with Barbara Kenny. He blundered forward, away from the den of deputy headteachers, all crawling after the horrible Dr von Brandt. He looked back through the glass doors, only to see the reptilian sneer of Ms Haken-Hughes. She waved her bony, ivory like index finger back and forth in a mocking manner, like a huge crocodile trying to hypnotise its prey.

*BEEP ---- BEEP ---- BEEP ---- BEEP!*

The harsh siren of Oakwood Institute blared, declaring that it was time for afternoon recess. Ms Haken-Hughes vanished back into the wilderness of the headteacher's quarters. But Christopher quickly forgot all about her serpentiform smile because his hunger had other ideas. He had completely missed lunchtime, and he felt it. His stomach growled painfully. He staggered towards the edge of the balcony, feeling weak. Beneath him, a swarm of Oakwood pupils filled the Artery. They all moved in an orderly fashion, like worker bees in a hive receiving command after command from their queen. Every single pupil held an Incaendium device in their hands. No verbal communication occurred amongst the flock of pupils.

"Chris! Mate" Stevie pounded up towards her poorly looking friend. It was as if she had been waiting, all this time, waiting on him leaving the lair of the horrible headmaster. "Here, have this!"

Before Christopher could say anything, he had some tasty paneer cheese toast thrust into his mouth. It was delicious; just what he needed. He faltered back towards the wall, allowing the food to energise him. He smiled, but then he quickly remembered his Nana. He felt like someone had punched him in the stomach.

"My N…Nana!"

"Chris, your arms!" Stevie grabbed a hold of her friend's forearms with concern. "What in Ganapati's name are these marks?!"

Christopher looked down in concern. There, just below his biceps, lay two ghastly bruises. Thankfully though, Stevie's welcome food began to fill his friend with more energy. His thoughts became clearer. The concern for his grandmother jumped to the forefront of his mind.

"S…Stevie I have so much to tell you, but I…I have to go. M…My Nana's h…had an accident."

Stevie understood her friend. She quickly scribbled down something onto a chewing gum wrapper taken from her pocket and handed it to Christopher. "Here, take this. It's my number. Please, text me later, or better still, call me and tell me how things are." Automatically, she took her cap off and placed it onto her friend's head. She thought that it might help stop his shivering.

Christopher smiled at Stevie's kindness. He was so grateful for their kindling friendship. He instinctively moved forward and hugged her. The two friends embraced tightly, grateful that they had found each other in their own awkwardness. Perhaps it was the moment that caught Stevie, but just there and then, she looked more feminine than Christopher had ever seen her. But he could also see that it was just a glimpse, a remnant even, of what she was about to leave behind before she transitioned into who she really wanted to be.

"Christopher?" It was Kerry. Smarting tears made her eyes look like beautiful shimmering emeralds. "I've been calling and texting you since last night, but you haven't returned any of my calls or messages." She feared the worst as she saw Christopher hugging a beautiful girl with beaming brown eyes.

Christopher pulled back from Stevie, aware of what his friendly cuddle might appear like to Kerry. Thankfully, Stevie instantly read the situation and moved towards Kerry.

"Hello," Stevie declared, in the deepest tone she could muster, offering her hand to Kerry. She had been practising her voice and it paid off. "I'm Stevie – Chris's new friend. I was just hugging him because his Nana's in hospital."

Kerry felt both sad and happy at the same time. She was pleased to hear – and see – that Stevie was a friend of Christopher's. Kerry now understood. She could see something charming in the little, short-haired, boyish-girl; so, Kerry was glad to meet their acquaintance. However, an eruption of sadness and anxiety still bubbled to the surface of Kerry's mouth.

"Your Nana, Christopher. What's happened?!

"N...Nana K...Kathy's had a fall. Th...that's all I know. My f...f...father w...will be waiting." Christopher almost choked out his final few words. He was ever so glad that Stevie had instantly taken care of any misunderstandings because he did not have the energy to justify anything. He could barely explain what had happened to his Nana, never mind the last few hours of the dark pool, the cruel hands of the Kenny or the serpent.

"Yes, so he must go now!" Stevie demanded, steering both Christopher and Kerry downstairs towards the foyer of Oakwood Institute.

Usually, Kerry did not like anyone bossing her around but, in this case, she could see that Stevie had Christopher's – and his Nana Kathy's – best intentions at heart. Kerry encouraged Christopher, along with Stevie.

"Th...thanks." Christopher uttered. He wanted to stay and spend more time with both Kerry and Stevie. Just being in their company made everything more bearable.

"You'd better go," Kerry said, hugging Christopher as she almost pushed him out into the daylight. "You have my number, so you'd better text me this time," she added.

Christopher looked back at Stevie and Kerry standing in the artificial stone entrance. They were both smiling. Stevie winked at Christopher before declaring, "don't worry, I'll look after Kerry."

# CHAPTER 28
## ~ *BIRDIE AND THE BELASCO* ~

Christopher staggered down the concrete steps of Oakwood Institute's threshold. The fine rain had transformed into a greasy drizzle, coating everything in an uncomfortable and sickly hue. Christopher longed for the beautiful sight of Sam. His striking appearance would have been such a welcome sight in amongst the murk that lay in front of his master. Surely, the white Siberian would be in the back of Aiden Brenton's car, eagerly waiting Christopher's arrival. After all, there would have been nobody else at Milaw House to look after Sam.

Just before Christopher reached the last few steps, he stood for a moment, gazing at the car park in front of him. A maze of cars lay ahead: they all looked like filthy cockroaches trying to find their way through an infinite maze of dirt. But, right there, under his nose, in the most prestigious of car park spaces, lay his father's black Belasco. It looked like a scarab beetle, scrambling its way to the top of other menial insects.

Something else caught Christopher's eye. In amongst the black and grey tones of the car park, the colour red flared. A tall, pale figure with fiery hair stood at the driver's side of his father's car.

The pale hand of Aiden Brenton appeared. He passed something out of the window – it appeared to be a little black box. The receiver of this dark object held her ashen white hands out. She opened the box. Then she jumped up and down several times before twirling around on the spot.

It was Candice Hayden.

Christopher sprinted down the last few steps at the front of Oakwood Institute. He had to find out the reason why Candice was speaking to his father. But when he looked up, the red leviathan had vanished. Christopher stopped. He quickly surveyed the drab surroundings of the school. There was no flicker of that fiery hair anywhere. It was like Candice had suddenly turned invisible.

A cold breeze cut through the air, slicing through the damp mugginess that had been lingering for far too long. Christopher shuddered. This time he really was not looking forward to seeing his father. He could not shake off the vision of the three-headed serpent.

"CHRISTOPHER! HURRY UP!" Aiden Brenton was already standing outside his black Belasco sports car. "Look at the state of you. Get in, before someone sees you with me! And take off that ridiculous looking baseball cap!"

Christopher reluctantly removed Stevie's hat. He placed it in his bag and then moved forward to open the front door of the passenger side, but it would not budge. He looked up, across the roof of the car, only to find his father sneering at him.

"You're sitting in the back. *What* made you think that I would allow you to sit in the front?!" Mr Brenton laughed at his son in such a condescending manner. The back door slowly opened in response to a button he pressed on his Incaendium phone.

Christopher wanted to kick the car with all his might, but he swallowed down his anger and stepped into the darkness of the back seat. He said nothing to his father.

The inside of the car was even more stand-offish than its exterior. Black leather upholstery blended in with all the interior's fittings. It was hard to make out anything. The windows were black, except for the flashing scarlet lights radiating from the ridiculous gadgets on the dashboard. Even the front windscreen had a strange dark tone; it was a miracle that Aiden Brenton could see where he was going. Bluish-grey smoke floated heavily in the air. It was stifling. It caused Christopher's throat to burn and his eyes to water. Aiden Brenton was smoking a Gran Habano: a ridiculously priced cigar that he would only roll out on special occasions.

It was like he was celebrating something.

Christopher felt like he was in a hearse, going to his own funeral. He could barely move in the cramped space of the two back seats.

"It's one of the perks of having a sports car," Aiden Brenton interrupted his son's morose thoughts. "It's what make this Belasco fly. Less passengers equals more speed."

Christopher looked at the side profile of his father's face as they sped along the road. He did not recognise him from such an angle. His features appeared to be more pointed than he remembered. They looked so angular in the raven darkness of his car's interior. Christopher felt like he did not belong with him. He had so many things that he wanted to say – or shout even – to his father. But one burning question sat uncomfortably at the edge of his lips: *what did you give to Candice Hayden?* However, Christopher bit his tongue and plunged his hands deep into his blazer pockets. He decided to keep quiet for the time being. At least he still had his Papa's key and pen. His focus first – and foremost - was his Nana. Sam also hounded his thoughts. Where was his trusted Siberian?

"It's rude to stare," Mr Brenton asserted, aware that his son had been looking at him all this time. "What's the matter? Have you nothing to say? Again. We never really got to finish our little conversation, did we? I think you were about to –".

"WHAT'S HAPPENED TO MY NANA!" Christopher's anger and concern broiled to the surface, melting away any stammering. This was one question that he had to ask.

"Mwah, ha, ha," Mr Brenton chuckled callously. "I'm impressed by your anger."

"J…just tell me. Is Nana Kathy o…okay?"

"You'll see her, all in good time." The black car stopped. "All in good time."

Aiden Brenton flicked his rear-view mirror so that he could see his son. Christopher met with a dark, penetrating stare and it made him feel very uneasy; so, he quickly glanced away. He looked outside instead, searching the dim windows for an answer. He wondered why the car had halted.

"This is not the hospital!" Christopher declared effortlessly, again, with no stutter.

*SLAM!*

Without any warning, Aiden Brenton left his son sitting the in sullenness of the coffin like car. Christopher felt anger pounding at his temples. He could not believe that his father could make such a casual pit-stop on the way to see his Nana Kathy. Rage broiled all the way down to his fingertips, but instead of allowing its dark power to take over, he sat back in the confines of his father's car and inhaled deeply. At first, it was difficult because of the stale cigar smoke lingering in the dead air, but then he tried to imagine a serene place, full of healing, just like the other world he had visited in Ferncross Library. Christopher envisioned a forest full of dancing lavender, reaching out to him, soothing his outrage.

Thankfully, it worked.

Tranquillity washed over him. Christopher's head felt clearer. He squinted his eyes at the dark glass of the passenger seat window. Beyond the gloomy interior, he could just make out muted shapes and forms. Two dark figures stood outside, one much smaller than the other. They were deep in conversation. Their angular shapes looked like sharp shadows flickering in the flares of an unruly fire. Christopher instantly recognised the taller of the two forms as being his father, but there was something familiar about the other. Christopher looked down at the window switch. Curiosity caused him to place his index finger onto the black button. He had to hear what his father was talking about and why he had stopped so abruptly on the way to the hospital.

"*I'm not sure Mr Benton,*" quivered the smaller man. "*The data has already been captured - and sent to the surveillance department.*"

Christopher leaned closer to the gap in the window. From behind the black veil of the glass, he could just make out some detail of the smaller man. A slight arch in his back made him look so insignificant next to Mr Brenton. Christopher almost felt sorry for the small man.

"Well, you had better make it possible. My company owns *everything*, from the CCTV cameras right down to the digital data they record." Mr Brenton leaned in, towards the small, dainty looking man. "*Send the data to my email, and then erase the footage from the database. And do it quickly!*" His whisper sounded more like a snarl.

Even in the darkness of the car, Christopher could see that the measly looking man was shaking. The trembling figure looked a lot like Officer Ruiz.

"So that will be all my good chap," Aiden Brenton declared, before patting the scrawny looking man on the back.

Christopher had witnessed such false politeness before; it was all part of Aiden Brenton's act. Sadly, hundreds – if not thousands – of innocent souls had fallen prey to his superficial charm. Like a hive of mindless worker bees, they would buzz around him, providing his artificial core with honeyed compliments; then, when he grew tired of their devotion, his wrath would appear, causing their wings to melt like candle wax.

A heart-breaking knot twisted at the pit of Christopher's stomach. His poor mother had been one of those bees.

"I hope that you weren't eavesdropping – *yet again* – on my little conversation there."

Christopher's blood ran cold. He did not hear his father step back into the car. "I…I was t…too hot. I had to g…get some air."

"Hmmmmmm … is that so?" Aiden Brenton turned round to face his son. He was lighting another one of his Gran Habano cigars. "Well, it was nothing, so forget what you heard." He then callously blew some cigar smoke into his son's face and started laughing.

The bluish-white spiral slithered up Christopher's nose, causing him to cough and wretch violently. He shut his eyes to block out the burning pain.

"Ha, ha, ha … a little smoke never hurt anyone." Aiden Brenton clearly had no sympathy for his son's poorly state.

It was all too much. Christopher fumbled for the door handle and clicked it open. He leapt out onto the pavement, choking, suffocating, gasping for air. He fell to his knees and grasped at his throat. But it was no use. He felt like all the air had been crushed out of his lungs. Christopher looked towards his father for help, but he was still sitting in the stygian sports car, smoking an extremely expensive cigar.

Sparkling fireflies flickered around Christopher's vision. He struggled to see the pavement in front of him. He focussed hard on the most mundane of objects in front of him in case he was having yet another Tiramavee. He pushed his fingertips to the ground, feeling its solidity. Yet again, he recalled his counsellor's advice: *one, two, three. Deep breaths.* Christopher slowly returned from the darkness. He sat upwards, but he kept his fingers on terra firma. Its roughness felt strangely soothing, like walking over hot coals; it was a reminder that he was still alive. He looked to his left, to where his father was sitting in the black car. Behind the inky blackness, the silhouette of his angular nose looked so supercilious. Christopher wanted to shout, scream, and howl at his father - all at once. It was like Mr Brenton was deliberately trying to cause his son to fall prey to another fainting fit.

"GET BACK INTO THE CAR CHRISTOPHER!" Aiden Brenton demanded. The full snarl of his smile was in clear view now that his window was down. "Stop making such a fool of yourself. I thought that you were in a hurry to see your *darling Grandmother.*" The last part of Aiden Brenton's statement was spiked with such sarcasm.

Christopher's heart pounded in his ears. He was about say something unpleasant to his father, but he was stopped by a little fluttering behind him.

"Here son, let me help," insisted a bright, tiny voice. It sounded so familiar.

Christopher was lifted to his feet by the welcome force of tiny helping hands. He suddenly felt as light as a feather. It was like time had halted. Mr Brenton sat as still as a tomb in the front of his car.

"Don't let that bully of father get to you son. He is only trying to ignite your anger," the little voice added, as Christopher was hoisted back into the car.

Christopher spun around in astonishment. His vision was met by the kind little face of Primrose Ruddock, or Birdie, as she liked to be called.

"And try not to worry about your Nana", she announced, winking at a wide mouthed Christopher. She carefully shut the door and then fluttered away from the black, beastly Belasco car.

# CHAPTER 29
## ~ *SAINT WILHELMINA* ~

Aiden Brenton drove in silence all the way to the hospital. Christopher was glad. He had nothing more to say to his father; he just wanted to see his Nana Kathy. Despite Birdie's words of hope, Christopher felt an overwhelming sense of dread. The journey there felt like an eternity and it made Christopher worry even more about his Nana. He wondered why she had not been transported to the nearest hospital.

Saint Wilhelmina's Hospital lay just on the outskirts of Leicester. Upon arrival, Nana Kathy had been taken straight to the operating theatre. That was all Christopher had heard, so he was anxious to hear how she was.

Four huge ionic pillars stood proudly at the entrance of the stately looking edifice, welcoming Christopher in with protective hands. It looked more like something that had been constructed in Neoclassical times, which made sense given that it was one of the oldest hospitals in the area. A bronze plaque on the outside declared that it had been *Gifted to the Town of Leicester by a Generous Benefactor.*

Christopher ran ahead of his father, not caring about the consequences. Two huge bronze statues stood at the foot of the grand staircase, stopping him in his tracks. A pair of harpy eagles met his vision. Both birds were perched on the splendid white marble plinths in front of Christopher. They looked so impressive with their outstretched wings. They were simply magnificent. Something lay trapped under both of their enormous talons. Christopher moved forward to have a closer look. On the statue to the left, the harpy eagle held a raven beneath its claws; on the statue to the right, the other harpy eagle held a snake beneath its claws. Christopher nearly feel to his knees at the sight of their power.

"What grotesque looking statues," Aiden Brenton scoffed, one step behind his son.

"I think they are brilliant," a little voice cheeped, before Christopher could say anything in return to his father.

It was Birdie.

Christopher ran towards the little woman and flung his arms around her tiny waste. Even though he had only met her twice, she was exactly the person he needed to see.

"B…Birdie, how's my N…Nana?" Christopher's words tripped out of his mouth. He was about to ask her how she had made it so quickly over to the hospital, but the evil stare of his father caught his vision.

Birdie wiped the matted hair from Christopher's eyes. "*Try not to worry*," she whispered. Then she looked up at Aiden Brenton. "You could have at least brought a change of clothes along for your son Mr Brenton. He looks like he's crawled out of the darkest depths of the murkiest waters."

"And you are?" Aiden Brenton asked, in a deploring manner, raising one of his dark eyebrows.

"You know who I am. I don't need to remind you." Birdie then lifted Christopher's bag from her shoulders and carried the weight for him. "Come on Christopher, let's go and see your Nana."

"So, *do I* get to tag along in this heartfelt reunion?" Aiden Brenton looked like a snake about to bite at its prey.

"No. No, you don't. You are not allowed to see Kathy. So, you will have to wait here. Or better still, wait in that monstrous car of yours."

Birdie and Christopher left Aiden Brenton standing in the grand staircase of Saint Wilhelmina's Hospital. He looked like the reaper, ready to sow his oats of destruction.

****

Before Christopher could see his Nana Kathy, a doctor led him into a private room. Birdie accompanied him, holding his hand for support. The light green walls and tree murals did nothing to appease the young boy's failing spirit. He missed his Nana and he longed for the friendly cuddle of his trusted Siberian dog.

"Mr Muir, my name is Dr Ra," started the friendly doctor. His warm, amber coloured eyes glowed in the afternoon sunlight cascading through the window. "But you can call me Sonny if you want to. Can I call you Christopher?"

Christopher nodded his head in response. He wanted to say more, but words failed him. He looked at Dr Ra and smiled.

Dr Ra's amber eyes lit up in response to Christopher's smile. The young-looking doctor stroked his thick, dark beard. "I wish I had better news for you at this time, but I am afraid it does not look good for your Nana."

Christopher's heart sank down, deep into the pit of his stomach. The room swirled. Birdie wrapped her arms around him tightly. He nodded, encouraging the young doctor to continue. Even though it was the worst thing he could hear, Christopher just had to know the prognosis.

"When Mrs Muir – sorry, I mean your Nana - arrived in theatre, she was barely conscious. She suffered something called a subarachnoid haemorrhage, which is a life-threatening type of stroke. We reckon that the bleed on her brain was caused by the impact of her head hitting the ground. Myself and my team of brain experts set to work quickly though - we operated and managed to stem the bleeding. But, unfortunately, because of her injuries, we were forced to protect your Nana – for the time being. So, we had to induce a coma." Dr Ra paused, allowing Christopher to take in all the details. But the look on his face made the young doctor instantly regret such gruesome detail.

"I…I eh, I don't f…feel so well." Christopher held his head tightly and tried to focus. This was not the time for another blackout. He clenched his jaw and sat back in his chair. Suddenly, a hot steaming mug of something was placed into his lap. The fragrant, minty smell brought him around. It was lavender tea.

"Drink this," Birdie urged.

Christopher engulfed the purple tea without hesitation. The warm, woody sensation embraced him, soothing his hammering heart. His vision quickly returned to normal. Dr Ra was gazing at Christopher with a concerned look. Birdie was still holding his hand.

"I'm sorry Christopher, but do you understand the implications? I had to be honest with you just in case the worst happens. Your Nana is very sick. But we are doing everything we can."

"Wh...when can I s...see her?" Christopher tried to swallow down the swelling at the back of his throat. He felt like everything was caving in on him: Sam had vanished, and his Nana was struggling to escape the clutches of death.

"You can go straight through now to see her. But I must warn you, she will look quite different." Once again, Dr Ra tried to explain the reality of everything to Christopher.

"Th...thanks," Christopher stammered, before standing up. "P...please, show me th...the way," he added, trying to be fearless.

"You're a brave boy, Christopher," Dr Ra said encouragingly. "Just remember, I will accompany you, so you can ask me anything."

Dr Ra led the way through to where Nana Kathy was situated. She was in intensive care, so only one visitor was allowed in at a time. Christopher thanked Birdie, not expecting her to wait, but her response surprised him.

"I'm staying put son. I will be right here. Plus, I have a few things that I need to talk to you about." Birdie then pulled her friend's grandson close again for another embrace. Tears gathered at the edge of Birdie's eyes. "Now go and see your Nana," she insisted.

Time crawled forward. Christopher was glad of Birdie's presence; she was such a welcome force compared to his father's wrath.

"Are you ready?" Dr Ra asked.

Christopher nodded and stepped forward. Two ornately carved wooden doors separated him from his Nana Kathy. It brought all the horrible feelings, visions, and memories back from his mother's death. But, a thousand voices whispered to him, ushering him on, telling him to *be brave*.

Christopher found his Nana Kathy lying in an empty cavern of exhaustion. She was hooked up to all manner of strange bleeping machines and tubes. Wires pierced her paper like skin from all angles, searching for a vein to inject life back into her listless form. Only a small section of her lavender hair was visible underneath the thick bandages wrapped tightly around her head. Dr Ra was right: this did not look anything like Nana Kathy. Christopher now understood Dr Ra's warning.

"N...Nana," Christopher started, holding his grandmother's hand, "it's m...me, your grandson."

The heat in the room was unbearable. Christopher struggled to just keep himself above the level of consciousness. But he knew he had to. *This isnae the time to be havin' a tiramavee son*, he could almost hear his Nana say.

But she said nothing.

"She can still hear you. It might not seem like it, but just keep talking to her. Studies show that talking to a coma patient can help with recovery." Dr Ra's words melted into doubt.

"Wh...what happens next?" Christopher was surprised at how pragmatic he was, given that his beloved grandmother, his only real remaining caregiver, was – perhaps - about to pass on to the other side.

"I can't say, as of yet. For now, she needs to rest. Then we can assess the extent of the damage." The words of Dr Ra's last sentence rang out, like an ominous siren, warning everyone about an impending tornado.

Christopher struggled to swallow the news that his Nana might never regain consciousness. The room swirled again.

But he focussed on her frail form lying on the crisp white sheets of her hospital bed.

"*If they ask me, I could write a book, about the way you walk and whisper and look,*" Christopher started singing to Nana Kathy. He wanted her to hear the words of his Papa's song. "*I could write a preface on how we met, so the world would never forget.*" Christopher sung the notes perfectly, with no stuttering.

Nana Kathy's hand twitched. She grasped a hold of her grandson's hands tightly.

"See, I told you," declared Dr Ra. "Keep going Christopher."

"*And the simple secret of the plot, is just to tell them that I love you, a lot,*" Christopher tried with all his might, singing the song, ensuring that he had not stuttered once. He hoped that it would be enough to bring his Nana out from her dark chasm of unconsciousness.

But there was nothing.

Nana Kathy fell further, deeper into the darkness of death's clutches.

# CHAPTER 30
## ~ *THE GODDESS OF HOPE* ~

Christopher held his Nana Kathy's frail hand. Her skin looked almost alabaster in the fading light. Only fifteen minutes had passed, but time held a cruel grasp of everything. There had been no more movement, no speech, no life.

She lay motionless.

"*Nana?*" Christopher whispered – again – into his grandmother's ear. He was certain that she would recognise his voice and wake up. But only a white veil of emptiness prevailed. Christopher was glad that Dr Ra had given him some quiet time alone with his Nana Kathy. Despite her silence, he appreciated the opportunity to just be with his beloved grandmother.

"Nana? It's me … Christopher. Can you hear me?"

Nana Kathy's left hand trembled slightly beneath her grandson's grasp. There was a strange warmth - almost damp feeling - in her fingertips. Christopher was taken aback by given her usually chilly hands. He could almost hear her say *cold hands means a warm heart you know*. He hoped that this was a sign of life powering its way through to his Nana's fingertips. He hoped that Dr Ra was right. He hoped that these would not be the last waking moments he would spend with his Nana.

"I love you Nana," Christopher declared, again, without any stutter.

No words fell from Nana Kathy's mouth. No twitches. Nothing.

Christopher slumped back into the surprisingly comfortable wooden chair. The unusual timber arms appeared to wrap around him, offering some longed-for comfort; it was nothing like any other hospital chair he could ever recall. He gazed outside the huge square window at the side of Nana Kathy's bed. The day was turning into evening and it sparked a huge display of strange colours over the thick, leaden sky. Angry storm clouds swirled above. But in amongst the sickly green billows, a golden statue stood bravely on one of the hospital's ornate white domes. She looked happy, despite the approaching squall. Ironically, she was positioned on the top of a golden weathervane, one that would usually dictate the climate. But this weather bureau was different. Her poise held such confidence, as if she could predict the future before the wind even whispered anything. One hand pointed forward; the other one held something delicate. It was hard to make out, so Christopher moved towards the window to have a closer look, but all the while, he kept a hold of his Nana's hand.

"That's our Goddess of Hope," Dr Ra pointed out to Christopher as he re-entered the room. "She's pretty magnificent, eh?" He suggested, trying to encourage his patient's grandson to say something.

"Wh…what's she holding?" Christopher felt stupid for asking, given the serious nature of his Nana's health. There were other questions he wanted to ask.

"It's a pomegranate flower," Dr Ra replied, without any hesitation. "Legend has it that this flower is a symbol of fertility and eternal life. We always put our special patients in this room."

Christopher shook his head. He had no idea what the young doctor meant.

"Well," Dr Ra started, "put it this way, many patients that have been in this part of ICU have actually survived. We like to think that our golden Goddess has magical healing powers." He then smiled encouragingly before checking the readings on the machines hooked up to Nana Kathy.

"Wh…where's my Nana's glasses…" Christopher was cut off in mid-sentence by the sudden appearance of an unwanted stranger. A dark figure stood in the doorway of

Nana Kathy's hospital room.

"Excuse me, sir, this is Intensive Care. It is family only and one person per patient." Dr Ra uttered, feeling immediately threatened by the nefarious force of the man standing in front of him. He had not even heard the door open.

It was Aiden Brenton. The stale smell of cigar smoke filled Nana Kathy's hospital room.

"I *am* family, young man – *that* is my son," Mr Brenton declared, pointing a long finger at Christopher. "And I think that you are telling lies. You said that only one person is allowed, but why are there two people in this room?"

Dread, fear, and anger crawled all over Christopher's skin.

"I, eh, I am Mrs Muir's Physician," Dr Ra offered his hand, but Aiden Brenton brushed by him. "I am a neurosurgeon," the young doctor then asserted, moving over to the unwanted visitor. "So that makes me medical staff. We are not counted as visitors."

Aiden Brenton ignored Dr Ra's words. He moved to the foot of Nana Kathy's bed and picked up the wooden clipboard, hanging on the edge of the bedframe. "Such an old-fashioned way of recording details. My company, Incaendium, could help your hospital a lot." Mr Brenton smiled odiously at the young doctor.

Outside, the weather had taken a turn for the worse. Icy, hot hail rattled against the windowpanes. Thunder growled in the air directly above the hospital.

"No thanks," Dr Ra insisted, without even contemplating the matter. "I'll take that, thank you," he declared, snatching the clipboard from the unwanted visitor. "I'm sorry, but we haven't been formally introduced – you are?" He asked, aware that his handshake had previously been rebuffed.

"I'm Aiden Brenton. CEO at Incaendium." No handshake was offered. "And as I have previously mentioned, *that*, *there* is my son." Mr Brenton stared menacingly at Christopher. "Right, given the state of Kathy, you are coming to stay with me."

Sickness curled like snake inside Christopher's gut. He had not even thought about the consequences of his Nana's poorly condition.

Thankfully, Dr Ra sensed Christopher's pain. "Yes, that's all very well, but you will have to provide identification. Let's discuss this elsewhere." As he ushered Mr Brenton away from Nana Kathy and out of the room, he turned to Christopher and whispered, "*spend as much time as you want with your Nana. Take your time.*"

The click of the door sounded so final, leaving a hopeless feeling floating in the air. Christopher moved his chair towards his Nana Kathy's right ear, in the vain hope that she might hear his words or feel his presence. He decided that now was the time to tell his Nana about everything – even the uneasy bits. But before he told her anything about everything – including the discovery of the book, his Papa's pen, the appearance of Sam, or any of the other strange occurrences – there was one thing that he had to do. Christopher kissed his Nana's cheek. He told her that he loved her more than life itself.

\*\*\*\*

The family room in Saint Wilhelmina's Hospital was a welcome sanctuary for people in need of a quiet place. It was such an unusual room, one that baffled many architects and interior designers. Despite its small size, it sat like a room of infinite space in the hospital. Its pure white ceiling and striking thistle engraved cornicing created the impression that the room was huge, as if it stretched off up into the eternal heavens. The ornate tree frescos painted all over the walls created a friendly ambience. Arm-like branches reached horizontally across the small room; again, creating the feeling of a never-ending forest. A south-facing window flooded the room with welcoming light. But when

Christopher entered, the walls were a horrendous bilious colour from the storm outside. Disagreement hung heavily in the air, and it was almost reaching its boiling point. A strange mishmash of adults stood in front of him: Birdie, Dr Ra and Aiden Brenton. Two were strangers; one was not. But Christopher knew that he would be much safer staying with any one of the two strangers.

Aiden Brenton cut the silence. "So, I trust that when the documents arrive, you will have everything you need. My lawyer is in the process of sending them over right now." He finished by adding "*Dr Ra*," in such a contemptuous tone.

The words struck terror into Christopher's core. He knew exactly what his father meant.

"Well, despite the promise of Christopher's birth certificate or other such documents, I still think that he would be best placed with Mrs Ruddock," Dr Ra disagreed wholeheartedly with Mr Brenton. "Especially with what Mrs Muir specified when she was brought in."

"Nonsense," Aiden Brenton dismissed the young doctor's offering with a wave of his hands. "Mrs Muir, had suffered a head trauma, so she was in no state to declare anything when I saw her." Aiden snorted haughtily, as if he knew that he was completely in the right.

"What do you mean, *when you saw her*?" Birdie cheeped, "when did you see her? I was one that found her. I then went with dear Kathy in the ambulance."

"I… yes, I mean I saw her … saw her ambulance." Mr Brenton tripped over his words uncharacteristically. The mighty force of Birdie had managed to somehow whip away his cool and well-rehearsed façade.

"So, you were the dark figure skulking around the entrance to Milaw House? I saw *you* then, just as the ambulance pulled away. What were you doing?"

"I eh…I came t…to see her. To talk about Ch…Christopher." The dark greenish-grey light from the storm outside shone upon his face, giving him the appearance of death.

Another rumble of thunder rolled over head.

"Now I see wh…where I get my stutter from," Christopher could not help himself; he seized the opportunity to point out his father's weakness. Dr Ra smiled at Christopher.

"Shut up you impertinent boy! No one asked you to say anything!" Mr Brenton's violent outburst sent shockwaves throughout the hospital. He started pacing back and forth like a demented beast trapped in a cage.

Birdie moved over to Christopher and placed her protective hands on his shoulders. "I know one thing, Mr Brenton," Birdie bravely declared, "no father should ever speak to his son like that. Right now, Christopher needs looking after, and you are in no fit shape to do so. Kathy wanted her grandson to stay with me, so that is how it will be."

*Clap --- clap --- clap!* Aiden Brenton's applause sounded louder than the hail battering against the window. "Well done, Mrs Ruddock, I congratulate you on your brave announcement." Aiden Brenton had stopped pacing up and down. He was now grinning menacingly at both Birdie and Christopher. "But don't tell me what I *can* or *can't do*, or *how to raise my son*. He is coming back, to stay with me."

"Noooooooo!" Christopher wailed loudly.

"Is everything okay in here?" The bearded face of a friendly looking security guard appeared around the door of the family room.

"Yes, yes, everything is fine." Aiden Brenton was the first to speak. He moved forward and offered his handshake to the security guard. "How do you do. I am Aiden Brenton, CEO at Incaendium, but you can call me Aiden. What's your name?"

The bear like, bearded security guard stepped inside. He almost filled the room with his broad shoulders and huge arms. His dark blonde moustache twitched above his lip. He could sense that something was not right, but out of politeness, he shook Aiden Brenton's hand. "I'm Artie Otso, the chief security guard at Saint Wilhelmina's Hospital." He quickly turned away from Mr Brenton and glanced around the room. Concern was etched deep in his steely blue eyes. "Dr Ra, can I speak with you outside?"

"Yes, of course Artie. Let's go to my office." Dr Ra looked at Christopher with a worried expression before turning his attention to Mr Brenton. "I think that, given everything that has happened, you should wait downstairs in the reception room, Mr Brenton. I will let you know when I receive your lawyer's email, along with Christopher's documents."

"I tell you what, why don't I show you the way," Artie politely but firmly insisted, ensuring that the dark force of Aiden Brenton had no option. "Dr Ra, I will speak to you in your office after I have escorted Mr Brenton down to the reception room."

"*Yes, of course, Artie,*" Aiden Brenton interjected, mimicking Dr Ra's reply, coating his anger with a layer of artificial sugar.

Artie Otso clamped his bear like hands around the sinewy arm of Aiden Brenton and then insisted "this way, Sir," leaving Dr Ra, Birdie, and a very troubled looking Christopher in the family room.

\*\*\*\*

Dr Ra's office was in the heart of the hospital. Artie Otso and Dr Ra were still inside talking; Christopher sat patiently outside. Birdie had flapped down to the hospital's canteen, insisting that she should buy her *friend's grandson some tea*. He knew that his Nana was right: Birdie was the best carer for him - for the time being. Despite their short acquaintance, he felt like he had known her all his life.

Christopher did not mind waiting because he felt safe. Knowing that his so-called father was somewhere else, banished to a place way below in the depths of the building, almost made Christopher laugh out aloud. Dr Ra's office had a spectacular view, so it helped to pass the time. It was on a balcony overlooking the huge hallway below. It was the centre of the magnificent building – the rotunda. Christopher stood up and peered over. The floor below had an intricate design of mosaic tiles. In the centre there was an eight-pointed gold star. It was so breath-taking. Christopher felt like he was looking through the lens of a wonderful old kaleidoscope. The hall was full of different people, all busying about with purpose. He shut his eyes for a moment, allowing the imprint of the golden star to shimmer just that bit longer. It reminded him of something that he had seen before, long ago.

When Christopher opened his eyes, the hallway was empty, all except for one solitary figure. Even from the great height where he was standing, there was no mistaking the plaited flaxen-haired beauty standing directly below him. It was Avias Deryn. She was standing in the middle of the eight-pointed gold star. She was swirling around in a slow circular movement with her eyes closed and she appeared to be chanting something. Christopher stood on his tiptoes, peering further over the balcony, in the vain hope that he might hear what she was intoning.

"CHRISTOPHER! GET BACK SON!" Birdie came flapping towards her friend's grandson. Despite her hands being laden with food from the canteen, she still managed to flutter over to him at full tilt. Before Christopher could say anything, she grabbed him by the waist and pulled him back to the wooden chair outside Dr Ra's office. He did not even see her put the plates or drinks down.

"D...Don't worry Birdie, I w...wasn't going to j...jump." Christopher quickly realised what Birdie was panicking about. "I'm d...devastated about my N...Nana, but I wouldn't d...do that."

"Thank goodness," she cheeped. "I feared the worst there. Here, eat this," she handed Christopher a cup of vegetable broth and a plate full of sandwiches.

Christopher's stomach growled loudly. He had forgotten all about the importance of eating, yet again. "H…how m…much longer do you think we will have to w…wait?" He shoved a whole sandwich in his mouth and washed it down with a huge mouthful of soup. After he swallowed, he peered over the balcony in search of Avias Deryn. But she was nowhere to be seen. The hall had returned to its usual busy self.

"Ahem, Mrs Ruddock?" Dr Ra asked politely, peeking around the doorway of his office. "Sorry to interrupt, but can I speak with you?"

The tone of Dr Ra's voice caused an uneasy atmosphere. The usual golden colour in the surgeon's eyes had faded.

"C…can I come in t…too?" Christopher hesitantly asked, trying to swallow the remnants of his cheese and pickle sandwich.

"Christopher, you don't need to hear any of this. It's more important for you to spend some time with your grandmother before saying goodnight. Come back here in half an hour. Hopefully, this will all be dealt with." Dr Ra smiled at Christopher, trying to cover up his real feelings of worry and concern.

Christopher's heart tumbled lower in his chest. Something was wrong. Very wrong.

****

Almost twenty-five minutes of silence had slowly passed. Christopher held his Nana Kathy's hand tightly. Thankfully, the storm had ceased, along with the hail. The sky looked exhausted, spent out even, as if the heavens had nothing left to give. Even the Goddess of Hope appeared to have lost her sprightliness: she was now facing away from Nana Kathy's window. Being one for superstition, Christopher thought that this meant a bad omen.

"Can I get you anything?" The sweet voice of a young nurse interrupted Christopher's thoughts.

"N…No thanks. I need to g…go soon." Christopher was aware that he only had a couple of minutes left before he had to return to Dr Ra's office.

"Well, just let me know. I'm Nurse Forbes, but you can call me Lana." She smiled at Christopher warmly and placed a glass of water in front of him. She had such unusual blue eyes.

Before Christopher could say thanks, the jovial nurse trotted back to her station. She sat back at her desk and smiled. She had what Nana Kathy would call *a right bonnie wee face.*

But Nana Kathy still lay silent.

There had been no more tremors, no sign of life. Christopher hoped it was because she was so tired. He slumped further back into his chair and sighed heavily.

*Clang.*

From somewhere below, Saint Wilhelmina's grand clock chimed, signalling its half hour declaration. Christopher picked up his glass of water and swallowed its welcome contents; he hoped it would wash down the huge pill of sadness stuck in his throat. He moved closer to his grandmother and kissed her goodnight.

Nana Kathy's forehead felt like a cold marble statue.

Christopher walked slowly and heavily away from his Nana's bed. He could not bear to leave her. His eyes prickled with tears, blurring his vision. It was all too much as he stumbled forward, towards the nurse's station at the door.

"Try not to worry, your Nana is in good hands," Nurse Forbes encouraged Christopher. Her curly brown hair framed her heart-shaped face, giving her the appearance of a sweet little llama.

"Th…thank you Nurse Lana," Christopher stammered.

Outside, the thunderstorm had passed, so the sky above was clear. The golden light of the evening had cast a blinding aura across everything in the room. For a split second, a flashing orb of light flickered at the bottom of Nana Kathy's bed. Christopher rubbed his eyes. But when his vision returned to normal, nothing was there.

"Christopher, try to relax," insisted the little, curly-haired nurse. "I'm working the night shift, so I am your Nana's protector for the night. Here, take this." She handed him an amethyst stone. Its pointed purple crystals called to him immediately as he held it firmly in his hands. "It will send you off into a good night's sleep, no matter where you are. Just put it under your pillow. Now go and get some sleep."

Christopher knew that he would not be able to sleep. He would rather spend the night in Saint Wilhelmina's, right beside his Nana. He held the lilac tightly in his right hand. It felt solid, real, truthful. It was a reminder of what living life meant. "I eh…, n…need to…"

"You need to go now." Nurse Forbes urged Christopher. "I will be here in the morning when you return," she added, blinking her blue eyes in a meaningful promise.

Christopher touched his chin with his fingers and then brought them forward, towards Nurse Forbes. He was signing *thank you*, a deeply ingrained gesture, something encouraged by his mother when he was a young boy.

But Nurse Forbes thought that Christopher was blowing her a kiss, and so she caught his kind gesture with both hands. "Go now," she mouthed, "I'll look after your Nana."

Just as Christopher left the room, Ella Fitzgerald's voice sang softly through the old wireless at the nurses' station. The words of "Into Each Life, Some Rain Must Fall" waltzed sadly over towards Nana Kathy.

# CHAPTER 31
## ~ *THE OLD GOAT* ~

When Christopher returned to Dr Ra's office, the door was firmly closed. Despite a blast of voices, volleying out from behind the young doctor's door, Christopher still knew that this was his nest of safety, high up on the balcony of Saint Wilhelmina's Hospital. He sat down with a sigh, hoping that he would be staying with Birdie until his Nana was well enough.

Inside the young doctor's office, stood Dr Ra himself, Birdie, and Otso Artie. Aiden Brenton's dark presence also haunted the room, along with his lawyer, Giles Mammon: a rather old goat of a man, who was fast approaching his winter years.

"So," bleated the white-haired lawyer, "here are all the papers you need, along with the temporary child arrangement order. For *Christopher Brenton*." Giles Mammon then clicked his black suitcase shut and trotted back from Dr Ra's desk. The solicitor's three-piece, black-and-white, pinstripe suit made him look like a prohibition gangster from the roaring twenties. He clattered his teeth heavily, accentuating how much his lower jaw and row of narrow teeth jutted over his top lip. It was such an annoying habit that Aiden Brenton had grown to endure, especially after how much the old goat of a man had helped him out of many dark spots.

Dr Ra and Birdie were speechless. Artie Otso stood in the corner of the room with his muscly arms folded, staring hard at the two unwanted visitors.

"Thank you, my good man," Aiden Brenton tapped the wiry shoulders of Giles Mammon. "*I think that they understand everything perfectly now.*"

"No, no, we don't!" Birdie piped up. Anger puffed up her little chest and caused a rosy flush to spread across her cheeks. "Kathy, Christopher's grandmother, was awarded child custody after Margaret passed. There was a reason why you did not get custody. Plus, Kathy declared that I should look after her grandson until she is well enough. And Christopher changed his second name to Muir."

"On the contrary," Giles Mammon interrupted Birdie's whirlwind of arguments. "Christopher is still legally named *Christopher Brenton*. Aiden Brenton *is* Christopher's father. I have all the paperwork to back up such details. Here. have a look." He then flashed his pale white hand in the air as if to dismiss any of Birdie's reasoning. "So, we have no option now but to bring in *Christopher Brenton*. He must be told."

Dr Ra fell into his chair, staring at the documents in front of him. He felt wronged. Defeated. He was lost for words. Otso, the security guard came over and stood behind the young doctor.

"Well, you can at least give me a few minutes with my friend's grandson. Alone. I will bring him into the office." Birdie appeared to the only one taking the lead.

"Very well, Mrs Ruddock, do as you wish." Giles Mammon looked at Birdie and shook his head.

Aiden Brenton sneered silently, like a king cobra about to bite brutally into its prey.

\*\*\*\*

Dr Ra's office door shut firmly behind Birdie. Christopher instinctively ran towards her and flung his arms around her tiny frame. At that moment, she was the closest thing to family that he had.

"P...please tell me that I c...can come and s...stay with you t...tonight, and n...not my f...f.... Him." Christopher had a feeling, deep down, that his question would be met by his worst fears.

"Christopher," Birdie started, stroking his hair dark hair away from his eyes. "Whatever you are told in there, I promise that I will find a way. Your Nana asked me to be your protector, and that is what I will be. Tonight, will just be a short blip. But I will be with you. Everything will be okay. I promise." Birdie's brown eyes were full of hope.

"O…okay, Christopher stammered. Despite the honesty in her voice, he found it difficult to believe in what the tiny woman was saying. He tried to put a brave front on, but inside he was melting into nothing. He had a bad feeling about it all.

"I have also something to tell you," Birdie added, "but I will wait until the bright light of tomorrow morning."

Christopher said nothing. He just sombrely shook his head in agreement. He just wanted to survive the rest of the evening. Spending the night without his Nana Kathy or Sam would be like a living nightmare.

Birdie held Christopher's shoulders and steered him through the door, towards Dr Ra's office.

\*\*\*\*

Giles Mammon was the first figure that Christopher set eyes on, and it made him want to about turn and run away screaming. The terrifying white points of his receding, widow's peak made him look like a snarling beast with white horns.

"Welcome, young man. Your father has been waiting for you. On your return." Giles Mammon brandished his cloven-like hand to and fro, in front of Christopher, in a hypnotising manner. "Here." He patted on an empty seat beside Mr. Brenton.

Christopher felt like he was sleepwalking forward, step by slow step, following the silver goat-skull ring on Giles Mammon's fifth finger.

"This is not right," Birdie tutted. "Christopher does not want to be with you, Mr. Brenton. I should know. You've somehow masterminded all of this. I will get to the bottom of it. You'll see!" Birdie's brown eyes were full of tears.

Silence twisted throughout the room. Christopher

226

robotically sat beside his father. Aiden Brenton smiled obnoxiously at Birdie and Dr Ra.

"So, that will be everything then." Giles Mammon nodded at his menacing client, Aiden Brenton, before pointing his snout towards the door of Dr Ra's office.

"Yes, it will," Aiden Brenton agreed.

Christopher followed his father like a servant, following his master. He stepped away from the safety of Dr Ra or Birdie.

# CHAPTER 32
## ~ *DIABLO* ~

Aiden Brenton sidled out of his car and moved towards his shadowy, sentry-like abode. A tall concrete-encased house stood menacingly in front of him. It looked so unfriendly, very out of place next to the other houses on the street. Christopher was in no rush to join his father, so he slumped back further into his seat, into the darkness of the Belasco car.

Christopher felt hollow inside. Everything had been snatched away from him, almost in the blink of an eye. The pain of his loss had really hit him hard upon returning from Saint Wilhelmina's Hospital: Aiden Brenton had stopped at Milaw House so that his son could pack the things that he needed, but when Christopher ventured inside, alone, his heart shattered into pieces. The house seemed so cold, so empty, so lifeless. Nana Kathy was the beating heart of Milaw House; without her presence, everything appeared to be bereft of life. Christopher had searched every room, every cupboard even, in the futile hope that Sam was hiding somewhere. But his beloved dog was nowhere to be seen. Even the garden looked spiritless. All the flowers had closed their petals as if they were preparing for a long spell of nasty weather. The lavender buds appeared to be dying. Christopher had not entered the old lean-to. He could not bear to see it in such a derelict state again. The last time was enough.

When he returned to his father's car, Christopher faced the worst challenge of all. As if to add salt to his already aching wound of loss, Aiden Brenton forced his son to go back into Milaw House to retrieve his Incaendium device.

"Do you like it?" Aiden Brenton interrupted his son's melancholy thoughts. My company designed and built it. It didn't take long." Mr Brenton stared at his concrete fortress with affection. Christopher had never witnessed such

228

admiration in his dark eyes before. "And they paid for it," he added, smiling wryly.

Christopher instantly hated it. He could not believe that his father owned yet *another* property. Perhaps though, the worst part was that it sat right in the village of Fernlock, and it was just a few streets away from Milaw House. Christopher stepped out of the car and moved towards the grotesque-looking building. He recalled his Nana talking about the housing development site. Most of the locals in Ferncross contested against it, Nana Kathy being one of them, but their efforts melted into nothing. Christopher had never even considered that his father's business was in partnership with the building company.

"Wh…when were you g…going to tell me th…that you lived around the c…corner f…from us?"

Mr Brenton laughed at his son's question. Instead of answering, he held his phone towards the house and pressed a button. Something beeped then clicked. The front door opened slowly. A red light from the hallway snaked its way out into the evening's darkness.

"Perhaps, if you jog on through to the back of the house, you might recognise something, something that might put a smile on your face."

Christopher sprinted towards the front entrance. He instantly thought of Sam, hoping that his trusted dog would be in the back garden waiting on him. A dark corridor slithered through from the front of the house right through to the back door. Christopher stopped running and stared at the walls. He had never seen such dark wallpaper before. It was hideous but, at the same time, hypnotic. He reached out and touched its velvety texture. There were no pictures anywhere; instead, a strange array of animal skulls punctuated the dark wall. Two of them really caught his eye: a goat's skull and a huge monstrous looking stag. Christopher almost swallowed his breath.

"Deathly dahlia." Mr Brenton declared, as he stepped inside the serpent-like hallway.

Christopher wondered if his father was speaking in some strange code. He turned to face him, trying to figure out what he meant.

"It's the name of the wallpaper. I see that you like it." Aiden Brenton then moved his right hand and condescendingly gestured to Christopher. "But stop touching it."

"Wh…where's my dog?" Christopher demanded as he pulled his hand away from the wall and the gruesome display of animal trophies. He hated that his father had such power over him. It made him want to smear both hands all over the wall, to spite him. But, again, Aiden Brenton ignored his son's question. Instead, he issued another command.

"Go on out into the back garden. Wait for me there; I need to make an important call."

The evening crawled on. Despite the end of the storm, dark clouds gathered above his father's house, creating the impression that another squall was on its way. A huge plot of land lay at the rear of the house, and the area itself was big enough to accommodate another residence. There appeared to be some flora and fauna, but it lacked the life needed to call it a garden. Black dahlias and dark baccara roses fringed a triangular-shaped artificial lawn. In the centre, there was a huge fire pit. Christopher almost gagged at the smell emanating from it. Dark moths fluttered between the sharp blades of fake grass. He looked around the inhospitable looking garden, searching for Sam. He longed for the white flicker of his bushy tail, but only darkness prevailed. All of a sudden, Christopher heard a rustling between the dark flowers. He looked behind him, but his eyes were only met by dead foliage. A carpet of discarded, brown leaves capered about on the hard-concrete path at the back of the tall, gaunt looking house. Their decayed appearance sat very out of place, given that it was still only early Autumn.

Christopher looked beyond the sallow leaves. There,

behind the dark glass and concrete patio, stood the creepy figure of Aiden Brenton. He held his Incaendium phone tightly to his left ear as if others were listening in on his conversation. He looked angry. His face was crushed up into a tight ball of fury, ready to explode. Fear pushed Christopher a few steps back from the window. Aiden Brenton stared at Christopher and grimaced. In the fading light, his lips formed a black, almost corvid-like beak. He then vanished into the murkiness behind the glass. Another uncontrollable shiver shot up Christopher's spine. He felt so alone in his father's sad excuse for a garden. He could just hear his Nana Kathy declaring *whit a pile of hellery!*

"*Chris-topher.*" Aiden Brenton called to his son in such a familiar, ghastly tone. It was so powerful, just like before, when he fell into the depths of darkness. His voice held such a horror-like quality. Christopher began to shake uncontrollably. But he automatically followed the unearthly tones of his father. "Here. Put this on." Aiden Brenton handed his son a dark, cloak like jacket. "Take that damp blazer off." Without thinking, Christopher handed the scarlet blazer over to his father. His Papa's key and pen were still in his pockets. Aiden Brenton disappeared back into his dark, concrete abode.

Christopher was alone again in the garden. He stared out into the darkness, thinking of his Nana Kathy. But then something caught his attention: the sombre blossoms in front of him flickered violently. He jumped back, afraid at what might be lurking behind the fake looking foliage. It was not Sam. A black snout appeared from the darkness, flying towards Christopher with aggressive force. In the shaded moonlight, the strange hound looked sleek, black, and brutally beautiful. It then bared its razor-sharp, yellow teeth. A guttural sound emerged from its snarling jaws.

*Grrrrrrrrrrrrrrrrrrrrrrrrrhhhhhhuurrrrrrrrrrrrrrr*

All at once, the black beast leapt towards Christopher and pinned him to the artificial grass. It snapped at him viciously, as if it was about to tear the flesh from his face.

"DIABLO! HERE BOY!"

The beastly, black dog pounded over towards his master, Aiden Brenton. It rolled over onto its back, allowing him to pat his belly. It the pale moonlight, it looked like a little puppy playing. Christopher scrambled to his knees and made his way over to the two fiendish looking figures.

"Ah, I see that you have met my Doberman pup, Diablo." Aiden Brenton patted the sleek black coat of his dog.

Diablo growled at Christopher, baring his teeth. This was no pup.

Christopher was speechless. He was still reeling after being forced to the ground by his father's dog. "I...I'm quite tired. I w...would appreciate it i...if you could s...show me wh.... where I am s...sleeping tonight."

"Nonsense. I was just about to cook some food for us."

Christopher looked at his watch. Mickey Mouse's small hand was nearly at number ten. It was way past teatime. He could just hear his Nana Kathy shouting at his father *this is hot chocolate time, ya eejit!*

"I tell you what, you go and sit by the fire pit with Diablo. I will cook us up a storm." Again, there was something so persuasive in Aiden Brenton's voice, compelling his son to follow his instructions. Diablo followed his master's son, like an obedient spy.

*Beep ---- boof.*

The fire pit in Aiden Brenton's garden sparked, then burned brightly. Its orange and yellow flames licked upwards, just below the black grate, like a trapped animal snared by its dark cage. Christopher looked behind him. His father was standing on the concrete slabs, holding out his Incaendium device towards the fire pit. He then vanished back into his dark castle.

Diablo stared menacingly at Christopher. The beastly dog's eyes flickered with rage. He sat upright, as if he was tensed and ready to attack again. Christopher felt as though the dog already had him pinned to the spot, but this time it was with his stare. Christopher began to tremble again. He longed for his trusted dog Sam to be by his side once more.

"Don't take any notice of Diablo, he's just sussing you out" Aiden Brenton said, returning with a steaming mug of something. "Here, take this," he commanded, passing the drink to his son.

Christopher inhaled the sweet vanilla essence emanating from the mug. It brought a strange smile to his face, as if he had inhaled some laughing gas.

"Go on, drink it!" Aiden Brenton insisted, almost losing his patience with his son again.

Christopher brought the mug up to his lips and swallowed its warm, sweet contents. At first, it tasted like hot chocolate; then it became more like warm, melted vanilla ice-cream. He could feel the hot liquid sliding all the way down into his stomach.

And then everything around him became blurred.

"Wh…wh…what h…have you g…g…given me?" Christopher mustered, stammering more than usual.

"Mwah, ha, ha," Aiden Brenton chuckled, as he sat across from Christopher. "Relax, it's called Chocolate Cosmos. It will loosen you up a little. No more panic attacks."

Aiden Brenton was right. Christopher no longer felt leaden heavy with worry or concern. His mind felt fuzzy. He knew that he should be worried about something or someone, but he could not remember what. Or who. Instead, he just sat there, smiling like a sleepy child on Christmas Eve.

"The concoction is taken from a plant called Cosmos Astrosanguineum – a plant that's almost extinct in the wild." Aiden Brenton threw two huge steaks onto the grills of the fire pit. "It's poisonous, but I have extracted the toxic part. I think." He then looked at the stupid expression on Christopher's face and began laughing. Diablo let out an unearthly growl, as if he also found the prospect of Aiden Brenton poisoning his son hilarious.

Christopher could just make out his father's pointed features through the flames. He too started laughing uncontrollably. The thought of being potentially poisoned would be enough to instantly set him off into a huge Tiramavee, but the effects of the Chocolate Cosmos had wormed its way right into his central nervous system.

In the pale moonlight, Aiden Brenton's face looked like something else. With all of his might, Christopher tried hard to remember where he had seen such a terrifying expression before. And then he remembered.

"You…you're th…that th…three h…headed s…serpent!" Christopher howled at his father, with more confidence than usual. But instead of shouting in fear or anger, the young boy continued to laugh, pointing at his father and shouting, "I kn…know who you a…are".

Aiden Brenton's face turned ashen grey. He was no longer laughing. He stared at his son through the dying embers of the fire pit. Diablo's growl intensified into a snarl.

"Shut up, you stupid boy! I am only glad no one else is here to witness this." Aiden Brenton snapped. "Here, eat this!"

Christopher looked down at the triangular plate handed to him. A thick, almost raw sirloin steak sat under his nose. The smell and sight of it were enough to make him nearly vomit. Red juice oozed from the course meat. It was all too much; Christopher could not stomach it. He turned to his side and threw up violently. He flung the plate down and staggered away from the rotten flesh-like smell radiating from the fire pit. Out of nowhere, a fang of pain pierced into his arm. Cold liquid coursed through his veins. Christopher felt like he had been injected with ice, causing him to shiver uncontrollably. But then the cold liquid turned hot, as if it had reacted with his blood. His veins burned. His body convulsed. He tried to shout for help, but no sound came from his mouth. He rubbed and rubbed his eyes, trying to focus on the vision that lay in front of him.

*Chwistooooooooo!*

It was Sam. The beautiful, white Siberian put his paw out towards his master. His cerulean eyes were full of concern. Christopher fell to his knees and hugged his dog tightly. When he moved back, he could see old Oli standing behind Sam. Christopher rubbed his eyes again, in complete disbelief.

"*Shhhhh*," whispered Oli. "*You've not much time my boy. You need to get out. Get out of here now. It's not good for you here. Your father is a dark influence on you.*" The old man's voice sounded weak, as if he was trying to communicate over white noise.

"Wh…what do I do?" Christopher whimpered, aware that he was like a prisoner, trapped in his father's sad excuse for a home.

But Christopher never received a reply; the white-haired helper and Sam vanished, almost as quickly as they appeared.

*WHACK!*

Christopher felt a searing pain at the top of his skull, as if he had been struck with a heavy object. He fell back, into the glacial like grasp of near death.

# CHAPTER 33
## ~ *CHOCOLATE COSMOS* ~

Christopher awoke to the sound of his father's voice. The frigid hands of panic wrapped around his neck, making it hard to breathe. His heart thumped out of time beneath his ribs. Something was not right. But he had no idea why: his mind was blank. Christopher heard the last remnants of his father's one-sided conversation.

"Yes, that's correct, Titus, my son won't be in school today. Or for the rest of the week. *But I will drop by later.* We still have unfinished business to discuss." There was a moment's silence before he added a final "*goodbye.*" Aiden Brenton's difficult voice crept through the crepuscular shade of his dark fortress.

Christopher sat up slowly. His head ached, and he still felt very fuzzy. He slowly surveyed the room that he was lying in. He appeared to be at ground level: through the gap in the curtains, he could make out the barricade of the front fence, keeping everything out. Despite his father's house being a newbuild, the room smelled musty and damp. Red wallpaper bedecked the walls with a repeating black design. It looked hideous. On closer inspection, Christopher thought that the image resembled two snakes strangling an eagle. He shuddered. He felt, so he threw off the black blankets that were almost strangling him. They smelled of old cigar smoke; they were thick and scratched his skin. A label at the top corner of the harsh duvet had almost carved a V-shape into his bicep. The sharp tag had the words *Best English Mohair, by Impetus*, brandished upon it. Christopher pushed the itchy covers away from his pale skin. He suddenly became aware that he was almost naked, apart from his pirate monkey underpants. He rubbed his head, trying to recall what had happened to him.

A black Doberman pincher padded around to his side

and growled at him.

"Are you *actually* awake?" Aiden Brenton's question sounded more like a command, criticizing Christopher for his sleepiness. He stood at the bottom of the scarlet Chesterfield sofa where his son lay, in a crumpled mess.

"Eh, y…yes. Wh…what happened…why am I not at M…Milaw House with my Nana?" Christopher felt like he had no memory. He did not understand what was happening. There was no recollection of Sam or old Oli, never mind any of the other important – and yet strange – things that had been happening to him.

"Well, after I served up that delicious – and very expensive – steak, you decided that you didn't fancy it, so you wandered off to the edge of my garden and started talking to yourself. And then you fell and hit your head. So, I dragged you, erm, I mean, lifted you in here."

Christopher rubbed the crown of his head, waiting for his memory to return. But nothing happened. Instead, a huge lump bulged beneath his fingers. When he withdrew them, he was horrified to find his hands covered in blood. The black Doberman slobbered forwards and licked away any remnants of Christopher's blood.

"So that's why you are going to stay home today. I think that, for the time being, until you feel better, you should be home-schooled." Aiden Brenton placed a shiny black laptop onto Christopher's knees. He then vanished behind the leaden door to some other cavern-like room in his dark fortress.

Like a submissive servant obeying its ruler, Christopher lifted the laptop from his knees and flicked it open. Its red glare instructed him to stare at its screen whilst it scanned his retinae. Christopher followed its command. He then sat like a robot, adhering to the remainder of its directives.

Aiden Brenton returned with a plate full of charcoaled sausages and fried eggs for his son, along with another cup of Chocolate Cosmos. Christopher ate everything, washing it all down with the deadly, sickly sweet concoction.

Somewhere in the kitchen of Milaw House, another petal fell from the withered rose.

# CHAPTER 34
## ~ *THE GREAT ESCAPE* ~

Minutes melted into a mindless mist of nothing. Outside, life was bustling in Ferncross village; inside, Christopher sat in front of the black haze of his new Incaendium laptop, tapping and clicking away furiously. Diablo, the black Doberman, sat faithlessly by his side.

When Aiden Brenton left for work, he ordered Christopher to complete a stack of Incaendium business modules. He insisted that they would help him become *a stronger young man, just like his father*. Under usual circumstances, Christopher would have cast the laptop aside and refused to complete any work. His focus would – should – have been his Nana Kathy, lying in the hospital. Unconscious. But this morning, something was very wrong.

Christopher continued to sit, mindlessly reading the red writing on the black screen. He had nearly completed the first module: *How to Succeed in Business, Regardless of the Repercussions*. The scarlet letters drip-fed strange messages into his brain as if they were enough to hold off any need to move or think. Diablo still sat unfaithfully by his side.

"Christopher! Christopher!" A little voice chirred through the gap in the window.

But Christopher still stared at his screen.

"Christopher, come to the window!" Desperation cracked at the fringes of the speaker's instructions.

But Christopher did not move.

And then the little voice began whinnying loudly, like a World War Two air-raid siren.

It was more than enough to shake Christopher from his dark trance. He instinctively threw the scarabaeus like laptop down and moved towards the window. It fell onto the floor, causing the screen to crack. He felt like a weight had been lifted from his shoulders. And then he remembered everything, but before he could do or say anything, Diablo snarled viciously and leapt towards him. Within seconds, the beastly dog had him pinned to the ground. He tried to push his growling muzzle away, but the hell hound was far too strong. Christopher's life flashed before his eyes.

"Here doggy, doggy, doggy!" The little voice commanded. "What's this?"

Diablo sprang away from Christopher and pounced towards the foot of the window. A huge, juicy steak lay in front of the deathly dog's salivating mouth. Without hesitation, he sunk his teeth into the meat and swallowed it almost whole.

*Thud!*

Diablo fell over before the meat had even hit his stomach. His mouth fell open and his tongue lolled to the side. Christopher clambered to his feet, grateful to still be alive. He prodded the dog with his foot. It lay motionless.

"Hurry, we don't have much time!" It was the little voice again.

Christopher pulled the red curtains back, desperate to see who was talking to him.

It was Birdie.

\*\*\*\*

Birdie's red Mini whooshed through the streets of Ferncross. Her nimble hands crunched through the gears, revving, and thrusting the vintage car forward, out towards Saint Wilhelmina's Hospital. The tiny black window wipers struggled to clear away the heavy rain battering against the front windscreen.

"I...is Diablo d...dead?" Christopher asked worriedly.

"Ha, ha, no." Chirruped Birdie. "That big pooch will just be in a bit of a daze for a few hours. I mushed up just enough of my valerian root to put him into a comfy sleep. Along with a strong sedative. His eyes were bigger than his belly."

Christopher felt like crying and laughing at the same time. But, instead, he sat quietly, staring in awe at the tiny figure beside him. For such a small woman, she could really pack a punch.

"Thank heavens I found you when I did. You looked like a little orphan, all wrapped up in strange blanket." Birdie smiled sadly at her friend's grandson before adding "Your father is a swine!"

"H…how did you know where I w…was? And h…how did you g…get by the h…high fence?" Christopher thought that this little woman must have special powers. It was the only explanation.

"I flew. Plain and simple."

Perhaps Christopher's ideas were not as ridiculous as he thought. But before he could ask any other questions, Birdie chipped in again.

"So, your Nana – you have to hear this. She is out of her coma. It all happened very quickly – and very unexpectedly. That's all I know right now, so we have to get there and find out more."

Christopher's heart leapt up into his throat. Joy, confusion, and fear swirled around in his stomach all at once.

# CHAPTER 35
## ~ *CANIS EST TUTUM* ~

Christopher found himself back in the family room of Saint Wilhelmina's Hospital along with Birdie. Less than twenty-four hours had passed, but Christopher felt like months had drifted by since he was last in the strange little room. Spending the night at his father's house had thrown him completely off balance.

"Try not to worry," Birdie expressed, sensing the concern broiling up inside her friend's grandson. "We'll soon hear something."

But Christopher could not help it. He was a born worrier. Anxiety crawled all over his skin because he could not see his Nana Kathy right away. She was away for a series of scans and tests; that was all the information he received upon entering the ward. Although his Nana had regained consciousness, he was still deeply concerned that there would be other complications. It made him think of his old primary teacher, Mrs. Baker: one day she was fine; the next, she had fallen prey to a stroke. Sadly, when she recovered consciousness, she could not speak, and she had lost the power of her left side.

"It was awful," Christopher unconsciously said out loudly, whilst scratching the strange scab on his arm at the same time.

"I think one of our skin specialists should have a look at that," suggested a familiar voice. It was Dr Ra. Christopher did not hear him enter the family room.

"How are you?" The young doctor asked, concerned about Christopher's pale complexion and darkness lurking beneath his eyes. "I take it that you did not sleep well last night," he added. He was still upset that Christopher had to spend the night at Aiden Brenton's house. He feared how much it had affected the teenager's appearance. "Perhaps we should run some blood tests on you, so th –".

"How is my N…Nana?" Christopher cut Dr Ra off mid-sentence. He did not mean to be rude, but he was desperate to know everything.

"Well, as you know, we have carried out some further tests on your grandmother. We will not have these results until later today." Dr Ra paused before then adding, "something like this has never happened before. Well, I haven't witnessed anything like it. Your Nana has completely regained consciousness. When I arrived this morning, she was eating her breakfast."

Christopher's heart leapt up into his mouth. "Wh…what about her sp…speech? Or m…movement."

"We don't know everything yet, but your Nana's speech seems fine, along with her mobility. And she was singing a song before we took her down for the tests." Dr Ra smiled and laughed a little. "Your Nana is quite something."

Christopher sat motionless. It took a few minutes for the news to sink in, but when it did, he bounced out of his seat and started jumping up and down. Birdie flapped up beside him and joined in. But exhaustion quickly put a stop to his celebration. Dizziness forced him to sit back down. Birdie took his arm. Dr Ra moved his seat directly across from the poorly looking teenager.

"How long have you had this for Christopher?" Dr Ra asked, worried about the angry looking wound on his forearm.

Two bloody punctures marks tarnished Christopher's forearm. Christopher felt nauseous as he looked at it. Dr Ra studied the inflamed wound closely.

"Have you been bitten by something in the last twenty-four hours?" Dr Ra asked Christopher hesitantly. He feared something terrible had occurred at Aiden Brenton's house. "Does your father own a snake?" He added, certain that this would count as child abuse.

Christopher wanted to tell Dr Ra all about the horrible experience he endured at his father's house. He also wanted to explain everything else: from being strapped to the metal stretcher, to then fumbling through obscurity, before ending up in the darkest depths of water. And then there was the encounter with the three-headed serpent. But when he heard the description of it in his head, Christopher thought that it would be enough to have him sectioned.

Christopher decided to keep quiet. He merely shook his head at Dr Ra.

"Well, I am going to prescribe you some antibiotics and run some blood tests just in case you were bitten. And I will have a nurse put a dressing on that for you." Dr Ra had a bad feeling. Something told him that Christopher was afraid to say anything incriminating against his father.

"C...can I s...see my Nana now?" pleaded Christopher, glad that he could change the subject with a more pressing issue.

"Yes Christopher, of course you can. Follow me."

Dr Ra led the way, with an eager Christopher following suit, and little Birdie fluttering behind.

\*\*\*\*

"Nana!" Christopher half shouted; half sobbed as he entered her ward. He ran towards her and hugged her tightly. She smelled like fresh lavender on a summer's morning. "I th...thought that you w...were going to die," he mumbled almost incoherently. He then began sobbing uncontrollably into her neck like a little toddler needing consoling after hitting his head.

"There, there son. It's all right," Nana Kathy whispered to her grandson, whilst stroking the hair on his head. "I'm no' going anywhere. No' for a while yet. Here, let me have a look at your wee face."

When Christopher sat back on her bed, he could not believe his eyes. His Nana's cheeks flushed with her usual rosy glow, and her brown eyes sparkled. The rain had finally stopped. It was enough to stop his blubbering.

"It's the emulsion, eh?" Nana Kathy chuckled, trying to put a smile on her grandson's face. "It catches us all when we least expect it."

"Wh…what h…happened? C…can you remember a…anything?" Christopher had so many things that he wanted to ask her; he did not know where to start.

"We have quite a bit to talk about son. It'll be more than just a wee chinwag - I can tell you that. But no' in here." Nana Kathy winked at her grandson and patted her nose. "But one thing's for sure, your no' going back to stay with that bampot of a faither of yours." She then reached forward and held Christopher's hand tightly. Her eyes became glassy with tears. "He's a nasty lying walloper. And I have his cards marked. So, when I get the *all-clear* later, we're going back home. To Milaw House."

"Not so fast," Dr Ra had returned to Nana Kathy's room. "We need to see your scan results first before we can make any decisions." The young doctor then turned his attention to his patient's grandson. "Christopher, I hate to interrupt your time with your grandmother, but I have organized some tests for you." Dr Ra moved towards Christopher and handed him a brown envelope. A look of unease crawled over his face. "I want you to take this and go to Wing B downstairs. They will look after you. When you are all done, you can come straight back here and see your Nana."

"Whit tests? Is there something wrong with my grandwean?" Nana Kathy sat upright on her hospital bed. She did not like the look on the young doctor's face.

"It's okay Mrs Muir, I don't want you worrying. Christopher appears to have a bite on his arm. I am sure that it will all be fine though." Dr Ra tried to hide the alarm in his voice.

"If that ba -," Nana Kathy started, but then readjusted her words, "Eh, I mean, if that bampot, called Aiden Brenton, has done something to my Christopher, then I'll have him thrown in prison. And I'll throw the bloody key away myself!"

"Now, now Mrs Muir, just you sit back and try to get some rest. You need to take it easy." Dr Ra moved closer to his lavender haired patient and checked her pulse. "Your heart rate is still quite high, so I want you to try and calm down. Try and get some sleep."

"Sleep? Are you kiddin'? What I need is some lavender tea and to be back home with Christopher."

"Did someone say lavender?" Birdie popped her head around the heavy door of Nana Kathy's hospital room. "If I could just use the kettle, then I could accommodate my good friend's request".

"Birdie!" Nana Kathy shouted. "Jeesy peeps, you're a sight for sore eyes! Come ben the room."

Against Dr Ra's advice, Nana Kathy jumped out of her hospital bed and flung her arms around her old friend. Christopher almost laughed aloud at the sight of his Nana and Birdie flapping around each other. Before Dr Ra could say anything about the one-visitor-to-a-patient rule, Christopher nodded to the young doctor. He hugged his Nana. He was so glad that she appeared to be very much like her old self again. She clung to her grandson tightly before releasing him. She then handed him a piece of crunched up paper. Christopher instantly opened it and stared at the familiar handwriting.

The note read *Canis est tutum* Instead of a full stop, there was a tiny paw print, signalling the end of the sentence.

Christopher looked up at his Nana with a look of confusion. She smiled at her grandson and winked.

# CHAPTER 36
## ~ *VENOM* ~

Wing B resided on the ground floor of the hospital. It was a long corridor leading off from the grand hallway. Christopher felt sick at the thought of having his blood taken. He sat trembling as he remembered the last time: his mum thought that he had glandular fever, so she had to coax him to see the doctor. The mere sight of the needle brought on a fainting fit. When he came to, his mum was by his side, telling him that it was all over. The memory caught at the back of his throat. He held his Nana's note tightly in his left hand. It brought him comfort.

"Hello young man," a bright and friendly voice clucked. "I thought that I would find you here." It was Nurse Forbes.

The sight of the little brown-haired nurse stilled his galloping heart. "Oh, N...Nurse Forbes, I am s...so happy to see you. B...but you must be so tired." Christopher was suddenly very aware that the friendly nurse had already put in a full night shift; how did she even have the strength – or energy – to take his blood or even dress his wound.

"I'm here to pay you a quick visit. Nurse Maclaggan will be along in a minute to see to you. I have something to tell you." The little, curly-haired nurse jutted her head towards him as if to seal the importance of her words.

Christopher just nodded his head, fearing what she had to say.

"It had been quite a difficult shift because one of our other patients in the ICU nearly passed. It was a bit of a struggle, but we got there in the end, and thankfully he pulled through. I shouldn't really have told you that, but I feel that it might explain the strangeness of what I saw next." Nurse Forbes looked at Christopher with a strange appeal. She continued without even giving him the chance to say anything as if she was in a hurry. "I felt more tired than usual, so when dawn arrived, I felt very sleepy. So, when I looked up and saw a beautiful, blonde-haired lady standing at the edge of your Nana's bed, I dropped my mug full of coffee onto the floor. It smashed into pieces, making such a clatter. But it didn't stop your Nana's striking visitor. I stood, like a gaping fool, watching the bewildering events unfold in front of me. I didn't say anything. I swear I'm telling the truth. Please believe what I have to say next." She reached forward and grasped his hand tightly. Christopher had forgotten all about his blood tests. He now sat on the edge of his chair, eagerly awaiting what Nurse Forbes had to say.

"The beautiful blonde woman started screaming at the top of her voice. It was so charming and yet so deafening at the same time. I had to cover my ears. And then she stopped. But here is the strangest part of all. My radio started playing an old jazz song; it sounded a bit like Billie Holiday. But I'm not sure."

"C…can you remember the w…words?" Christopher instinctively asked, encouraging the little nurse to finish her account of what happened.

"It was something about writing a book. I know, that sounds silly, doesn't it? But I was so taken aback by the blonde lady at your Nana's side, so I didn't pay much attention to the radio, or the song." Nurse Forbes' cheeks flushed with what looked like embarrassment. Again, she did not wait for Christopher's reply. "I suppose I now only realize how strange it was that my radio started without me even touching it." She paused for a second before adding, "But, here's the most unbelievable bit. Before the song finished, your Nana hopped out of bed and started dancing. And singing! I stupidly hit the panic button to call for assistance because I just assumed the worst. I don't know what I was thinking of, to be honest. But just as I pressed for assistance, the beautiful, blonde-haired lady vanished. When the crash team arrived, Nana Kathy was perched at the end of her bed, swinging her legs. She told the doctors that she was fine. She then turned to me and said that I had a right, wee bonnie face." Nurse Forbes giggled nervously, covering up her tense laughter with her small hands.

Christopher fell back into his chair, laughing hysterically. The look on the little nurse's face filled his heart with a strange joy. She too had been a witness to a small part of the craziness he had been experiencing all along.

"Here's the last thing that I have to say. At the end of my shift, I chatted to your Nana briefly. She was so interested in me – she wanted to hear all about my family. It was lovely. She told me that I would see her again. But just as I was leaving, I saw something very out of place."

"G…go on," Christopher encouraged, longing to hear the rest of her explanation.

"When I turned away from your Nana, I just happened to glance out of the window. I nearly fell back at what I saw. A huge golden eagle filled the huge frame of the window. It appeared to be smiling at me".

\*\*\*\*

Christopher's blood tests came and went without any fainting fits. He was too busy thinking about Nurse Lana's words, that, and the fact that his Nana had rallied round back into the world of consciousness.

When Nurse Maclaggan returned with Christopher's antibiotics, he found his patient smiling away to himself. The carroty-haired nurse chuckled, "well, it's good to see that you are feeling better. Dr Ra said that you nearly fainted upstairs in the family room." Despite Nurse Maclaggan's huge stature, his gentle mannerisms created the impression that he was just as small and cuddly as a Highland cow's calf. He took his time dressing the strange wound on Christopher's arm.

"Y…yes, but I'm okay n…now. Th…thanks." Christopher did feel better. Just being away from the horrible presence of his father made him feel human again.

"Well, I'll let you know when your results come back. In the meantime, no running marathons or anything." Nurse Maclaggan smiled at Christopher and then handed him a purple lollipop. "And that's for being a brave boy."

****

Christopher had finished his lollipop by the time he had climbed the steps back up towards the ICU. He could not wait to see his Nana again. He could not bear to think about living his life without her. So, he promised himself that he would look after her more. Guilt sat low in his stomach still. He could not shake off the terrible feeling that he had somehow caused his Nana to fall off the ladder. It was eating away at him. "I'll apologize right away," he thought as he pushed the door to enter his Nana's room. But Nana Kathy was nowhere to be seen. Her bed had been stripped and cleaned, waiting on another patient in need. There was no trace of her anywhere.

"Wh...where's m...m...my Nana?" Christopher sputtered; his voice tight with panic. Tears blurred his vision. He suddenly had the terrifying feeling that he had imagined everything.

"Hello me dear, are you Christopher?" A plump faced nurse asked.

"Y...yes," Christopher quickly replied, desperate to know what was going on.

"Oh, good. I'm Mabel, and I am delighted to meet you. It's nice to put a face to a name. Your grandmother has told me all about you. Listen to me, blethering on, I expect you want to know where she is. Well, she's moved to Ward Unwin. It's on the first floor. You shan't miss it if you follow the signs."

Christopher almost fell back with relief.

"She's quite a remarkable lady, your Nana," Nurse Mabel added. "I've never seen anything like it in all of my forty years of nursing. I bet your glad she's no longer in need of intensive care."

****

When Christopher reached Ward Unwin, he found Birdie and his Nana giggling away like a couple of schoolgirls hatching a plan. Birdie was wrapping a lilac scarf around Nana Kathy's head to cover up her bandages. They had not yet noticed Christopher. He stood in the doorway, watching them, smiling.

"Quick, give me the mirror so I can have a wee look," Nana Kathy asked her friend.

Birdie handed the mirror over and began giggling all over again.

"Jeesy peeps! I look like Mystic Kathy. All I need now is a wee crystal ball!" Nana Kathy handed the mirror back to her friend. Just as she began unravelling the head scarf, she noticed her grandson. Her eyes lit up. "Christopher! Come ben the room. Thank God, you found us okay."

Christopher jumped over to her bed and hugged her tightly. He would never tire of showing his Nana Kathy how much he loved her. "I'm s…sorry Nana." He decided that now was his moment to apologise. "It's a…all my f…fault. Y…your accident, it was m…my fault."

"Ach away with yourself, don't be daft. It wisnae your fault at all. I know who's to blame for this," Nana Kathy was cut off by her little friend.

"Christopher, you'll never guess what," Birdie began, trying to change the subject, "your Nana has been given a clean bill of health. The doctors are baffled. They have never seen the likes of this happen."

Christopher felt like cheering and clapping, but his Nana's words stopped him.

"Aye, but I'm no quite oot the woods yet Birdie. I'm just waiting on one test result to come back. Let's wait and see what they say. Who knows, they might even find my brain." Nana Kathy tried to make light of the situation.

"B…but that's great n…news though N…Nana. I'm so happy."

"Och, never mind me, what aboot you son. What did they say about the wound on your wee arm?" Nana Kathy's eyes were full of concern.

Christopher explained the little information that he knew. He wanted to say more, but there really was nothing else he could add. What he really wanted to talk to his Nana about scared him; he was terrified about what she would say about the pool of darkness and the three-headed serpent. The appearance of Dr Ra disturbed his musings. The young doctor was carrying a clipboard full of scribbled notes, and he was wearing a grave expression, so Christopher decided to keep his mouth shut for the time being. He thought that perhaps it would be better to tell his Nana when they were back home in Milaw House. "Mrs Muir, how are you feeling?"

"I'm fine. Never felt better. Fit as a fiddle, whatever that means," Nana Kathy laughed, trying to smooth over the palpable change in atmosphere.

"I have good news for you. Your last scan indicated no damage to your brain. In fact, it's like you never even suffered a subarachnoid haemorrhage. It's a miracle. You're a walking miracle, Mrs Muir. You're free to go home this afternoon." Despite the fantastic news, the young doctor still looked sombre.

"Oh, thank you, Dr Ra!"

The young doctor did not acknowledge her words. Instead, he turned to Christopher. "Young man, your results have also come back. I don't know how to tell you this, but your blood samples contain viper venom. You have been bitten by a snake."

# CHAPTER 37
## ~ *CHRISTOPHER'S HEALING POWERS* ~

"Christopher, please, try to remember. This is important." Dr Ra sat opposite him at the foot of Nana Kathy's bed.

Christopher felt cold and clammy. The shock was sinking in. He did not know where to start; or even how to explain what had happened after he drank the strange vanilla brew at his father's fortress. He tried to speak, but his throat felt dry. "M...my f...father." Was all that he could muster.

"That walloper! I knew it. I bloody knew it! Well, when I get my hands on that swine called Aiden Brenton, he'll no' know what's hit him!"

"Mrs Muir, please try to relax. I don't want you to suffer too much stress." Even though Nana Kathy showed no signs of her injury, Dr Ra reminded her that she had suffered a near fatal fall, less than twenty-four hours ago. Content that she had listened to his advice, the young doctor turned back to Christopher. "Can you tell us exactly what happened?"

This was it. This was Christopher's chance. They had to believe him now that there was evidence because it was right there in his bloodstream. Strangely though, his body had not reacted in any way to the snake venom. His heart, kidneys, liver, and lungs all appeared to be functioning normally. The words, *you appear to be immune to its venom*, crawled around in his head.

Christopher swallowed down his apprehension and began his story. "It all s...started out in his b...back garden."

"Huh, garden? That bloody fool couldnae grow a weed," interjected Nana Kathy. She was furious at what Aiden Brenton had caused. "Sorry, continue son," she nodded, aware that she had spoken her thoughts out aloud.

Christopher then moved onto the macabre details of the fire pit and the almost raw and bleeding steak, but just as he was about to describe the strange vanilla-like tea, a seething, burning sensation ignited from his bandaged wound. It felt like someone was holding a hot poker to his forearm. "AHHHHHHHH! P…please help. M…my arm!"

Birdie flapped from one end of the hospital bed to the other, while Nana Kathy sat with her arm around her distressed grandson. Dr Ra remained calm and acted with ease. He undressed Christopher's wound carefully, so that he could inspect the source of pain. What lay beneath shocked everyone in the room.

The bite mark had completely vanished.

\*\*\*\*

Dr Ra shook his head in bewilderment. He had never seen such a vicious wound heal so quickly before. There was no redness, no scarring, nothing. Even the rosiness had made a welcome return into Christopher's cheeks.

Birdie had stopped fluttering about; she was now hovering above Nana Kathy and Christopher, looking at the miracle that had occurred in Saint Wilhelmina's hospital for the second that day. Christopher rubbed his arm, amazed that the angry wound had vanished.

"Well, this disnae change things." Nana Kathy was the first to speak. "The fact is, that horrible gowk of a man did something terrible to my grandwean. Birdie saw it. She said Christopher looked like a poor wee waif when she rescued him. I'm reporting him. I'll wipe that smug smile off –"

"Mrs Muir, calm, remember." Despite Dr Ra's stress, he still urged his nearly discharged patient to relax. "I think what we need here is a bit of normality, clear thinking and a plan of what to do next."

Nana Kathy grabbed Dr Ra's suggestion with both hands, but she interpreted it in her own way. "Aye! We do. Hmmmmm," she thought, whilst taking her glasses off and holding them up to the light. She rubbed a few specks of dust away and then declared, "that's it!"

"What's it?" Asked Birdie, curious to know what her old friend had conjured up so quickly.

"Normality. You said it, Dr Ra. So, here's what we will do. Firstly, Christopher, you will return to school – this afternoon. It'll just be for a wee while, just until my master plan starts cooking. As long as he is well enough Dr Ra?" Nana Kathy asked, hoping that the young neurosurgeon would agree.

"Eh, yes, technically speaking, Christopher is well enough, but –"

"Great," Nana Kathy exclaimed, not even giving the young doctor a chance to say anymore. "Christopher, Birdie will drop you at school and she'll be there to pick you up at the end of the day. In the meantime, I'm off home, back to Milaw House. Dr Ra will drop me there, just to make sure I'm *calm*." She smiled warmly at the young doctor, before declaring, "Aiden Brenton, I'm coming for you, and you've nae chance."

# CHAPTER 38
## ~ *THE ARREST* ~

Thanks to Birdie's speedy flight in her little red Mini, Christopher arrived at school just at the end of lunch. He had just enough time to make his way to class, without anyone really noticing him. His father still had his blazer, but at least Christopher had the rest of his uniform.

'Out of a fired ship, which by no way, but drowning could be rescued from the flame..." Mrs Bridget Ash started her lesson in her usual way, reading out a few lines of mundane poetry.

Christopher scrambled to find his usual seat, keeping his head down, avoiding eye contact with anyone. *Normal*, his Nana Kathy had insisted, *act normal son*. The events of the past few days had been far from normal.

"Oi, mate! Chris!" A little jab of an elbow followed the friendly voice. It was Stevie. She leapt out of her seat and threw her arms around Christopher. "I thought you were dead!"

"Sit down young man," the bland, flat voice of Mrs Ash droned. She held no authority; she did not need to. The other eighteen Oakwood students did not lift their eyes from their Incaendium devices. 'So, all were lost, which in the ship were found, they in the sea being burnt, they in the burnt ship drowned..." The lifeless voice of Mrs Ash sullied on.

Stevie clambered back to her seat and smiled at Christopher. Her light brown eyes looked almost golden, as they glistened with tears of happiness. She then frantically scribbled something onto her notepad. When she had finished, she ripped the paper from its hinges. Christopher stared at Mrs. Ash, pretending that everything was *normal*. But everything was far from *normal*.

*Plip.*

A scrunched-up ball of paper landed on Christopher's desk. He opened it, curious to find out what Stevie had written.

"*What's going on mate? You look terrible. How's your Nana? I missed you!*"

Christopher turned to Stevie and smiled. He hoped that his smile would be enough to reassure her that everything was okay. But it did not work. Stevie shook her head and raised both hands in confusion.

Christopher searched for his Papa's pen so that he could write a message back to his little baseball-capped friend. He fumbled in his trouser pockets, hoping that it would be there. But the gold-tipped ballpoint was nowhere. Panic gurgled at the back of his throat. He then remembered that his blazer was still at his father's house, along with Oli's key and his Papa's pen. But despite his alarm, Christopher tried to focus on his Nana's instructions: *act normal son.*

"*Here,*" Stevie whispered, throwing a pen to him.

Christopher grabbed it and quickly scribbled a message on the back of the scrap that Stevie had thrown to him. Just as he added a full stop, Mrs. Ash snatched the crunched paper out of his hands. It was a miracle that she could see anything with the huge eye patch plastered over her face.

"Too much to explain. I will tell you at recess. Missed you too." Christopher's message to Stevie fell blandly from the letterbox mouth of Mrs Ash. "Well, at least you know your difference between your prepositions and adverbs," she monotonously declared. She pocketed the note.

Christopher smiled as normally as he could at his insipid English teacher.

\*\*\*\*

Afternoon recess arrived, along with some of Birdie's home-made banana bread.

"I th...thought we were done f...for there," declared Christopher, as he handed some of the delicious baking to

Stevie.

"Never mind that, what the heck is going on with you?" Stevie asked, keen to find out what had been happening to his friend.

The two friends had forgotten all about the school rules; without realizing, they had wandered towards the Artery: an area for Year Nine and above during recess.

"S…Stevie, you won't b…believe this, b…but my Nana is okay." Christopher began explaining above the noise of all the other students. He told Stevie all about his Nana's miracle, and how she had survived a subarachnoid haemorrhage without any horrible effects. "A…and here's the b…best bit," he continued. "The Nurse, L…Lana, in charge of my Nana, said that she s –"

"Christopher!" Kerry Robinson appeared from nowhere from the throng of scarlet blazers. She flung her arms around him. "Are you okay?" she asked, pulling away, embarrassed by her over-enthusiasm, "you look tired."

"That's what I said," Stevie agreed.

"I…I'm fine," Christopher was still trying to act *normal*.

"No, you're not," Kerry said, touching his cheek with her hand. "I missed you, I feared the worst."

Christopher lifted Kerry's hand from his face and smiled at her. He automatically fell back into a trance just looking at her beautiful emerald eyes.

"His Nana is fine," Stevie awkwardly interjected, aware that she was the third wheel in his friend's romantic reunion.

"That's great news," Kerry squealed, now aware of Stevie's presence. "Christopher, I have to tell you something," Kerry started, the tone in her voice signalled importance. "Last night, I had the strangest dream. I dreamt that Avias Deryn visited your Nana in hospital. It was so real. I was like a spectator watching everything, but when I tried to speak, the mighty Deryn squawked at me and flew away. When I looked up, your Nana was dancing."

Christopher lifted his hands to his mouth in awe. But before he could reply, a horrible voice snarled at the three friends.

"Who gave you two permission to stand here - in the Artery? And why are you back at the Institute today, Mr. Muir?" Titus von Brandt's series of venomous questions pierced through Christopher's eardrums. "I met with your father earlier, and he said that you wouldn't be back here for at least another week." The horrible headmaster glared at Christopher through his blue lenses.

"I…I, eh —" Christopher struggled to find an explanation.

"He's all better now Sir!" Stevie jumped to the rescue and then masterfully changed the subject: "Sir, can we stay here and talk? We aren't causing any hassle, and there are only a few minutes left of recess anyway."

It took a second or two before Stevie's question fully registered with Titus von Brandt. His face turned scarlet as if his blood was boiling. Veins protruded from his temple. "No, no, you can't! Now get back —"

The deafening sound of the Institute's buzzer cut off the horrible headmaster's words. A flock of scarlet blazer-clad pupils herded off in different directions towards their next class. Kerry was one of those pupils, waving sadly at Christopher. She was mouthing something to him, but he could not understand what she was saying. Titus von Brandt stood still in the middle of the artery as if he had just parted the red sea. He stared at Christopher with such malicious intent but never said anything.

"C'mon Christopher, let's go," Stevie said, hauling at her friend's arm. "Now I know what saved by the bell means," she chuckled as they scampered away from Titus von Brandt.

\*\*\*\*

The remainder of the afternoon dragged by. Tiredness nibbled away at Christopher's concentration, so it was no surprise that he switched off during double Maths.

However, he managed to stay true to his Nana's request: he acted normal and kept his head down. And thankfully, Titus von Brandt was nowhere to be seen.

"What a way to end the afternoon? Death by Trigonometry." Stevie rolled her eyes back and lifted her hands out horizontally as if she was a creature of the living dead. She then started laughing, but she soon stopped when she realized Christopher was not partaking in her jest. "Chris, mate, are you okay?"

"Y...yes. Sorry S...Stevie, I was miles away th...there. I g...guess I just can't wait to see my N...Nana again."

Christopher scanned the car park at the front of Oakwood Institute for Birdie's car. But it was nowhere. Fortunately, though, neither was Aiden Brenton's black Belasco. He smiled at his little baseball-capped friend, trying to hide his apprehension.

"Don't worry Chris. I have a good feeling. And look mate, here's your girlfriend now," Stevie nodded her head in the direction of Kerry.

"*Shhhh*," Christopher whispered, his face flushed with embarrassment. But Stevie was not far wrong: Christopher longed to be Kerry's boyfriend.

"Finally! I can talk to you without the prying eyes of the von Brandt. Did you see the way he was staring at you?" Kerry then flung her arms around Christopher again and whispered in his ear, "*I was really worried about you.*"

When Kerry pulled back to look at Christopher, he was smiling from ear to ear.

"Perhaps we should all hang out – at the weekend?" Stevie asked, conscious that she did not want to ask Christopher and leave Kerry out. "As I suggested before, you could come over to my dad's restaurant. We could have a huge Indian banquet for three!"

But just as Christopher and Kerry were about to answer, a little voice cheeped in.

"Christopher? Are you ready? We really should get going." It was Birdie. She felt terrible for interrupting

Christopher with his friends. "I'm sorry to drag you away. Perhaps you could see them later?"

"No, that will most certainly NOT be happening!" It was Aiden Brenton.

Kerry, Stevie, and Birdie gasped in horror. Christopher said nothing; he felt as if his father's presence had pinned him to the spot. His blood felt like it had congealed within his veins. His forearm throbbed, as if the bite wound had opened again. When Christopher looked up, his father was towering over him, like a huge rook about to attack. Birdie fluttered behind the monstrous figure of Aiden Brenton, but her attempts to move him out of the way were futile. Christopher was almost certain that he would be returning to the horrible fortress like abode with his father.

"I left you with Diablo, back at Chez Solas! So, what are you doing here? You had important work to do. It is just as well I knew where you would be!" Aiden Brenton grabbed Christopher's arm and started hauling him down the steps outside Oakwood Institute.

"How did you know where he would be? Have you implanted some kind of tracking device into your son's arm or something?" Birdie asked, trying to form a barricade on the steps with her tiny frame. Stevie and Kerry stood beside her.

Birdie's words struck a chord: Aiden Brenton stopped talking. He stopped moving. But before anyone could say anything else, a stocky policeman interrupted. A scrawny looking officer in blue accompanied him. Christopher immediately recognized both from before, especially the measly looking one. "Aiden Brenton?" the stalky policeman asserted, moving towards Christopher's father.

"Yes, yes, what is it?"

The remainder of the Oakwood pupils hanging around outside moved towards all the commotion. There must have been about thirty of them, moving in, closer and closer, like a pack of bloodthirsty hounds looking for some other form of entertainment. They all looked up towards Aiden

Brenton and the policemen. Like a sea of mindless machines, they held up their Incaendium devices and started recording.

The tawny bearded policeman, called Inspector Gass, sliced through the pent-up tension. "Aiden Brenton, you are under arrest."

Christopher stumbled back in shock. Birdie quickly flapped over to his rescue and stood beside her friend's grandson.

Inspector Gass continued: "I am arresting you on suspicion for intent to inflict grievous bodily harm. You do not have to say anything, but it may harm your defence, if you do not mention when questioned something you later rely on in court. Anything you do say may be given in evidence …".

"Can I at least call my lawyer, Giles Mammon?"

Aiden Brenton sneered darkly at Birdie and Christopher before being hauled away towards the police car.

# CHAPTER 39
## ~ *LITTLE BOY IN BLUE* ~

It was a short drive to Ferncross police station. Aiden Brenton sat silently, staring at the reflection of the scrawny officer at the wheel. From time to time, the measly looking constable would glance up at his rear-view mirror, but it was not to check the traffic; it was more like he was trying to communicate something to Aiden Brenton. Inspector Gass picked up on this, and it made him feel somewhat uneasy, but he kept quiet for the time being. He thought that he would address the matter later.

Giles Mammon was already at the police station when Aiden Brenton and the officers arrived. The goat-like man was propped against a shelf in the waiting room with a newspaper under his arm. He looked like he had just drunk his fourth whiskey of the day whilst waiting on his horse to win its next race. Inspector Gass took an immediate dislike to the lawyer.

The interview room was dark and small. An angle poise lamp shone directly onto one side of Aiden Brenton's face, creating a stark contrast of dark and light. It made him look like a murderer from a black and white horror film.

"So, what's this about grievous bodily harm, Officer," Aiden Brenton paused before adding, "Gass."

"I think that you will find that I do the asking of questions here. And it's Inspector Gass, *not Officer.*" The tawny bearded Inspector then declared, "time of interview commencing is seventeen hundred hours."

The scrawny policeman, Officer Ruiz, sat beside Inspector Gass. They looked like an odd pair. He did not offer much to the interview; instead, he sat doodling strange squares and cubes on his policeman's notebook. Inspector Gass kicked him under the table. Aiden Brenton smirked as if he found it all very amusing. But his sneer quickly faded.

"So, we have evidence that places you, Aiden Brenton,

at the scene of the crime." Inspector Gass began, but he was interrupted once more.

"What evidence? You need conclusive proof to incriminate my client." Giles Mammon raised one of his eyebrows towards his terrifying widow's peak.

"Oh yes, I do," Inspector Gass retorted, "and if you interrupt me again, then I will have you removed from this interview." He then continued, hoping that no one else would stop his flow. "We have CCTV footage from the street security cameras. It says it all. At precisely four minutes past two, Mrs Kathryn Muir was on her front lawn, trimming the garden hedge. Exactly two minutes later, you appeared on the pavement nearest to her property. You crawled along, below the hedge line, presumably so that Mrs Muir could not see you. When you were close enough, you kicked the step ladders, causing her to fall from a great height onto the concrete path. You waited precisely ninety-two seconds before checking to see if your victim was conscious. You then ran away, back in the direction of your car."

Silence waited awkwardly in the air.

"I think you might recognize this?" Inspector Gass slid a black and white photograph over in the direction of Aiden Brenton: it was a picture of a car registration plate that read *AB1*.

"Yes, that's all very fine and well," Giles Mammon snorted, "but a picture of a number pate still does not incriminate my client. Do you actually have the footage?"

Inspector Gass nodded to Officer Ruiz, directing him to call up the incriminating footage on the Incaendium laptop. The scrawny officer looked somewhat panicked, like a cat caught in a car's headlights. He then whispered something into his superior's ear. Giles Mammon and Aiden Brenton looked at each other, wondering what was happening. Officer Ruiz crept out of the interview room.

"Interview suspended at seventeen ten hours." Inspector Gass sat back in his chair and folded his arms. His expression was hard to read. He did not want the suspect or his solicitor to know what was happening.

**\*\*\*\***

"I don't see how you can keep my client in custody if you have no evidence." Giles Mammon felt agitated at the length of time they had been waiting.

Inspector Gass squirmed in his seat. He could not believe that Ruiz had left him so that he could *go to the toilet*. That was more than fifteen minutes ago. A pocket of sweat gathered on his huge back, causing his shirt to stick to his skin. But as he was about to call for assistance, another officer stepped into the room. She looked nervous. She squeaked something inaudible at her bearded superior and then sat down beside him.

"Interview resumed at seventeen thirty hours," croaked Inspector Gass. He reached for his water but quickly decided against it when he noticed that his hand was shaking. Instead, he folded his arms again and nodded to the young, blonde officer called Dowling. She pushed her spectacles higher up onto the bridge of her thin nose and then shoogled the mouse adjacent to the laptop. The Incaendium logo flashed quickly before the login page appeared. Officer Dowling entered her details, in full view of Aiden Brenton and Giles Mammon. Inspector Gass was still too full of rage to have noticed her naïve actions. The svelte blonde officer then called up the footage and clicked play. Inspector Gass exhaled heavily. But the screen went black. There was no CCTV footage. Nothing.

**\*\*\*\***

"WHAT DO YOU MEAN, THE FOOTAGE DOES NOT EXIST ON THE DATABASE?! THAT'S IMPOSSIBLE!" Inspector Gass slammed the door of his office. It was loud enough to cause an earthquake throughout the village of Ferncross.

"Eh, we have no idea, sir. Officer Ruiz was supposed to oversee it all. We thought that…" Officer Dowling trailed off into silence. The look on her superior's face terrified her.

*"Where is that little toerag?"* This time Inspector Gass spoke quietly but forcefully. He was leaning over his desk like a huge, tawny bear. "I thought he was behaving strangely," he continued, spitting out his words, causing little specks of spittle to land on his desk.

Officer Dowling sat in silence, secretly trying to wipe away some of the rogue saliva that had landed on her glasses. It made her feel sick. She tried to concentrate, but her obsession with cleanliness began screaming in her ear. It was all too much. The Inspector was too overbearing. Without warning, she clambered to her feet with such force it caused her chair to fall back. She scurried away back to her desk. The other officers stared in shock.

Inspector Gass appeared at the doorway to his office, shaking his head. Tidal like sweat marks seeped out from under his armpits and across the crease in his huge belly. He looked every officer in the eye and then growled. "What did I do to deserve such an incompetent team?" He particularly focussed on Officer Dowling. "I want every one of you to stop what you are doing. I don't care how important it is. I want you to find that bloody Officer Ruiz. And the missing footage!"

"Eh, when boss?" Officer Dowling squeaked, feeling more confident now that she was not sitting in the direct fire of his sputum.

"RIGHT NOW!" He shouted before slamming his office door behind him. *"How am I going to explain this one to the Superintendent?"* He thought before piling an enormous apple pastry into his mouth.

\*\*\*\*

Aiden Brenton stood outside Ferncross Police Station,

inhaling the early evening air.

"So, I believe that makes you a free man, Aiden. They have nothing on you. Nothing." Giles Mammon bleated happily.

"Did you get the login details?" Aiden Brenton asked, without even thanking Giles for his services.

"Yes, here," the old goat replied, grabbing his client's hand, and shaking it. He slipped a small piece of paper into Aiden's palm containing the police system login details.

"That will be all then, for now, my good man," Aiden Brenton added, as he dropped the paper into his suit pocket.

Giles Mammon trotted off towards his old silver Buck. The car looked almost as ancient as he did and, it creaked like a pair of geriatric knees as he opened the door. Aiden Brenton turned away in embarrassment.

Aiden Brenton's car was a short distance away. Giles Mammon had arranged for one of his assistants to transport the black Belasco over to Treefoil Road. It was close enough to walk to, but out of earshot of Ferncross Police Station. He paused for a second before stepping into his car.

*"I'll get Christopher back into my possession if it's the last thing that I'll do,"* he spoke softly as if someone was listening to him.

A scrawny blue cat was circling Aiden Brenton's heels. It mewled pathetically, bunting into his shins as if it was looking for praise and attention.

Aiden Brenton smiled ominously and patted its head. "Well done, my little boy in blue," he whispered to the pathetic looking feline.

# CHAPTER 40
## *~ CHRISTOPHER MUIR: DECEMUIR SACRORUM LIBRI ~*

Milaw House breathed a sigh of relief. Nana Kathy's beating heart thrived at the building's helm once more, steering it towards happier times. She sat with her grandson in the front room, explaining the terrible ordeal of her so-called accident. Christopher was horrified, but the *tik---tock* of the old grandfather clock in the hallway had a soothing effect on him.

"Awe son, it wisnae your fault." Nana Kathy reassured her grandson. "That walloper of a man's in for it. I hope that they throw the bloody key away!"

"I c…can't believe it, b…but at the same time, I c…can believe it. There's s…something evil in him." Christopher struggled to find words to describe his feelings.

"It's just as well I saw him before I slipped away. I'll never forget the look on his face. Pure hatred. He checked my breathing - to see if I was dead, and when he thought I was, he left!" Nana Kathy stood at the huge bay window, staring out at the front lawn to the place where it all happened. Christopher shuddered. He moved towards his Nana and put his arm around her shoulder. "Wh…what do you m…mean, s…slipped away?" He felt a lump growing at the back of his throat.

However, Nana Kathy skipped over his question. "You know son, I saw your Papa. I'm no' too sure if I had checked oot properly at that point," she turned to her grandson and smiled. "But he was right there." She pointed to a place on the lawn.

Sadness gurgled at the back of Christopher's throat.

"But I'm here now. And I'm no checking oot for a long time yet." Nana Kathy insisted, seeing the tears forming at the corners of her grandson's eyes. She tickled his only dimple on his left cheeked and laughed. "Right, that's enough of that dreary chat. We have some other bits 'n' bobs to talk about."

The doorbell of Milaw House cut into Nana Kathy's announcement. Terror scuttled up Christopher's back. He feared Aiden Brenton's dark presence had returned, once again, and from the look engraved upon Nana Kathy's face, it was clear that she felt the same way.

Nana Kathy was first to move, but Christopher insisted that he should be the one to open the door. The two figures stood in Milaw House hallway, full of dread, wondering whose dark shadow lay behind the Charles Rennie MacIntosh glass. The grandfather clocked stopped recording time. It fell silent.

Christopher stepped forward and turned the doorknob.

The welcome and white vision of old Oli filled the doorway. He looked taller than Christopher remembered.

"My boy!" He declared as he trotted in with his stick. "You've grown in so many ways," he added before fumbling towards Nana Kathy. "And you, my dear, you're a sight for sore eyes. Some of us were worried, but I knew you would eventually come good." He smiled, grabbing out for her hands, and then they began waltzing around the hallway in time to some invisible music.

Christopher smiled at the two white figures. He breathed a huge sigh of relief. But just as he was about to shut the front door, it flew wide open, so much so that it thumped off the wall. Before Christopher could say anything, a huge dog surged towards him and pinned him to the ground.

It was Sam, and he slobbered his master with lots of doggy kisses.

"I bet you're glad to see him," Nana Kathy laughed, patting the Siberian's thick white nape.

****

"B…but when? H…how even? I thought that I h…had imagined it a…all. Even S…Sam. I was t…too scared to say." Christopher was still in shock at the return of his beautiful Siberian and his Nana's revelation. He sat on the rug in the front room, cuddling into Sam's coat. The beautiful white dog was fast asleep in front of the fire.

"It's a long story son, a very long story. Some of it will take a wee while to unfold and you'll learn more aboot it as you grow. For now, though, you only need to know a couple of things. A day at time. Let Sam be your guide. He is your protector." Nana Kathy smiled at the sight of her grandson's arms wrapped around the beautiful white Siberian. She sat contentedly, sipping a hot cup of lavender tea. "You know I've always said that you're just like your Papa Tommy? Well, it's true. You're part of a very important but very ancient bloodline called the *Decemuirs*."

Christopher's mouth fell agape. He instantly recognised the name. "B…but what does it m…mean?"

"It means a great deal," old Oli nickered, who was sitting across from Nana Kathy. "You'll eventually choose what that means to you, but in the meantime, think of yourself as being a keeper. A custodian of sorts. Someone who is responsible for keeping evil at bay." Oli smiled at Christopher.

"B…but I still don't understand," Christopher faltered.

"I think you do son." Nana Kathy offered. "You've assumed your role already, a wee bit quicker than I'd anticipated, may I add. The same thing happened wi' your Papa Tommy." She winked at him.

"The p…pen and the b…book." Christopher quickly stumbled. The jigsaw made more sense. "The h…horse and the l…lean-to. But you s…said to s…stay away from it?"

Nana Kathy chuckled. "Aye, yes, I did. I was only trying to protect you. I was worried that you were a wee bit young for it all. You weren't ready. Those Tiramavees are a wee warning sign that your body isnae quite ready for it all yet. It takes time." Nana Kathy nodded her head a little before reaching over to a worn paper bag by her side. She placed it upon her knee.

"So, who l…left the d…door open?" Curiosity clutched at Christopher.

"Me," old Oli chuckled, before Nana Kathy could answer. "I knew that you were ready my boy. That's why I just happened to be there that day in Balsamea Square. I was keeping an *eye* on you," he laughed.

"Aye, you did, you wee cheeky bugger," Nana Kathy declared to Oli in a playful tone.

The old man laughed. "Christopher my boy, you are a Decemuir, you proved that when you passed through the gateway in Ferncross Library. You did that on your own. Now other gateways will open for you, but they might take some time. In the meantime, do you still have your Papa's pen and key?"

Christopher did not know how to tell Oli that they were in his father's possession. He tripped over his words in his mind before replying. "Oh, Oli, Nana … I d…don't know how to tell you, b…but h…he – my f…father – he still h…has them." Christopher felt awful. He felt like he failed.

Oli and Nana Kathy sat in silence. Sam sat upright and howled a little.

"Don't worry son. That's no' your fault. It's that walloper of a faither of yours – it's his fault." Nana Kathy paused for a moment. "We'll get them back. You'll see. In the meantime, you should have this." She lifted a worn book out from the bag. "Christopher, son, this is yours now." She handed him *The Book of Almost Anything*. "You should use it wisely and carefully. You should only write in it when you feel the time is right, because whatever you write in here will come true. But you must use it for the good of this earth."

"Yes," Oli agreed. "As a Decemuir, you need to keep the bad forces at bay. You will have other powers too, ones that have not shown themselves yet. But they will soon."

Christopher opened *The Book of Almost Anything*. He sat in admiration, staring at its wonder. He turned the pages, one by one, gazing at his Papa's handwriting. There appeared to be a whole catalogue of events recorded, page after page of stories that he did not see when he first entered the old lean-to. The last page of writing was his own story of *Sam the Siberian*. The next page was blank. And then, at that very moment, Christopher realized that his story was only just beginning.

The rose in the kitchen blushed in the setting sunlight.

# ABOUT THE AUTHOR

K H Dawson is the author of the exciting new novel "The Book of Almost Anything". She lives with her wife and daughter - and of course, her ginger cat Tigger.

Dawson fell in love with reading at an early age, all thanks to her grandmother and parents. Her passion for literature led her to Glasgow University where she successfully completed a degree in English Language and Literature. Dawson then went on to achieve a Postgraduate Certificate in Education (English Secondary) the following year. From there, she worked in various schools, before settling in a local Lanarkshire school, where she has been sharing her enthusiasm for English literature and language ever since.

K H Dawson began writing her first novel, "The Book of Almost Anything," in 2014. She had a vision of what she wanted to write, and even early on, she realised that her novel would be the first part of a trilogy.

So, almost six years on, K H Dawson is delighted to announce the completion of her novel "The Book of Almost Anything."

Printed in Great Britain
by Amazon